HONORABLE
MEN

HONORABLE MEN

>×××××<

Louis Auchincloss

HOUGHTON MIFFLIN COMPANY • BOSTON

1985

Library of Congress Cataloging in Publication Data

Auchincloss, Louis.
Honorable men.

I. Title.
PS3501.U25N4   1985   813'.54   85-5257
ISBN 0-395-38812-0

PRINTED IN THE UNITED STATES OF AMERICA

P 10 9 8 7 6 5 4 3 2 1

FOR

JOSEPH V. NOBLE

A great director of the
Museum of the City
of New York and
a great friend

                    My Mother, you wot well
My hazards still have been your solace: and
Believe't not lightly (though I go alone,
Like to a lonely dragon, that his fen
Makes fear'd and talk'd of more than seen) your son
Will or exceed the common, or be caught
With cautelous baits and practice.

                    CORIOLANUS

I

><><><

ALIDA

I TAKE to pad and pencil, I suppose, because I don't really know what else to do. All my life I have been made periodically restless by the never quite quashable notion that I could write, and I have somewhere a box of old notebooks whose first pages are covered with the scribblings of unfinished stories and discontinued journals. I seem to have been doomed to the purgatory of opening lines, of bright initial flashes lost in the dusty spaces of a failed imagination. And this purgatory leads to a hell of negation, for the habit of stopping short is bound to spread, and what do I have to show for my half-century of life but the memory of good times ("same old good times," as we used jadedly to put it), the legend of a too much publicized debutante year and a reputation for pulling people apart in words when I could not do so in fact? Should not something more be said of the girl who married the last man to be tapped for Bulldog in the Yale class of '38?

· I ·

Well, today at least, I have done something. Almost three decades after Chip's nomination to that esteemed secret society I have resolved to leave him. When he comes home to Georgetown after his long day in the State Department he will find my letter, if I have not telephoned him first. It will not surprise him. It may even relieve him. He will no longer have to defend his idiotic war to a wife who "simply doesn't know what she's talking about." He will now be able to cut himself off entirely from the critics of his foundering Armageddon and from the last person who has the patience and persistence to remind him of all the associates in government who, one by one, have resigned from this demented administration. He can now give himself up to the cloudy trophies of mass suicide. I even see him, like the faithful Seyton in *Macbeth*, standing, stalwart and handsome, beside his desperate, lonely chief. They say that LBJ, sleepless, rises at night to pore over battle maps of Vietnam. Perhaps Special Assistant to the Secretary of State Charles Benedict is there to help him try to muddle out some specter of hope from the latest wires from the Far East.

But now that I have read over the preceding paragraph, I see that it is already time to pull myself up. And before I have fairly started! Because if I am to fill this notebook and not close it unfinished, like the others, it must be under the constant reminder that I have nothing to be smug about and that my greatest danger will always be in rejoicing — if that be not too strong a word — at the mortification of a man whose integrity and public spirit have always aroused my basest jealousy and resentment. It may be gratifying to watch one's moral superiors fall on their faces, but it is also a good idea to look around and see whether there is anyone left to lean upon.

And what, after all, in the name of all that's holy, have *I* to boast about? I can hardly point to my marriage. My son, Dana, at twenty-two, is a college dropout, unemployed, trying to beat a heroin hook and living in Stockholm because he refused to be drafted. My daughter, Eleanor, a lawyer working for an antiwar organization, has her life better organized, but I cannot bring myself in my heart (whatever lip service I may make to the modern deities of toleration) to accept her long-standing relationship with the young woman doctor with whom she shares an apartment in SoHo. Of course, Eleanor retorts, when I mutter about the "fulfillment" to a woman of a husband and children: "You mean a husband like yours, Mummie? And children like yours?" What can I say?

And yet, as I stare at the paper in my typewriter, reminding myself of the injunction that I should be fair about this man who took over my life, something seems to rip inside me. What life, after all, has he left me to write about but the worn-out garment that I turned myself into for his adornment and that he has tossed aside? For however bravely I may talk about leaving him, don't I know that he was never really mine to leave? I have a sudden vision of myself as a gaudy little bug flitting haplessly into the corolla of a carnivorous plant and buzzing about while the petals slowly but inexorably close over its idle existence. So is that what I am proposing to do: write about the plant that ate me? I must have been a failure from the very beginning.

.　.　.

I suppose the Strutherses were all failures. Unless the term is not applicable to people who never tried to be anything more. Because of my great-grandfather Ashton Struthers, there was just money enough for his descendants to be idle, though at the rate it had been foolishly spent or ineptly lost, by the time I came along a distinct indigence was mixed with our now tarnished gleam. The house in East Eighty-first Street was inconveniently narrow, though it boasted a pompous beaux-arts façade and a marble stairway that dwarfed its tiny rooms, and its fake Louis XVI chairs and consoles were badly in need of repair. The shingle summer cottage on West Street in Bar Harbor, Maine, had not been painted within anyone's memory. And the portrait of me with my younger sister, Deborah, in red velvet matching dresses against a gleaming background of chinoiseries had been taken back by the artist when his bill was not paid.

The first Ashton had been one of Commodore Vanderbilt's "kept" judges, rewarded for decisions favorable to New York Central. This was always perfectly well known, but the Strutherses lived it down, or perhaps got around it by ignoring it, or even by not knowing it, for they knew very little. Because they never budged from Manhattan, except to a spa, and because they knew by instinct when and where to be seen, they acquired over the decades the reputation of being "old New York" and "exclusive." Indeed, the avid reader of social columns would have been apt to rank them higher than many families whose far greater fame and wealth had the effect of highlighting their equally crooked origins. In short, our reputation was made of spit and sealing wax.

Let me turn to my parents. Daddy always looked at you as if you had interrupted him in the performance of some slightly tedious but nonetheless necessary task. He was serious of aspect but wholly undistinguished; my friend Gus Leighton used to say he looked "like a dentist," by which I suppose he referred to Daddy's gray, square, bluish chin and the pale, expressionless eyes behind steel-rimmed spectacles. Even in a dinner jacket he had the air somehow of being about to loosen his tie and roll up his sleeves, preparatory to going down to the cellar to fix the furnace. You would never have supposed that his life was dedicated to the organization of testimonial banquets, charity raffles, athletic tournaments, subscription dances and the like. Yet such were his only passion.

He had worked as a customer's man in a brokerage house after his graduation from Harvard, but when he discovered that he earned only what he paid his valet, he dismissed the latter and retired. The rest of his life, on a steadily diminishing income (he was one of those cursed with the fatal illusion that the rise and fall of the stock market was caused by determinable rules), he devoted to serving as secretary on boards of clubs in New York and Mount Desert Island. He made himself almost indispensable to these organizations, and never suspected that he was not as important as any of the tycoons who made up their membership or that they did not consider him entirely their equal. He would have been deeply hurt had he heard their contemptuous references to "busy bee" Ashton Struthers.

Mother came of different stock. I don't think Daddy, who, the reader will have gathered, was hardly a perceptive man, ever appreciated how great a gap existed between her family and his. Or did he, like a Victorian baronet marrying a Jewish heiress, feel that his rank obliterated hers? Grandpa Gayley, an immigrant from Galway, was shanty Irish, but he made a fortune in dry goods, built a monstrosity of a house on the south shore of Long Island and married his eight sons and daughters into the Social Register. They had all had rather sexy Irish looks, which, like the Gayley money, they lost early.

Mummie, at fifty, which is somehow the age at which I always think of her, was gray and soft, her round countenance and diminutive features only faintly suggesting the pretty colleen she must have been. She smoked endlessly and gossiped endlessly, dropping into the huge portmanteau of her knowledge of trivia the endless scraps of social information that she accumulated like a nest-building bird and never forgot: births; deaths; marriages; divorces; fortunes made, lost, stolen or given away; love affairs; perversions; blackmail; suicides; even murders. Why did she accumulate it all? And why did Daddy care about his clubs? My parents, like the birds and the bees, seemed united in dry, unending, unjoyous and unquestioning instinctive activity.

Of their two children only I constituted a problem. Deborah, two years younger, has been all her life a totally conventional, placid person. Fortunately, in marrying Tom Ayers she equipped herself with the money the Strutherses so dismally lacked. I think she had just intelligence enough to perceive that this was the one thing she needed to live the life her parents pretended to live, and with it she has been quite content.

I, on the other hand, conceived at an early age the idea that I had been deposited, like a baby cuckoo bird, in a nest to which I did not really belong. It seemed impossible that a soul bursting with so many romantic and idealistic notions could have been the seed of Gayleys or Strutherses. At Miss Herron's Classes I singled out the few girls who seemed endowed with something of the same spark, and we smoked secretly in our bedrooms, wrote passionate love poetry and sneaked away from dancing or calisthenics classes in the afternoon to see Clark Gable with Norma Shearer, or Clark Gable with Joan Crawford, or Clark Gable with Garbo. I would stare into my mirror and pull my hair back and strike absurd poses, wildly predicting the metamorphosis of that drowned rat before me into the pale, dark-eyed, languid, mysterious, ideal debutante of that era: bored, jaded, with long, dank black hair falling to her shoulders. Actually, I was developing into something not too different.

Nor was it all just sex and fantasy, though a lot of it must have been. I refused to believe that I was doomed to be as empty a woman as my mother or to be chained to a life hobby as vapid as my father's. I felt throbbing deep within me the impulse to become something much more daring and exciting and certainly more beautiful. When I should flap my wings at last and leave my dowdy nest, it would be as a swan, a black swan, not only a paragon of beauty, but a poet or writer or even an actress. I dedicated my afternoons to voice lessons and my weekends to scribbling. I found a retired Russian actress who coached me in Ibsen, and I had visions of the Lady from the Sea and General Gabler's pistols. My parents were complaisant so long as it did not cost too much. It never occurred to them to stress that what I really needed was discipline and hard work.

Only when I had a chance to play bit parts in summer stock did Daddy put his foot down. He said I was too young and that I would lose my reputation. When I appealed in desperation to Mummie, she passively agreed with him. I now hated them both. I saw them with the merciless eyes of seventeen. There was no sympathy in my heart, only a cold malignant rage.

Frustrated, I turned that summer to boys. There were plenty of them in Bar Harbor. I necked in the bushes at the Swimming Club dances, smoked cigarettes in a long jade holder and jumped at midnight from the high diving board in an evening dress that blew out like a parachute. But my precocity disillusioned me before my debutante year. I fell in and out of love with prep school boys and college freshmen; I found them too raw and puppyish. I decided that I was reserved for something much more passionate or perhaps not for passion at all. Why should I not be an Emily Dickinson and hide away from the vulgar world behind closed doors in a white gown and write deathless verse? But I could never seem to "taste a liquor never brewed" or "feel a funeral in my brain," no matter how late I stayed up after parties to make up rhymes.

I see now that it might have been better had I rebelled and become a communist, as did so many young people in the nineteen thirties — even in society. But politics was left out of my make-up; perhaps my ego was too strong. The agony of the Spanish Civil War did not move me; the rise of Hitler left me cold. I decided that I might be saved by a novel, and I wrote a dozen chapters about a Newport debutante who falls in love with a bootlegger.

It was not perhaps quite as bad as that sounds, but it was pretty bad. I showed it to Gus Leighton, a friend of my parents, but also of mine who had established himself as a kind of father confessor. He disliked the book and told me so, but he told me something else that changed my life. Let me introduce him.

He was a bachelor, in his middle thirties, who, had he ever had any great ambitions, seemed now to have successfully squashed them. Rumor had it that he had taken a master's degree in English Lit at Columbia in order to teach at a boys' school, but then had abandoned the idea when neither Saint Luke's nor Groton, the only two he deemed worthy of him, had seen fit to hire him. There was even a legend that he had been violently in love with a beautiful heiress and had turned his back on romance forever when she had refused him. For about fifteen years now he had lived at the Metropolitan Club in Manhattan and summered at the Malvern Hotel in Bar Harbor, dining out nightly and supplementing a modest income by a small but highly select public relations business. No one knew just who his clients were or exactly what he did for them, but his particular field was almost certainly social advancement: how and when the newcomers should entertain, what were the most useful charities for them to support, what clubs and summer colonies they should try for. To do him justice, I believe he took a dignified view of his shabby trade, persuading himself that he was coaching the new rich how to be ladies and gentlemen in the best sense of those hackneyed terms.

He was a large man, inclined to be stout, with thick, long, rather greasy black hair, a white doughy skin, a round puffy face and large, dark, commanding, often angry eyes. He dressed in black suits in winter and loud blazers and white flannels in summer. He knew a great deal about a great many subjects, but I never saw him presume to know more than he did. He was a force, at least in the small society in which he had chosen to live.

As I have said, Gus was not impressed by my novel. He was particularly disgusted by my bootlegger's "gun moll," who had gold fingernails.

"It is not, heaven forbid," he counseled me, "that I have any truck with the inane rule that a writer should write only of what he knows. What under that restriction would happen to *Paradise Lost* and most of Shakespeare? But where there are no facts, there must be imagination, and your gun moll, my dear, is not imagined — she is fantasized. You may be one of those unfortunates endowed with the artistic spirit yet not furnished with an outlet. I know something about that. The answer must be found in making your life a work of art. In making use of the materials you have to hand."

"And what do those amount to?"

"A good deal more than you think. You have a sharp eye for the second-rate in your parents' world. But you do not see it as others do. Cholly Knickerbocker speaks of your mother as a *grande dame* of Gotham."

"But that's all tommyrot."

"Is it?" Gus frowned, as if he were dealing with weighty matters. "Who is to decide? That a considerable body of even ignorant persons believe something to be a fact may be important. To you, anyway. Even supposing your world is rotten and doomed, even assuming it is about to be swept away by a red tide, it is still here and now and part of truth. Maybe a bigger part than you think. Doesn't Marie-Antoinette take up as many pages in the history books as Robespierre? Is Augustus Caesar more remembered than Cleopatra?"

"Must I get my head chopped off? Or take an asp to my bosom?"

"It doesn't matter how you die. It's how you *live*. Let me give you two examples. First, Theodore Roosevelt. He conceived of himself, dramatically, as a leader of men, and his image of himself gained world acceptance. Now move to our own day. Take Mrs. Neily."

"Who?"

"Mrs. Cornelius Vanderbilt. T.R. started with many disadvantages — asthma for one — which he overcame. Grace Vanderbilt was older than her husband and despised by his family, who disinherited him on their marriage. But she conceived of herself as a great hostess, spent whatever she could lay her hands on, and more that she couldn't, and made the world — or enough of it — see her as she saw herself!"

"But surely you can't compare a great President with an addled old party-giver!"

"Why can't I? I value the hand one is dealt and the bid one calls. What do I care whether it's for the White House or for social supremacy in Newport?"

"You mean they're equally vulgar?"

He shrugged. "Or equally valid."

"Very well, then. What bid shall I call?"

"Why don't you become the most famous debutante in America? You have the pale slinky looks that are coming into fashion. You're a New Yorker, which is essential. And your family can be made to look as grand as we choose."

"And what do we do for money?"

"It'll take less than you think. You'll need a party, of course, but I think Grandma Struthers will come through."

"Grandma? You're dreaming, Gus!"

"Leave her to me."

"And suppose it worked. What would I get out of it?"

"Fun! You'll see. I promise."

And that was how my fantastic debutante year began.

2

⋈⋈⋈

ALIDA

FOR SOME WEEKS I could not believe that Gus was really serious, but he obliged me in the end, with an almost legalistic formality, to accept or decline his proffered service. Of course I accepted. Even if it was only a game, why should I have denied myself the fun of it? He and I agreed to lunch together every Monday at his favorite restaurant, the Chenonceaux, review what had happened during the past week and make plans for the ensuing one. Our business was largely with the press.

The first and great commandment, Gus taught me, was never to pretend to a reporter that I was not earnestly seeking publicity. Obviously, they knew I was, or I wouldn't be talking to them, and they had only contempt for the hypocrisy of socialites who affected to have been surprised or tricked into obviously intentional indiscretions.

"Put your cards on the table," he told me, "and you'll find, on the whole, that you're treated fairly. Not always, of course, for the society reporter is likely to be someone who's failed to make it on the other pages. A man who's a sorehead or a woman who feels she's been discriminated against. Sometimes they're out to get their revenge on the silly asses whose inane parties they have to cover. But don't worry. The basic quality of this type of journalist is laziness. And on that laziness hangs my deepest purpose."

Gus paused to look inscrutable until I obligingly responded to my cue. "Which is?"

"Which is precisely to save him his labor. What I propose to get across to the evening press and to the fashion magazines is that if they all agree to cover one debutante, and make her the news of the day, they will save themselves the trouble of covering fifty. And you and I, my dear, have chosen that debutante!"

The funny thing was that his crazy scheme worked. It all started with a few modest social notes, slipped by Gus into news and gossip columns in the form of discreet releases. "Miss Alida Struthers is far from the usual type of debutante; she has written a novel, hopes to do a screenplay and prefers the public sands and buffeting breakers of Jones Beach to the exclusive waters of the Creek Club Pool." Or: "Everyone was at Newport last Saturday for the Frazer debut, except Alida Struthers, who was simply unable to forgo a morning sail to Block Island. 'It was the one perfect day we've had all June!' she cried." Or: "It is *not* true that Miss Struthers smokes hashish; she inhales a rare and harmless form of . . ." Or: "Alida Struthers keeps a pet macaw in her bedroom."

Accompanying these handouts were beautiful photographs, including one by Gus's friend Cecil Beaton. It did not take long for my publicity to accelerate until by Christmas it had become a minor avalanche. I was already on all the debutante invitation lists, but now I received bids from every socially ambitious mother in the Greater New York Area. Gus scrutinized these carefully and selected some surprising ones for me to accept.

"We can't stay just with the Knickerbocker families. We have to branch out. I'm picking the people whose parties will make news. No matter how sensational!"

I soon found that I was getting boxes of lovely things from fashionable stores and free tickets to popular shows, and I even, rather daringly for those days, endorsed a cold cream in an advertisement that was widely distributed. I was, of course, well paid for it. When I suggested to Gus that this sort of thing was bound in time to depreciate my social value, he cheerfully agreed.

"But by then you'll have got what you want."

"And what is that?"

"Anything!" he exclaimed, throwing up his arms. "It'll be time enough to choose when we get there."

He thought it desirable that I should have a team to back me up, and I selected two classmates from Miss Herron's Classes, Amanda Bayne and Dolly Hotchkiss, to whom I confided my project. Both were delighted to go along, hanging, so to speak, on my coattails. Amanda had dowdy old parents with very little money who were afraid of their beautiful daughter and gave her no trouble. Dolly, on the other hand, had a conservative banker-father who objected vociferously and who had to be (and usually was) got around, with the help of a mother who lived vicariously in Dolly. And we soon formed a squadron of some half-dozen college men who were intrigued at the idea of becoming nationally known and would cut any class at Yale, Princeton or Harvard to attend a dance or house party when I commanded. One of these was Chessy Bogart, an Eli who became a kind of protégé of Gus. Gus described him as one of the few members of the younger generation who had penetrated the falseness of every "ism" of our era, from the farthest right to the most extreme left. In time I was to realize that Chessy was just as bright as Gus perceived, if not brighter. But in those days I tended to regard him as a clown, my court jester.

How did my parents take it all? Very complacently indeed. Mother attributed the old guard's dislike of publicity entirely to its jealousy of new and more colorful arrivals, and as she had always pored over the social columns, she liked them the more for making a feature of her daughter. After all, a good deal of the glory redounded on herself. People were constantly telling her what they had read about me, and she almost purred. Daddy's reaction was less enthusiastic but still accepting. The male company that he so largely kept did not read the social columns, and my new fame was not so frequently flung in his face, but when his attention was called to a news item about me, his complete literalness and lack of imagination made him champion me against the shrieks of Granny Struthers and her old maid daughter, Aunt Fanny. For if I was described as "brilliant" or "beautiful" in print, Daddy assumed I must be. He tended to see the world in the same colors as did such reporters. Besides, he was delighted that it all cost him so little.

The one expense that could not be avoided was a coming-out party. I did not have to have a big one, but I had to have one, and my parents were far too broke even to think of it. Grandma Struthers was the only hope, and Gus had pledged himself to bring her round.

Granny and Aunt Fanny occupied a brownstone on East Thirty-third Street stuffed to bursting with the eclectic collection of the crooked judge, who had had a rather florid taste for huge German porcelains, academic historical scenes and Turkish bazaars, hung one over the other on dark walls. Yet if one looked carefully one could spot a fine medieval reliquary glinting in a Turkish corner, or a "right" Corot above the door, or even a Roman scene by Alma-Tadema. Had we only waited until now before selling the collection, we would have made a fortune. But, alas, Daddy let it all go for a song when Granny died in 1940.

She belonged to a generation that did nothing to resist age or hide the double chin and gnarled neck. She wore a pince-nez that made her look severe, a black choker and large yellow diamonds. She said "poyel" for pearl and "goyel" for girl, in the manner of old Manhattan, and would ask young people who had been to a ball if they had seen many attractive "toilets," so that ignorant people thought her vulgar. She affected to be spunky about her ailments and afflictions, but she was in fact an utterly self-centered valetudinarian. Aunt Fanny, endowed with a decayed, sexless prettiness, fluttered about her, fussed over her, asked people constantly whether they did not agree that she was "marvelous" and hated her. When Granny died, she left Aunt Fanny almost penniless.

But we didn't realize then that Granny was romping through her capital. We assumed that she was still rich and had to be cultivated for favors. Gus, however, did know it — how he discovered such things I never knew — and he used this useful piece of intelligence to crowbar the cost of my coming-out party out of her. It helped a good deal that he had known her since his childhood, his mother having been a flower girl at her wedding.

Much later he told me how he had done it. He called on Granny on an afternoon when he knew that Aunt Fanny was at her exercise class, and the conversation went something like this:

Gus: I hope you will forgive me, Mrs. Struthers, if I talk rather personally about your granddaughter. You might say it's none of my business, but didn't the ghost of Jacob Marley learn too late that mankind was his business?

Granny: Is womankind yours, Augustus? Are you a candidate for Alida's hand? If so, it's her father you should be addressing yourself to. Not that I mean to discourage you, dear boy.

Gus: Boy of almost forty! You needn't be that anxious to get rid of her. The poor child's going to do a lot better than a jaded old creature like me.

Granny: She's not a *parti*, you know.

Gus: How could she be, in these dark days, when we're all put to it to make ends meet? I sometimes think you must be a bit of a genius to maintain the style of living that you do maintain.

Granny: Well, of course, it's not easy. One has to keep a sharp lookout.

Gus: Just that? I know so many people who nibble on their capital.

Granny: But we were brought up not to do that!

Gus: We're not all saints, are we? Oh, come, Mrs. Struthers, don't tell me you've never sneaked a bond out of the tin box and sold it when no one was looking? Have you never been naughty? Never once?

Granny: Well, maybe just once in a blue moon. Things are so very dear!

Gus: Exactly! And I'm sure your son and daughter-in-law have, too.

GRANNY: Oh, them — for sure!

GUS: And between you all, I wonder whether poor Alida won't have to learn a trade.

GRANNY: I don't think I quite follow that, Augustus.

GUS: It's simple. How is a young woman brought up to believe that meals and bathrooms cook and clean themselves supposed to support herself when her immediate progenitors have gone to their reward — if reward, indeed, it be?

GRANNY: That's her progenitors' lookout.

GUS: But if they don't look? Isn't a grandmother a kind of surety on the bond?

GRANNY: What are you driving at? Why can't Alida marry some sensible young fellow and be a good wife to him?

GUS: Because she's been brought up to be perfectly useless. And to fall in love with youths who will either be after the money she hasn't got or afraid she's after theirs!

GRANNY: Am I responsible for the low moral tone of my daughter-in-law's house?

GUS: No! But you're responsible for not saving Alida if you can.

GRANNY: Can I? How?

Gus proceeded to tell her. And he actually got the party out of the old girl. She did the bare minimum, but that proved enough. We rented the Aquamarine Room at the Hotel Stafford, not the best place by a good deal but adequate, and Gus secured a number of concessions in the way of music and liquor when the merchants discovered what the press coverage was to be. It was an April party, late in the season, and it constituted its climax. Alida Struthers the next week was on the cover of *Life*!

When Gus came to our house one morning with an advance

copy, he kissed me and murmured, "Now I can chant my Nunc Dimittis."

"Well, you've had *your* fun." I gazed at the large photograph almost with incredulity. "When does *mine* start?"

I did not mean to be ungrateful. But in sober truth, what had I really got out of the whole thing? I had learned nothing that had not confirmed my low opinion of the games played by New York society; I had exhausted my body with late hours, smoking and drinking; I had made mincemeat of my self-respect; I had added nothing to my knowledge of the arts and literature; and I had not even fallen in love! When I looked back over those months of futile activity, I had only a sense of hundreds of bland young faces, of lips forming inane compliments or feeble jokes, and of laughs, smiles, giggles, an endless bray of pointless jocosity. Where was the heart of fools? Of course, in the House of Mirth!

Once, after a long lunch at the Chenonceaux with Gus, reluctant to go out to the rainy street, I gazed glumly over the emptying tables and sipped a second cognac.

"What are you doing it for, Augustus? Are you like the guardian in *The School for Wives* rearing an innocent ward to be the perfect spouse? If so, you're taking rather a new tack, aren't you? For instead of walling me up to preserve my purity, you've exposed me to every contamination on earth! But maybe that's just your perversity. Maybe you're the ultimate decadent. To want a spouse like Salome, a virgin who is totally corrupt!"

"No, I don't fly so high." Gus always took in his stride one's extremest flights of fancy. Did I attract him at all? It was hard to tell what lurked behind those dark, damp eyes, sometimes so scornful, sometimes so sad, sometimes simply so bored, so horribly bored. When he shut out the world, was he shutting out clamorous, intrusive females? Or perhaps grinning, leering boys who knew what he really wanted? Or did he simply want to be alone with his intensely intelligent self? "No, I don't aspire to the hand of my Galatea. She is too fine a property for the likes of me. But that needn't mean I can't have a candidate."

"Oh, you have one?"

"I think I may have."

"Whom I've met?"

"No."

"And when shall I meet this paragon?"

"Ah, but of course I'm not going to tell you. That would put your back up."

"Will you tell me after I've met him?"

"Only if I think you like him."

I admit that Gus was wise to make a mystery of his project. I found myself wondering now, every time I met someone at all attractive, whether this one might be he. And in a surprisingly short time it became an amusing game. I was constantly asking men I met: "By any chance, do you know Gus Leighton? Why? Oh, no reason. I was just wondering." But then, of course, it was always possible that Gus did not know his candidate personally. He might have made his selection merely by title: a duke or a maharajah. At any rate, as the fateful season ended and I faced the long, familiar summer of Bar Harbor with my parents and Deborah, I began to wonder if Gus's ambition for me might not be the only thing I had salvaged from a year of folly.

3

×××××

ALIDA

HENRY ADAMS, who was always concerned with the dichotomy of the one and the many, not only in the twelfth and twentieth centuries, but in the eras of his own life, professed to see unity in the sober, disciplined Boston of his childhood and multiplicity in the careless freedom of the countryside at Quincy. One represented winter and school; the other, summer and license.

With me it was just the reverse. Manhattan, with its bustle of traffic and much-touted pace of living, with its ruthless competition in social and business life, struck me as the licentious "many," while Bar Harbor, serene between its green mountains and the sapphire blue of Frenchman's Bay, seemed a unit that existed only for itself. Bar Harbor made sense, or nonsense if you preferred, which in the silver air of its few peerless Maine days (one ignored the fog that shrouded the island for half the summer) was all that seemed to matter. For there was no world outside Bar Harbor, or really much of a one in it besides the summer community and the shops and servants and boats and glittering old limousines that made up the crazy round of its idyllic days.

When I close my eyes I see the Swimming Club on West Street, with its terrace and lawn descending to the huge pool whose cement walls extended down the stony beach that was covered at high tide, as was the long sandy dike that connected Bar Island to Mount Desert. The club was the undoubted center of the "one," and here at noon the leading ladies of the colony foregathered at umbrella tables while boys in scarlet jackets brought on silver trays the first cocktail of the day. I used to think of those half-dozen tables under their brightly colored shelters as a kind of senate, for surely here, by these broad-hatted, silk-gowned women, with their pearls and high heels and low throaty chuckles, all the decisions of the community were made. If their men had some voice in the distant cities, they had none here — nor did they seek any, except in the management of the golf club, carved out by them as a small, independent principality.

My mother lived for that noon hour at the Swimming Club. Sitting with her needlework, a cigarette dangling from her always moving lips, she listened and chattered at once, missing nothing. She was the admitted historiographer of the island, even of the outlying and sometimes rebellious settlements at Northeast and Seal Harbors. I see myself coming up to her chair when it was time to go home for lunch (my generation never sat at the umbrella tables) and hovering there while she answered some such final question as "Did the John Stewart Kennedy fortune really all go to cats and dogs?" or "Florence, what was the true story about Ann Archbold's kidnapping her children?"

Life radiated out from the club to the "cottages" on West and Eden Streets, large shapeless shingle structures, sometimes brightly painted, with well-mowed emerald lawns, to the cozy shops on Main Street with windows invitingly full of imported luxuries, to the woods and the long blue driveways of the more distant villas concealed by spruce and pine, yet all familiar to us, including stone castles, Italian palazzos, Georgian red brick villas, but still for the most part shingle habitations, with dark proliferating turrets and porches. And then there were the "mountains," hills really, that one could climb on trails for breathtaking views of the ocean and mainland, or, in the case of Green Mountain, drive all the way to the peak behind the limousine of some little neat old lady in black or white who spoke to her chauffeur through a voice tube and had a glass vase with an orchid attached to the wall by her seat.

Politics and war were shut out of Bar Harbor. It was difficult even to read the newspaper. Yet it was saved from being too hopelessly silly or artificial by being only itself. When the husbands and fathers from New York talked of distant disasters after dinner over brandy and cigars, the ladies in the drawing room, resuming the discussion of the umbrella tables, knew that they were coping with the "real" problems.

I think that one of my principal reasons for loving Bar Harbor was that my parents seemed less ridiculous there. It was hard to take the values of New York too seriously, and the social game, the gossip, the endless mirth, seemed to fit in with the squawking of the gulls that awoke one on misty mornings and the reflection of the midday sun on the vivid shutters of the shops on Main Street. And so, in the long summer that followed my hectic debutante season, although my heart was filled with a sense of anticlimax, I could at least hope that it might be dulled by the euphoria of a Maine July.

Gus Leighton had taken his usual rooms at the Malvern, and he told me firmly that he was "off duty."

"But suppose Mr. Right comes along?" I protested. "Will he give us a second chance? Won't we have to pounce?"

"You know nothing ever happens in Bar Harbor. It's a Garden of Eden where everybody's allowed to eat the apples."

"And the poor snake is out of a job."

"Precisely. Which is why I have cast off my shiny green skin and intend to doze. Go thou and do likewise."

Of course, Gus was not serious about relaxing his social life. He dined out nightly. But although no one expected so elegant a bachelor to return their hospitality, Gus was meticulous about his obligations and would give a monthly dinner party at the Swimming Club that he called a "massacre" ("kill-off," he insisted, being too mild a term) to satisfy them. But as he would think over each boring hostess to whom he was indebted, and picture to himself what havoc she might create in an otherwise congenial gathering, he would end by striking her name, until finally his "massacre" had evolved into a delightful party of only those persons (always the most amusing) who had *not* invited Gus Leighton to dine in the preceding four weeks. When I asked him why he accepted so many bids from hostesses who simply wearied him, he wailed, "Because I have no one to answer my telephone, and I haven't time to think up an excuse!" He once showed me a notebook in which he had rated (or berated) the different entertainers of Bar Harbor, and I recall such brief jottings as: "Mrs. Hale. Fish house punch! Never again." or "Mrs. Twining. Took me out of a business double. Nevermore!" But he always did go again; a good Bar Harborite never kept a good resolution.

At Gus's first dinner party that summer I found myself seated next to Jonathan Askew, a tall, baggy bachelor of twenty-seven, whose mother, Lady Lennox, had recently (for tax reasons, according to my all-knowing ma) abandoned the United Kingdom for her native land and had repurchased her parents' old place, Arcadia, on a peninsula that gave her a double view of Frenchman's Bay. Askew, the sole issue of her earlier American match, was making his first visit to Mount Desert.

"What do young ladies like to talk about in Bar Harbor?" he asked me in a loud hollow tone, as if he were offering me a tray of goodies.

I knew right away that this had to be Gus's candidate. Askew, thanks to an ancestor who had invested first in the China trade and then in railroads, bore a famous name. He looked the part, too; he had a large aquiline nose, a high sloping forehead, curly auburn hair and watery gray eyes that stared at one blankly, haughtily, suspiciously. His voice was high and affected, and he moved his large body with a kind of arrogant clumsiness. He would have been perfectly cast in a Cecil B. DeMille film about a Roman emperor.

I took a firm line.

"Young ladies in Bar Harbor like to talk about different things at different times," I replied to his question. "When I have the honor of sitting next to an Askew, I feel inclined to ask what it feels like to be one."

"Oh, it's nothing so great." He took his status as much for granted as if he had been a prince or a movie star. "It's rather a bore, really. One can't see why one's all that different from another chap."

Chap. But of course he had been raised in England. "Aren't you afraid that people are after your money?"

His eyes widened. "The girls, you mean?"

"Aren't they all dying to be Mrs. Askew? Perhaps you should confine your attentions to heiresses."

"My mater says that makes no difference. According to her, the average heiress is even greedier than the poor girl. She would want what I have either to add to her pile or else as a guarantee that I wasn't marrying her for *her* money."

This was my first glimpse of the sort of mother Lady Lennox must be. I felt almost sorry for him. "So that it's impossible for you to be married except for mercenary reasons?"

"So it would seem," he agreed gravely. "Unless I were to find someone indifferent to money. Someone who had enough accomplishment in her own right to be above material needs."

"You mean a famous actress? An opera singer? A trapeze artist?"

"Would I have to go quite so far? What about a famous debutante?"

He was actually flirting! My lips parted in surprise. "But I thought they were the most dangerous of all! Why on earth would they become debutantes but to make good matches?"

"I should have thought a girl who appeared on the cover of *Life* could pick just about any man she wanted."

"Well, Mrs. Simpson's already got the King of England. So the rest of us will have to make do with simple dukes. And maybe here and there an Askew."

"Oh, come, you're pulling a fellow's leg."

"I've never been more serious. Do you realize what I've staked in this game? My coming-out party represents my inheritance from my grandmother. And at the rate Mummie and Daddy are going, they'll be totally bust in a few years' time. I can promise you, Jonathan Askew, that I don't relish the idea of becoming a waitress at Jordan's Pond or begging Miss Herron to take me in as an assistant in her kindergarten."

"But surely things can't be that bad." He looked bewildered. "You wouldn't be living the way you are if that were the case. And you wouldn't be . . . well, you certainly wouldn't be . . ."

"Telling you?" I finished for him. "To your face? Why not? I'm like the trick man who shows you his outstretched palms and lets you search his pockets before he picks a gold piece out of your ear. It's a question of skill. Professional skill. You'd better watch out, my friend. Or don't go out at night on Mount Desert Island without your mummie to protect you!"

I continued in this jocose vein, ignoring his pleas that I be "serious," until it was time to turn to my other neighbor. Askew was oblivious of the rules of dinner table conversation; he seemed to feel quite entitled to monopolize my attention. I had to show him my back to keep him from butting in. And after dinner, when he should have joined one of the ladies who had not been his neighbor at table, he made his deliberate way to the sofa where I was sitting.

"Really, Mr. Askew," I protested, "how is our host to entertain his guests properly if you are so unruly?"

Looking very cross, he actually left the party! When I got home at midnight Mother was still up with her eternal needlepoint, listening to the radio. She switched it off at once when I told her whom I had sat next to.

"He's staying with his mother, of course. I suppose he considers it slumming after Newport."

"Is he as rich as they say?"

"Who says so? The Askews believe in primogeniture. His cousin Matthew got the bulk of the fortune. Of course, Jonathan came into what he has early, when his father was killed playing polo. It was a long minority. I suppose he may have five millions."

"Well, isn't that enough?"

"For what? For a man who thinks he's entitled to fifty? I'm sure Jonathan feels he's been very badly treated indeed."

I should say here that Mother, for all her rapt concern with the social game, never once tried to make a match for me. She seemed to regard it as an entertainment that had no necessary relation to her family.

"What is Lady Lennox like?"

"She tries to be that tough, down-to-earth, damn-your-eyes British type. You know, heavy gold jewelry, tweeds, and dogs all over the place. She has one qualification for the role, anyway. A tin heart."

"You mean she doesn't give a damn for Jonathan?"

"She doesn't give a damn for anyone."

I was not really surprised when Askew called me the next morning. I knew when I had made a hit. He asked me if I would take him on one of my walks up a mountain. He explained that Gus had informed him that I knew them all.

"I'll pick you up at ten," I told him crisply. "We can do Jordan and then lunch at the tea house."

He huffed and puffed a good deal going up the trail, for he was obviously not used to much physical exercise, yet he insisted on talking all the way. As soon as he dropped the arrogant manner, which I divined was really a cover of shyness, he became confiding and rather sweet. He had never, so far as I could make out, done a thing with his life, or even seriously contemplated doing one. He had been brought up to consider that being an Askew was an occupation in itself, like being royalty. Yet he was not really conceited; he was almost humble about the little that his confused mishmash of European schools had taught him. I gathered that he had spent most of his life in the disordered wake of an aggressive mother. One of the things he seemed proudest of was that he had spent a whole winter in

London tutoring his younger half sister, Amy Lennox, because her psychiatrist had pronounced her too tense and indrawn to endure a strange teacher. Obviously, his mother was a horror.

"But you can't just be a family tutor all your life," I pointed out.

"No, I suppose I can't, can I?"

"Don't you think you could bring yourself to do something more creative?"

"It's good of you to ask. I thought I might write a history of the Askews. These society reporter chaps, you know, get those things all botched up."

"It so happens I do know something about that. But is there really so much point in unbotching it?"

"Well, facts are facts, you know."

"Do I?"

When I dropped him back at his house, we met Lady Lennox in the doorway, about to step into the little Bugatti in which she tore about the island at dangerous speeds. She was a large, much-powdered, false blonde, dressed in immaculate white. She leaned down to stare at me with glinting, mocking dark eyes.

"So you're the famous Alida Struthers! I'm relieved to see you've brought my boy back in one piece."

"Did you think I would eat him up?"

"Well, I'm not sure he could stop you — once you'd started!"

"Oh, come, Mother, that's no way to talk to Alida!"

She ignored him. "Come around some afternoon, my dear, and you and I will have a little chat alone. I was a debutante myself a century or so back. We might compare notes. Or is it just a case of *plus ça change*?"

I decided boldness was the only way. "What I'd really like is a tip on how you did it."

"Did what?"

"Married an Askew."

Lady Lennox snorted. "You'd better watch out, Johnnie boy! This one plays with her cards on the table! They're the worst."

I never did have that cozy chat with Lady Lennox, but I had several more walks with Jonathan. In fact, he attached himself to me as far as I would allow it, and he was constantly on the telephone when I would not. At the club he would join me and maintain a sulky silence if any other friends came by. If I sent him away, he would retire to the veranda and sit by himself, staring moodily across the lawn at me. And at the Saturday night dances he would have no partner but me.

My feelings were ambivalent. I liked him; I even pitied him; and I enjoyed our long, rambling, rather childish talks. We told each other endless silly stories about ourselves and laughed at our friends and relatives. Alone with me, he showed a naïve, sunny, confiding nature; his sulkiness and pride were only poses. He blandly announced that he was in love with me on our second walk and proposed to me on our third, but he made no clumsy efforts to kiss or maul me after I had told him firmly that I preferred to be let alone. And, of course, it was fun to have all Bar Harbor know that the scion of the Askews was at my beck and call. What an easy and obvious solution to all my problems!

On the other hand, it went against my grain to know that everyone in the summer community, nay, every employee of the Swimming Club, every merchant on Main Street, was convinced that I was using all the tricks in my bag to capture a man whom I would have scorned had he not been an Askew. How could I bear to be so exactly what everyone thought me, to fit into the pattern of our crazy social fabric as neatly and as inevitably as the parents for whom I had never felt aught but contempt? I had turned myself into a newspaper debutante, and now it began to look as if I should be a newspaper bride.

Lady Lennox seemed to penetrate my mind and to revel in reading it aloud to me. My dislike of her at last broke into the open one morning when I drove to her house to pick up Jonathan for our now daily walk. I had arrived a bit early, and as he was still upstairs dressing, I joined Lady Lennox on the patio, where she was finishing her breakfast. It was one of Mount Desert's peerless days, and the sparkling sea dazzled, but Jonathan's mother, blinking her black eyes at me, her powder caked in the glaze of the sunlight, seemed at once passive and dangerous, inert yet potentially agile, a lizard on a rock. When she spoke, she justified my uneasy apprehension.

"It won't be as bad as you think."

"What won't?"

"Marriage to Jonathan. He's not hard to handle, and you strike me as having already learned the knack."

"You take it for granted that I want to marry him?"

"Why on earth else would you bother with him?"

"Can't you see any good qualities in your own son?"

"Of course I can. A mother is perfectly qualified to appraise a son. So long as she doesn't succumb to middle-class maternal blindness. I can see that Jonathan is rather a dear — when he's not being stuffy and Askewish. But being a dear isn't what a girl like you looks for in a man."

"How do you know what I look for in a man?"

"Because I understand you. Remember: I was a debutante myself. And a poor one, too. And my parents were almost as bad as yours."

I had no interest in resenting this. "And you were after an Askew, too!"

"And one who was even less attractive than Jonathan. Max was actually unfaithful to me on the honeymoon. I was about to divorce him when he was killed on that polo field."

"That must have been a relief."

"It wasn't, in fact. Because it turned out that the money was all in trust for Jonathan. I had to spend my life in the Surrogate's Court trying to get a decent allowance. Fortunately George Lennox turned up. He had a few shares of a Canadian gold mine. Not many, really, but enough to exempt him from the British duty of wedding Yankee heiresses. Or perhaps he assumed, because I was a Mrs. Askew, that I *was* one. They're so careless about American facts and figures."

"Fortunately for you."

"Yes, my dear, fortunately for me. His death was untimely, too, unless you prefer to call it timely. He had received some rather nasty letters about me — all false, of course — at the time of his heart attack."

I rose, trembling. "Lady Lennox, I could almost marry Jonathan to make up to him for having a mother like you!"

I was answered only by her deep rumbling laugh. I don't know what more I might have said had Jonathan not appeared in the doorway.

"Hallo! What are you two yacking about?"

"Oh, just women's chatter, darling. It wouldn't interest you. Besides, he wouldn't understand it, would he, Alida?"

I turned away, tears now in my eyes, and shook my head angrily when Jonathan questioned me about it. We drove in silence to our trail and climbed in silence to the peak. At all times I kept a lead of several yards between myself and my puffing companion.

"For God's sake, Alida, what's wrong?" he demanded when

we were seated at last with our backs to a rock to contemplate the view. "What horrible things did Mother tell you?"

"It doesn't matter. I don't give a damn what she says or thinks."

"That's my girl. Neither do I."

"Oh, but you do! Don't kid yourself."

"I don't. I swear I don't!" And as I looked at him, it suddenly occurred to me that he might not. "If you marry me," he went on with a gasp, "you'll never have to see her. I promise!"

As I have said, it was a day of breathtaking clarity. I could see for miles over the untroubled blue of the Atlantic to the gray-white speck that was Egg Rock. I could see the whole village of Bar Harbor, with its neat white and yellow box houses, and the gray battleships of the visiting fleet, exactly like the toy vessels they are always compared to by observers at my elevation. I could see the long climbing forests in the neighboring hills and the black soaring dots of two eagles as high above us as we were high over the sea. Surely it was Lucifer who had lured me up there to show me the kingdoms of the earth!

"But supposing I tell you, Jonathan, that no matter how much I may like you, I'd never dream of marrying you without the money?"

"That's quite all right. Indeed, it's perfectly natural. How could you possibly afford to marry a man with no money? It's enough for me if you like me as well as my chips."

But this new humility only jarred me. "I'm not in love with you," I said roughly.

"I must hope that love may come later."

"When love comes later, it's not necessarily for the husband."

"Oh, Alida, don't be so cruel! Do you mean you could never imagine being in love with me? Am I such a toad?"

"No, no, of course not. But it doesn't seem to me that you're the type of man — however fine you may be — that I'm ever going to fall in love with."

"And what type is that?"

"I don't know!"

"Well, if you don't know, how can you tell it won't be my type?"

"I can't tell. I can only feel."

"Then that's the chance I'm willing to take. Is it anyone's business but mine what the odds are?"

Well, was it? I had a sudden blessed sense of relief as I leaned back against the rock to enjoy the view. Hadn't the devil been squared?

.   .   .

The next morning I joined Gus at the edge of the Swimming Club pool. We were both in bathing suits, but that didn't mean that Gus would do anything so drastic as go swimming. He would sometimes sit an entire morning without more than wiggling a toe in the water.

"Are you going to marry him?"

"The funny thing is that I might. Why did you pick him, Gus? He's not all that rich."

"He's plenty rich enough. He's got all you could possibly need. The world will provide the rest for a beautiful Mrs. Askew. You can't imagine what your life will be like."

"But isn't it just what I *can* imagine?"

"You've had the perfect training for wealth, which is very rare. You know all the things not to do. You will have carte blanche in houses, in decoration, in parties. You can take any line you choose. You can be political, artistic, theatrical, socialist, communist, royalist — it is up to you."

"You think Jonathan will have nothing to say about any of that?"

"Nothing you can't control."

"And yet it's all happening because I feel sorry for him!"

"That's an excellent beginning."

"Can you honestly believe, Gus, that what I feel for Jonathan is enough for a happy marriage?"

"It's more than many wives start with."

"But love, Gus! Love!"

"I'm sorry, sweetheart. I don't regard you as the loving type."

"Bastard!"

"On the contrary, it's a high compliment. From me."

"And it doesn't matter that I loathe his old 'mater,' as he calls her?"

"Doesn't everyone?"

"What remains then to be done?"

"To announce it! Announce it from here. I'll take care of the press."

"Hadn't I better talk to my parents?"

"By all means. But break it to them gently. They might die of joy."

. . .

Jonathan kissed me, very solemnly and very nicely, that afternoon when I accepted him. It was our first kiss, and I began to think everything was going to be all right. And then, of course, bing, bang, we were inundated by the publicity that followed Gus's announcement. It seemed as if the eyes of the whole country were directed on Mount Desert Island in one long, riveting stare. And I had a sense of a nasty chuckling in the clouds above.

Oddly enough, it did not make much difference in the routine in our days. Jonathan and I continued our daily walks, although I had to use all my knowledge of the island to slip away to trails where we were sure not to be followed by a reporter. Our first "public" appearance was two weeks after the announcement at the Saturday night dance at the club. It was a crowded event, because it was the weekend of an Atlantic race, and a large number of yachts and sailboats had congregated in Bar Harbor and Northeast. Many young men, not in evening clothes, bronzed from the sea, lent the party the noisy erogenous atmosphere of the fleet being in.

Someone leaned down over my chair and murmured in my ear.

"What's all this nonsense about your being engaged, sweetheart? Couldn't you wait till I came home from sea?"

It was Chessy Bogart, and standing behind him was the handsomest man I had ever seen.

"This is my friend Chip Benedict. He would like very much to dance with the future Mrs. Askew! Help me, Ally. He bet me a hundred bucks I didn't know you!"

"Will you split it with me?" I asked, still staring at his friend.

"Won't Askew give you pin money till the knot's tied?"

His friend was almost too blond. He might have been the hero of a film of propaganda for Nazi youth. The yellow-white hair parted to one side rose high over his scalp; it was soft and smoothly waved. His skin was very white, the type that reddens and never tans; he had thick muscles, no fat; large hands like Michelangelo's David's; a long face to top off his six feet; a Roman nose; a square chin. And his eyes were light blue, with a fixed stare. He wore white duck trousers and a red blazer, and he conveyed a sense of being afraid of inadvertently ripping them simply from an awareness that the limbs beneath the integument moved with so destructive a force. Chessy introduced us, and I rose.

The blond god and I danced, and I still said nothing.

"What are you thinking about?" he demanded. "Your fiancé? Does he mind your dancing with other men?"

"I was just thinking that I wished I were dead." My tone, however, was quite matter-of-fact. "Isn't that an odd thing to be thinking on the dance floor?"

"It's not much of a compliment to me."

"Isn't it?"

Over his shoulder I could already see Jonathan hurrying to cut in.

4

⋙⋙⋙

CHIP

CHIP BENEDICT had known from boyhood that he could always fool people. Why not? He had every advantage in that game. He was the only son of Mr. and Mrs. Elihu Benedict of Benedict, Connecticut, whose social sway over the eponymous town that manufactured their glassware was signalized, in nineteenth-century style, by the Colonial mansion on top of the residential hill between the railroad depot and the glassworks. Chip was accustomed to the admiring glances of the populace and the less feigned adoration of the loyal household servants (all parolees from the state prison). Yet he never lost an awareness that his blue eyes and golden hair, his air of brightness and the invitation of friendship that it seemed to throw off, formed a mask. And had the mask been torn away, the plaudits might have been silenced, to be succeeded by what? By jeers or even a hail of pebblestones? Not inevitably. That one was a fraud did not have to mean that one was vicious. Perhaps one had to be a fraud. Why? Did there have to be an answer?

Daddy would certainly go straight to heaven, if there was one. Nobody could be so benign, so gently ironic, so always in the right, and not be of the elect. And Mummie, too; though she was tense and easily vexed, Daddy could surely save her. And Chip's younger sisters, what were they but cherubim and seraphim? That was, if God really wanted three such sillies. But Chip was the pauper in Mark Twain's tale; he was dressed like a prince and treated like a prince, and it might be very dangerous to be found out. Suspicion lurked and sometimes boldly showed itself, as on the night when Mummie had thrown open his bedroom door and asked him, in an odd combination of challenge and trepidation, if he was "playing with himself." He hadn't been. That time. The chauffeur's boy did, he knew; also two friends at school; but even if they were damned for it, their punishment wouldn't hurt as much as his. Why? They weren't Chip Benedict.

He had always to be sure not to disappoint Daddy, whose patient demeanor and mild twinkle were supposed to conceal the tenderest of sensibilities. And he had to remember that a lifetime of filial devotion could never repay Mummie for her limitless capacity for caring. And he must set an example for the kid sisters and be democratic with the boys in the Benedict public school and, when he went off to the private academy in Massachusetts that Mummie's wonderful old father headed, he would have to be sure not to learn snobbish ways. Beyond that, beyond even Yale — far away, but the time would come; it always did — he would have to grow up and help Daddy with the company, though this was never said, because he had to pretend that he was perfectly free to be anything he wanted, except (with a chuckle) a bootlegger.

And all the while scarlet thoughts, putrid fantasies, and no love. No real love for anyone, except perhaps for Nanny, now remorselessly relegated to the sisters (boys weren't supposed to need nannies) and maybe just a little for Grandpa Berwind, who came to visit in Maine summers. Why were they always prating about love? Did they suspect one hadn't any in one's heart? Did they really have so much themselves? Sometimes he imagined that God cared only about "seeming," that this might be Chip's real function, that so long as he managed to look a part, he might be the part, that the appearance of worship, or at least of a decorous submission, was all the dusky deity required.

Chip was treated differently from his sisters by Daddy — he was taken on fishing trips and even on business excursions when Elihu Benedict visited other glassworks — but these privileges were burdened with the sense of how much more would be expected of an only son than of a mere gaggle of younger daughters. Elihu was a kind and patient father, and he knew how to listen to his children, but it struck Chip that he was always listening *for* something; that he was always in the process of tapping gently but firmly upon one's surface in the perennial hope, amounting by no means to a conviction, that he would ultimately find a hollow into which some of the paternal genius might be profitably poured.

This feeling was particularly vivid one June evening in Chip's fifteenth year when he and his father were sitting alone by the campfire in front of their cabin in the Canadian woods, looking out over the quiet moonlit lake. Elihu had twice used the expression "people like us," and his son was emboldened by the unaccustomed intimacy of their situation to ask "Daddy, what are people like us?"

"I suppose it's a foolish expression, really. What I think I mean is people who have been born with certain privileges and are therefore bound to contribute more than the average to their fellow men."

"But I don't contribute anything."

"Give yourself time, for Pete's sake! You're only a boy."

Chip considered this. "I suppose you and Mummie contribute all kinds of things."

"Well, we could always do more, that's for sure. But we make a stab at it."

"By having all those convicts in the house?"

Elihu glanced at him. Was he making sure that Chip was serious? "We try to give them a chance. Most people refuse to employ them. But if they can say they've worked for the Benedicts and produce a good reference, it helps. Do they worry you, Chip? I always check to be sure they're not violent types."

"No, no, it's not that at all. I wouldn't dream of being afraid of them. It's just that I . . . well . . . maybe I envy them a little."

It had been risky, and for a couple of minutes his father said nothing. But when he spoke, his tone was mild enough. "I guess I don't see why you should envy them, Chip."

"Because no one expects anything of them!" Chip was suddenly excited by his own nerve. "Because anything they do that's at all good is greeted with wild applause."

"My boy, do you think we expect too much of *you*?"

"Oh, no, sir, not really, no."

But now he was in for it. Elihu could not let this pass. Kindly, slowly, patiently, he proceeded to review his and Matilda's satisfaction with their son. It was evident that he had detected a leak in Chip's moral plumbing, and there would be no more fishing that night, no sleeping even, until it had been carefully soldered. And there was never any way to answer the question that now began to haunt the recesses of the boy's mind: Would this gaunt, strong man have loved his son had he really known him? He loved a fantasy — that was the gist of it.

With Matilda it was different. She loved Chip, yes, but she gave every sign of suspecting that her love *was* a fantasy. She might still have loved him even had this been proven, but it would have been at a heavy cost to her own self-esteem. She seemed to suffer from agonies of apprehension, as shown on that night when she had barged into his bedroom. What made her so suspicious? Why was she, devoted partner of her husband in the business of re-creating the moral world in a Benedict image, so afraid of cracks in the fortifications and traitors in the very bosom of the family? Sometimes Chip's heart went out to her; he fancied that he was the only person who comprehended the nagging anxiety lurking in the bland beam of those executive eyes. But if his mother secretly appreciated his sympathy, she never dared to betray it. It would have been to admit there was something to worry about. And again, also in that same summer of his fifteenth year, a horrible thing happened.

Elihu Benedict had purchased a small island near their summer home in Camden, Maine, on which he proposed to build a summer camp as a retreat from the intensifying social pace of the summer community. He took his wife and four children to inspect it one beautiful July morning; they brought a picnic hamper, and Elihu drove the motor launch himself. After the family had inspected their new domain, they gathered on a large flat rock by the water to eat their lunch. Flossie, the oldest of the girls, suggested that they should swim first, but Elaine and Margaret shouted at once that they had no bathing suits. It had been thought that the ocean would be too cold.

"It's no problem," their father observed. "Chip and I will go around that little point, and you girls can bathe here."

Matilda now demonstrated an unexpected freedom from convention. "How perfectly foolish, my dear. Why should we be so artificial? We're all one family. I can't imagine why we should be ashamed of the bodies the good Lord gave us. Let us all go in the water together right off this fine rock. And anyway, it's the only place on the island where you can get into the sea without walking on sharp stones."

The girls hooted with excitement at the prospect of such an adventure and started to peel off their clothes. Chip felt a cold band of terror tighten around his heart. It was not the prospect of seeing their pink backsides and boyish nipples that concerned him. He had peeked at these before. Nor was it even the vision of his father's nudity; he had seen those long thin limbs, that bony behind and gray pubic hair on fishing trips. But his mother! Could eyes abide it?

"I don't feel like swimming. I think I'll take a walk around the island."

"But you've seen it all, darling," his mother protested. "And the water looks so lovely. Don't tell me you mind our going in together this way. Isn't it the most natural thing in the world?"

The dreadful little girls immediately sized up the situation. They started to jump up and down, crying out that Chip was a sissy who was afraid to be seen naked.

"Be quiet, girls!" their mother chided them. She was already unbuttoning her blouse. But when she turned to Chip, he saw the concern in her eyes. She had at once recognized his shame and repulsion and was visibly upset. It was something bad in her son, something dangerous, something that had to be coped with at once.

"Look at me, Chip. I'm as bony and skinny as an old nag, but I'm healthy, thank God, and that's what counts."

At this she unhooked her brassiere, and Chip was aghast at the sudden glimpse of her breasts, as long and skinny and dangling as a pair of old stockings. Suppressing a cry of anguish only by slapping a hand over his mouth, he turned to rush away and collided with his father, who grabbed him.

"Chip, it's only natural!" he heard his mother wail.

"It's not! It's unholy!" he shrieked, struggling in his father's grasp. "It's wicked and horrible!" And he bit his father's hand so savagely that the latter released his hold with a cry of pain, and Chip bounded away into the woods.

An hour later, lunchless and hungry, he joined his family, silently waiting in the launch. Not a word was said by anyone on the trip back to Camden, but Chip knew that his sisters exulted at his meteoric fall from parental grace.

His conduct had been too shocking for further discussion, but his father the next day asked him very gently whether he would be willing to have a little chat with their summer doctor, a friendly old codger much admired by the Camden summer folk. Chip, knowing now that he might as well be hanged for a sheep, curtly refused. But to his relief and astonishment, there were no repercussions. His father, at least, knew when to lay off. And apparently he had been able to control his spouse.

In August the family went, as usual, to France and Italy, where Mr. Benedict visited and consulted with the principal glass manufacturers of those countries. That summer they stayed with one who had a château near Albi, and Matilda, who was a devoted sightseer, but who liked to see her monuments "in use," even if it happened to be a Roman Catholic use, took Chip to a service at the great fortress cathedral where the crusade against the Albigenses had been preached. She did not believe that a service in Latin could corrupt a youth, and besides, was not the choir famed for its beautiful singing?

Chip, seated with his mother beneath the marble pulpit, agreed that the choir, unseen behind the vast screen, was indeed fine, but when the Dies Irae was chanted, he could think only of all those men, women and children savagely butchered for believing that the world had been created by the devil. Who else would have made it? Looking about, he noted grimly that everything in the church celebrated the wrath and merciless-ness of the avenging deity. The pulpit itself was supported by two marble slaves whose writhing torsos put him in mind of the parolee servants at home. The latter, it was true, bore their burdens with happy smiles, but might not their bodies under white coats and aprons be as strained as those of the slaves? The choir screen behind which the angelic voices rang out was covered by a vast mural showing in gorgeous detail the suffer-ings of the losers at the Day of Judgment. The whole cathedral sang the glory of a power that was not any truer than the heresy that it had so cruelly suppressed; simply mightier. Chip's father had seen the trenches during the Great War on a Red Cross mission, and he had told Chip that *that* was hell. And yet Elihu insisted, as did Matilda, that the words in the creed "He descended into hell" referred to a limbo where there were no tormented souls. Huh!

"Do you think it hurt horribly to be burned alive?" He put the question suddenly to his mother as they walked after the service to where the car was waiting. "Or do you suppose the smoke asphyxiated you before it got too bad?"

"Good heavens, is that what you were thinking about during that lovely singing?"

He came as near as he ever had to snapping at her. The cathedral had made him almost desperate. "Isn't it what your religion is all about?"

"*My* religion, child? What are you talking about? I guess it's time, after all, that you went to boarding school. Grandpa will teach you that religion is love!"

5

CHIP

THEY HAD DELAYED sending him to Saint Luke's because they feared, even under the beneficent supervision of Grandpa Berwind, the contamination of boarding school. Yet they recognized that to have attended one would be almost a social necessity at Yale, and they figured that two years might be enough.

Chip was relieved to get away. He could breathe at Saint Luke's, away from Benedict and Benedicts, even though the other boys complained constantly of the restrictions. To him the long oblong buildings of gray limestone that formed a square around the dark Gothic chapel were relieved of the dreariness that others ascribed to them by the way they blended into the gray autumnal woods that stretched down a low incline to the sluggish river and the deserted boathouse and dock. Chip liked to walk along the bank alone of a Sunday afternoon, the silence interrupted only by cawing crows or the rush of a startled duck or the deep throb of the chapel bells, his heart moved, not unpleasantly, with a vague melancholy.

Indeed, had his grandfather not been headmaster, the two years at Saint Luke's might have been almost unalloyed pleasure. But there was never any getting away from this relationship or the obligations that it entailed. It was not that Mr. B, as Grandpa Berwind was addressed by all, singled him out for favoritism. Far from it. In public, in class, "Benedict, C." was treated exactly like any other boy of the three hundred, if not more gruffly. But there were also the private sessions, once a month, in the headmaster's study, where Chip was subject to the scrutinizing stare and careful interrogation of the grave little man whose undemonstrative but still felt love for his only grandson added uncomfortably to all that seemed expected of the boy.

"Have you heard from your dear mother? And your father? I trust they are well. They do not write so often now, knowing that you are here to supply me with their news."

So the sessions always started, and the personal note was then dismissed, reserved for summer vacations in Maine, when Mr. B, transformed into a chuckling grandpa, oddly attired in white flannels and a loud blazer, adored by younger sisters, would fill the Benedict household with bustling activity and merriment. For all his seventy-five years and plump, diminutive figure, he would still take his turn at the tiller in the catboat, light a fire out of nothing at a picnic and lead the family and friends in a singsong on Saturday nights. But at school, in chapel, in the pulpit, swaying to and fro to emphasize his moral points, the rich, melodious voice pouring forth his silver sentences, those gray eyes flashing in awesome sternness, he was a saint, an angel, God even. But why did Chip have to be the only boy with God for a grandfather?

Mr. B seemed almost aware of this at times, sitting in the big study with the pictures of crews and the prints of Roman monuments, with Chip on the other side of the desk-table, all subdued attention.

"It is not easy to be a boy, Charles. You will think of my own youth as something very far in the past, lost no doubt in the mists of antiquity, and yet it seems to me like yesterday. I did not, like your dear father, have the temptations of wealth to cope with. I was a poor boy in Worcester who had to help my father in his hardware store. Still, there were Saturdays, and I sometimes fell in with the bad boys of the town. But I always bore in mind what our good pastor, who took it on himself to put me through the theological seminary, used to say: 'When you marry, Peter, you will be a happy man if you bring a clean body to a pure woman.'"

Chip could not imagine sex with a pure woman. He had a momentary vision of his grandfather and the grandmother whom he had never known reaching gingerly for each other in a discreetly darkened chamber. Those thoughts again! But there was never the smallest doubt in his mind that Mr. B was right and that the boys who insisted in locker room sessions that a virgin husband would prove a sad hacker on the wedding night were wrong, or at least irrelevant. The world, indeed, was made up of a crude majority that was always wrong and a handful of saints. But the saints were saved.

Mr. B had not long been headmaster. The bulk of his lengthy tenure at the school had been as chaplain, and he had been elevated to the first position only upon the unexpected demise of his predecessor and then only as a temporary appointment, pending the selection of a permanent principal. But as the trustees had had difficulty in agreeing on a candidate, and as it was the consensus of the faculty and parents that Mr. B was doing a great job, the modest little gentleman of seventy was at last drafted for the supreme post. He could hardly refuse; the school had been his life. His wife had died forty years earlier, giving birth to their only child, Chip's mother, whose husband was the school's board chairman. So Mr. B had bowed his head and accepted the call and had then proceeded to administer his institution with a vigor and dignity that astonished the New England academic community. He seemed, single-handedly, to rebut the accent on youth of the nineteen thirties.

In the great depression every premise had seemed to fail. The words of the creed and of the commandments cracked on the marble wall. People began to ask if Saint Luke's and all the other preparatory schools were not anachronisms. But Mr. B was a beacon on a stormy night at sea. His light may have flickered in the tempest, but it was always visible. He preached from the pulpit of the school chapel and from others in schools throughout New England that the Sermon on the Mount was the same infallible guide it had always been, reminding boys that if their Father's house did not contain many mansions, He would have told them. Chip listened, rapt, to the lilting, hypnotic tone of the great sermons.

" 'Ask and ye shall receive!' Our Lord did not say, 'Ask and maybe ye shall receive.' He did not even say, 'Ask and very probably ye shall receive.' No, there it is, boys, plain and literal: 'Ask and ye *shall* receive.' But you must know what to ask for. Our Lord was not concerned with baubles. He was not promising tickets on the fifty-yard line to the Harvard-Yale game or a new motorcar on graduation. Certainly not. But if you want the big things, boys, if you want the crown jewels of life, if you want consolation when you lose a loved one, or hope when you are down, or if, God forbid, you ever find yourselves in the trenches and yearn for courage, then, boys, ask and ye *shall* receive!"

Chip did not make the error, because his parents and Mr. B were both on the side of the angels, of putting them in the same boat. He remembered overhearing one of his father's sisters saying to another that their brother had been a "great match" for the daughter of a poor schoolteacher. Not that he thought for a minute that either of his parents would have agreed with so vulgar an assessment. On the contrary, his father, who had been a senior monitor of Saint Luke's in his own sixth-form year, had always professed not only to have married "far above himself," but to have been bold indeed in taking from poor Mr. B the young woman who had constituted his entire family. But there was nonetheless detectable to Chip the faintest hint of amiable condescension in the way his tall, spare, bony, tweedy father greeted the clerical pedagogue. Elihu Benedict was like a warrior bound for the battlefield who kneels for the priestly blessing in full awareness that the church must depend on his sword. What was it but the ancient division between church and state, emperor and pope, except that Chip's father was not waiting in the snow outside Canossa and Mr. B hurled no anathemas?

Sometimes, too, when Chip, on his way to class or chapel, would spot across the campus the long, lanky figure of his plain but imposing mother, smiling graciously at Academe as she moved in easy strides beside the briskly stepping, diminutive figure of her venerable parent, the boy would reflect that even the women from the great outside managerial world were inclined to feel protective about the priests of the supposedly almighty.

But it was not up to him, Chip, to envelop himself in the

mantle of that immune adult region until he should take his place there. Saint Luke's now stretched to the horizon, encompassing all his vision. He thought that he loved his grandfather, if what he felt was indeed love, and he thought that his love was returned, but what good was that if it was based on fraud? Mr. B did not know Chip; he did not know the pollution and callousness of his grandson's mind. If he did, those gray, luminous eyes would fill first with incredulity, then with horror. The hands would be raised in surprise and shock, and Chip would depart into weeping and gnashing of teeth.

He got on well enough with his classmates. His blond good looks, his facility in athletics, his quiet amiability, ensured that. But his tendency to solitude aroused some antagonism in those who saw in the smallest aloofness from the crowd a note of criticism, even of snobbishness. Why did he spend so much time in the library reading the adventure stories of Dumas and S. J. Weyman? Why did he go on bird walks alone on Sunday afternoons? Had he not been known to sit by himself in the empty chapel listening to Mr. Tobin, the music master, practicing fugues on the organ? Did not even Mr. B, whose faith nobody doubted, imply that religion "took" only when two or three were gathered together in "thy name"? God and Christ had no use for loners, for the "moony"; they favored the playing fields. And, anyway, religion was for the old, the dying. The boys, like Chip's own parents, seemed to believe that the spiritual side of Saint Luke's, and even Mr. B himself, belonged to the category of elegant, precious things that it was the privilege of private school patrons to acquire and that constituted, indeed, a kind of badge of American upper-classness, but that could never be considered in quite the same category as the realities of the marketplace.

Yes, Chip saw this. And he heard enough of what was said in the locker rooms and after lights in the dormitory to know that the heated luxury of private fantasies that seemed at times about to burst the very walls of his head apart was not peculiar to him. Yet he still suspected that his visions were filthier, his Venusberg more obscene. It was true that Mr. B in sacred studies had scoffed at the Calvinist idea that a man could be saved or damned at birth. Mr. B was saved; there was no question about that; but did those who were saved necessarily know those who were not?

The headmaster himself took note of his grandson's escapes to solitude with a gentle but definite concern.

"You read many novels, Charles," he observed at one of their sessions. "Are you seeking something in fiction? Or do you simply like a good yarn?"

"I think I like, sir, to be taken out of myself for a bit."

"Well, that's understandable. A school is so full of ringing bells and barking masters that a boy must wish to get away from time to time. But stories can be an evasion. They can even be a kind of drug. I don't suggest that in your case they are. I simply put the idea on the table."

"Mr. Terhune, in English class last week, described Saint Luke as our first novelist. He said he was the author of the Acts as well as of his own Gospel."

Mr. B seemed to weigh this. "That is believed by many scholars. The style is similar and certainly very beautiful. But I trust Mr. Terhune did not suggest that Saint Luke *invented* his Gospel."

"Oh, no, sir! He said it was more like an historical novel."

"Oh, I see."

Chip had had a vague notion that if he could find a novel

in the New Testament, it might bring Gospels into a relation with the fiction that he was reading and that this relation might somehow be used to bridge the gap between his grandfather's pure visions and the boys in the locker room. But now he saw that Mr. B was not going to allow this. There was no bridging that gap. It yawned like outer space between the sun and bipeds on the earth's surface.

And then there occurred a violent episode that emphasized even more strongly the separate worlds in which he and his grandfather were destined to move. Chip was too strong and agile to have much trouble with boys who liked to implement even a passing hostility with their fists, and on the rare occasions when he had been so challenged he had acquitted himself in a manner that did not invite others. Indeed, it was felt by some that he did too well. The moment he realized that the wrong was on the other side, he gave in to a sudden eruption of violent rage that had a kind of joy to it. On one occasion he even had to be pulled off his opponent by the alarmed spectators. But in the Stratton affair he was not challenged, personally. He was a volunteer.

It happened in the gymnasium shower room. Stratton, a shy, inhibited boy who too obviously destested public nudity, was being made cruel fun of by a rowdy group of his formmates, who pretended to see in him a naked female intruding on the scene of their ablutions. When the intensity of his embarrassment caused him to have an erection, which he sought desperately to cover, his towel was snatched away, and he was pelted with bars of soap. At this point Chip intervened. By the end of the scuffle one boy, whose head Chip had bashed against the tile wall of the shower room, had to be taken to the infirmary, and Chip that evening found himself alone with his grandfather in the latter's study.

"I am sure you will be relieved to hear, Charles, that Johnson has not had a concussion. Will you tell me, please, how this unseemly brawl began?"

"They were being mean to Stratton, sir. I thought I'd better help him."

"How were they being mean to Stratton?"

"I'm afraid I can't tell you, sir."

"I see." How those pale gray eyes stared! Was it conceivable that Mr. B could visualize such things? No, it was not conceivable. "Why, Charles, did you feel that you had to help him?"

"They were being very bad, sir."

"But is it your function to correct badness? Shouldn't you have called a prefect or master?"

"But that would have been snitching!"

"Sometimes it may be manly to snitch."

"Anyway, sir, there wasn't time."

After a considerable silence Mr. B continued gravely, "Why is it, my boy, that you feel compelled to correct so violently the badness in others?"

"I don't know, sir."

"Is it possible, do you suppose, that you may be seeking to correct some badness in yourself?"

"I don't know, sir," Chip repeated, miserably.

Mr. B's sigh seemed to indicate that he gave it up. "Well, remember, please, that you are strong. Think, before you raise your hand to another, that you may hurt him sorely. I do not wish, Charles, to hear of another incident like this."

When the great west window in the chapel, showing the warrior saints in all their fiery glory, Saint Joan, Saint George, Saint Louis, and the fighting kings, David, Joshua, Saul, was dedicated to the memory of the twenty Saint Luke's boys who had perished in the Great War, Mr. B, who had shared their hell as an army chaplain, was particularly eloquent.

"It is not fashionable today to say there is a right or a wrong side in war, much less to claim that God Himself ever chooses sides. But I impenitently believe that God *was* with the Allies in 1917. It was my privilege to have been at the front with our boys and I knew He was with us! It was not that grave wrongs had not been perpetrated by the Allied Nations in dealing with their empires and with other countries. But when our troops went over the top to stem the advance of German aggression, *then*, at that point anyway, boys, God was with us! You couldn't have been there, you couldn't have seen what they did and how they died, without feeling it! Oh, true, God never forgot the Germans, and He loves them, too — every bit as much as He loves us — but He didn't want them to win!"

At that moment Chip wished that he could have been one of those boys who had fought and died in France. So brave an ending might have redeemed him. For surely among the millions who had perished in the mire of the trenches there must have been some who had burned with his lusts: lust for naked girls, lust for naked boys, lust for self; and afflicted with his doubts: doubts of Mummie, doubts of Daddy, doubts of God. He had no doubts of Mr. B, but wasn't Mr. B an innocent? What did he know of hell?

6

><><><

CHIP

CHIP HAD an initial distrust of the boys from New York City, who made up almost half his class, but it was a feeling that he could relax in favor of any individual who proved to be friendly. He had been brought up not to accept the superior airs of the big city; his parents had always emphasized that to hail from Benedict was every bit as good as being one of the teeming millions of Manhattan, if not better. Nor was this simply a question of being a bulky frog in an exiguous puddle. It was a question of living in a fine, clean, God-fearing town, surrounded by a beautiful countryside and blessed with breathable air, as opposed to a gray metropolis reeking with false pride and falser values. And, anyway, the Benedicts could call themselves New Yorkers, if it came to that; the company maintained a floor in a hotel on Madison Avenue where they could stay whenever they wished.

But New Yorkers had a horrid way of making people feel

like hicks; Chester "Chessy" Bogart was a perfect example of this. He came from undistinguished origins — he was a scholarship boy — and although an adequate athlete on the rare occasions when he chose to be, he was short, with a square bulldog countenance, thick black hair and malicious, grinning dark eyes. Yet his self-confidence was supreme; he made fun of everybody and fought like a tiger when his victims tried to beat him up. He sneered at all the accepted school values, used filthy language and earned the grudging respect of some of his classmates by the graphic way in which he described how he had "had" two girls at a summer camp when he was only fourteen.

His mocking overture of friendship to Chip was certainly unconventional: "I guess you're the kind of guy my old man sent me here to meet. Handsome, wealthy and aristocratic!"

Chip was mildly shocked. He had been reared to believe that it was vulgar to refer to people's money. And if you did, you said they were "rolling," never "wealthy."

"Why is Benedict any more aristocratic than Bogart?" he demanded.

"It isn't. But God knows what we were before we were Bogarts. And now brace yourself, Tarzan. My old man's a dentist. And a dentist in Brooklyn, too! I guess the trustees like to use some of their scholarship pennies to give this joint a flavor of democracy. Not too much, of course. Just the right amount."

Chip did not think that his parents would take to Chessy, but hadn't they sent him to Saint Luke's to meet "different sorts of boys"? He decided to let Chessy join him on weekend bird walks, though the latter seemed to care very little for birds. He did care, however, about sex, and he talked of it with an openness that Chip found exciting. So long as he did not have to respond — and Chessy was perfectly willing to do all the talking — he thought it might be less wicked. Chessy was particularly vivid about the monastic aspects of school life.

"What sense does it make to lock us up here, months at a time, with no woman under forty allowed to set foot on campus, except some guy's sappy kid sister for Sunday lunch? I ask you, Tarzan, have you ever seen such a collection of bilious crones as our cleaning women? They say your grandfather inspects each candidate for the job. That old boy must have a depth of concupiscence to spot so precisely the attributes in a female that would make the most sex-starved boy vomit!"

"I wish you'd leave my grandfather out of it," Chip retorted. "And I wish you wouldn't call me Tarzan."

"It's only a pet name. And only in private. I like you, Benedict. You're naïve, but you're straight. Which not many guys in this snob academy are."

Chip was touched in spite of himself. "I like you, too, Chessy."

"Good. Maybe we'll make something of it. What else do they offer us here?"

"I don't think I follow you."

"Oh, yes, you do, Tarzan. Yes, you do! You'll be ready for a chimpanzee before the winter's out. Hell, your grandfather can rumble on till the cows come home about 'doing dirty things,' but if he doesn't let somebody out of this place from time to time, or let somebody in, he can take the consequences. He was young himself once. He ought to know."

Chip did not respond to this, and the following weekend he arranged to be too busy in the gym for their walk. Yet he was appalled to find his imagination aflame with the idea of "doing dirty things" with Chessy. At times the erotic images that filled his mind would be so vivid as to make concentration in the classroom impossible, and on one occasion he failed to respond to a master until the latter had thrice called his name.

"Come, Benedict, daydreams, daydreams! The Christmas holidays with all your little girl friends will come around soon enough!"

The class tittered, but Chessy's smile was a leer.

And then one night Chessy slipped into his cubicle and tried to get into his bed.

"Get out of here!" Chip whispered fiercely and swung at him. Chessy dodged, snickered and returned to his own cubicle.

After this Chip withdrew from all close association with his erstwhile friend. They greeted each other when they passed in the corridors, and they sometimes walked in company from the chapel to the schoolhouse, but Chip kept the conversations brief and impersonal and avoided any reference to the cubicle episode. Chessy, though, seemed to divine that such reticence must mark a major temptation. He would sneak up behind Chip and hiss in his ear: "You know you want it just as much as I do, Tarzan. Why hold out?"

The riveting, humiliating idea that his weakness had been uncovered, that for all his outer fortitude it was apparent to Chessy that he yearned for another visit to his cubicle, that "Tarzan" was a fraud and a phony who feverishly pined to do everything Chessy wanted to do, ultimately exhausted him. Nothing at last seemed worth the tension in which he lived. The next time Chessy came to his cubicle, he allowed him to slip into his bed.

. . .

The peculiar horror of the next weeks was that Chip could not seem to focus steadily for more than a few minutes at a time on what had happened, with the result that the shock of his guilt was a constantly repeated blow. He would be walking in the morning to chapel, or returning from the gymnasium against a reddening sky, or ascending the broad varnished stairway to the dormitory to don the stiff collar and tie required for supper, and he would feel a gasp of hope, as if, sinking in the ocean, he had just grasped the spar of safety, or, awakening from a nightmare, he had felt the blessed damp beads of relief on his brow, only to have the spar collapse, the illusion vanish, and know that he was doomed. The present was hopelessly spoiled, and also the future, even the years at Yale that his father had always assured him should be the happiest of his life.

Chessy was astonished at the violence of his friend's reaction. When Chip told him, the morning after the episode in the cubicle, that they must no longer be friends, he protested vigorously, running after Chip's retreating figure and grabbing him by the arm.

"Look, don't be an ass. It didn't mean anything. It's just till we get home and can see girls. Isn't it better than masturbating?"

Chip looked at him in horror. "I don't want to talk about it. I'm going to treat it as if it never happened. Maybe it didn't. Maybe it really didn't!"

"You mean we just dreamed it?"

"Yes!"

"You must be crazy!"

"It would kill my parents. If you ever breathe a word of it, I'll swear you're a liar!"

Chessy whistled. "Breathe a word of it? Do you think I'm proud of it?"

"It was your idea."

"And I had a ready pupil! Boy, how ready!"

Chip left him without another word. Chessy was like one of those little devils in the choir screen at Albi whose job it was to prod the damned with pitchforks. It was not his fault; it was his function. Chessy at length accepted the situation with a shrug and found his way to more hospitable cubicles.

Chip now had no close friends, but he found some relief in his semi-isolation. Without intimates he had no spies; without spies he could, in his own way, relax and learn to live with the grim but silent companion of a guilt that he knew now would never leave him.

Listening to his grandfather's sermons, watching the sunlight through clouds making first jewels and then dark blobs of the scarlet and green robes and turbans in the great west window, he would find himself lulled into a kind of torpor by the mellifluous phrases.

"There are those today, boys, who will tell you that a man is not truly the master of his being. The thief, they will maintain, cannot help reaching his hand into another's pocket; the adulterer is the prey of his own lust; even the murderer is propelled helplessly towards his victim by a rage that overpowers him. Our leaning to sin is a compulsion, like alcoholism or drug addiction. But always remember this, boys. Those who argue thus seek to deprive you of your own free will, of your very soul! For without sin, how can there be virtue? Without the struggle, where is the reward? Any man can do anything that he wills to do. What is an alcoholic but one who has chosen to destroy his will? But if he has destroyed it, must he not once have had it to destroy?"

Towards the end of March a sluggish spring brought mud puddles to the campus, and a white sky made the bare branches of the elms seem like bones. The winter had been so long and cold that it seemed too late for leaves. The boys were bored, the masters irritable, the wait for spring had become interminable. And then the one thing that everybody hungered for occurred: a scandal.

It had long been recognized by the more experienced members of the faculty, and even imparted to some of the sixth-formers who acted as monitors with semidisciplinary powers over their juniors, that Mr. B had to be insulated from certain campus misdemeanors of which he took too somber a view. Mr. B was a saint, it was conceded, but saints were sometimes impracticable. Taking the name of the Lord in vain, for example, and smoking were practices so common in many of the families from which the boys came that expulsion on their account, or even suspension, might have made the school ridiculous to the New England academic world. Accordingly, it was tacitly understood by the disciplinarians at Saint Luke's that swearing or smoking would be punished without being reported to the headmaster. Any boy, it was felt, who uttered an oath in Mr. B's hearing, or took a puff in his presence, was too great a fool to be protected. And to some extent sexual offenses fell into this category. A master or monitor might learn to look the other way if he suspected activities that amounted only to masturbation. Sodomy and oral sex, however, were different matters. Yet there was no such uniformity among the faculty in this area as in that of swearing and smoking, and if a young idealistic master happened to bump into even the mildest form of Mr. B's "dirty things," the fat might be in the fire.

Unhappily for Chessy Bogart, just such a master was on duty in his dormitory when a boy was reported sick during the night. Hurrying to the cubicle of the afflicted student, young Mr. Boyd, a devout teacher of sacred studies, ill-guided by his pocket flashlight, entered the wrong cubicle and discovered Chessy in bed with another boy. It was only too evident even to his chaste vision what they were doing, and the next morning every boy at Saint Luke's knew that the two culprits had been summoned to Mr. B's office.

Chip, who as a fifth-former had his own study, went there during an hour's break between classes to avoid the gossip. He knew that at least a dozen other boys had been involved in the same activity in that dormitory, and he wanted to avoid the feverish speculation as to whether other "arrests" were likely to follow. He felt a sudden calmness and clearheadedness. Now that all the world was mad, it was perhaps time to be sane. He had a curious sense that the worst was behind him, that he had, to some extent anyway, been through his purgatory. He even suspected that there might be offered to him an unusual way to redeem himself. When the inevitable knock came to his door, he was ready for it. He even had a moment to reflect that his pulse was actually normal.

"Charles, are you there? May I come in?"

"Come in, sir."

Never before at school, except in his grandfather's own office, had he been addressed by the headmaster as "Charles." The door opened, and the little man, very grave but somehow not formidable, came in.

"Let me sit here by your desk, Charles." The voice was kinder than Chip had ever heard it. The deep, deep eyes were fixed on him. "I suppose you have heard what has happened. Two boys in your dormitory were caught by Mr. Boyd doing things with each other that no decent boy would do. I have no wish to be more specific. The boys will be expelled. That is not why I am here. I am here because one of them, Bogart, told me he had done nothing that others had not done. Oh, he was very bold about it! He declared that if I were logical, I should expel half the school. He even went so far, Charles, as to imply that he had done these things with you. Is that true? Have I been living in a fool's paradise?"

Chip felt almost lightheaded in the rush of his sudden assurance. "It is not true, sir."

There was not even a flicker of relief in that steadfast gaze. "I didn't believe him for a minute. It was obvious that the wretched boy thought that I would never expel my grandson and therefore would, morally, not be able to expel him. He was wrong, of course. I would have expelled a grandson who had done what he had done. But that need not detain us further. I want you to go to my house, Charles, and remain there until the two boys have left the campus."

"May I ask why, sir?"

"Because I am afraid you might be tempted to beat up Bogart. I can understand how a clean young man would react to so base an accusation."

Chip rose with his grandfather and walked with him to the shingle house behind the chapel that was the headmaster's home. And that was all.

There were no repercussions. It became known that Chessy had tried to implicate Chip, but his motive was obvious, and no one saw any reason to disbelieve the denial. Chip seemed to have been cleared by the very gods themselves.

There were times when he wondered whether a drama so inner had any reality. Each week that passed made his nocturnal experience with Chessy seem less true. And as for his lie, what good would the truth have done his partner in evil?

He had saved the peace of mind of his parents and possibly the very life of Mr. B. For he had felt at last the full weight of the old man's love.

There was a distinct change thereafter in the way Mr. B treated him. He never called him "Benedict" now, even in class, but always "Charles." It was as if Chip had passed through his period of probation, triumphantly, and could be recognized before the world as the staff on which the aging headmaster would confidently lean. Teachers and boys both seemed to sense this, and as Chip, gaining confidence, and even a kind of happiness, took in the new friendliness of the campus, he became popular. When at the end of the spring term he was elected head monitor for his second and final year, the gratified headmaster wrote his daughter that he could now sing his Nunc Dimittis.

But, for all his pride in his only grandson, Mr. B's health failed rapidly during Chip's final year at school. It was felt by the senior masters that the tall, blond youth who presided so serenely at assembly, who read the lesson in chapel with such admirable clarity and seriousness, who administered justice to the younger boys with such humanity and understanding, was a kind of gray eminence to the declining chief. It was to Chip that they came before presenting some delicate problem to Mr. B — the need to relax an outdated rule, the question of a new privilege sought by the boys and already granted by other schools — and Chip would explain the matter tactfully to his grandfather, who seemed quite willing now to relax his clung-to prejudices in favor of this new enlightenment.

The announcement of Mr. B's retirement was scheduled to be made at Chip's graduation, which would almost have made it an occasion of too much sentiment. At any rate it was not to be, for the old man had a stroke a month before Prize Day and lingered only a week, immobile and hardly able to articulate a word. As the end approached, Matilda Benedict relinquished the post by her father's bedside that she had occupied for three days and most of three nights and indicated to Chip that he should hold his grandfather in his arms for the last minutes.

Mr. B tried to touch Chip's head, perhaps to bless him, and then expired, whispering a name that was presumably his.

Afterwards, Chip's mother followed him into the next room, where she found him sobbing brokenly.

"But, my darling boy, you must try to remember that you made him happy!" she cried, almost in surprise at such violent emotion. "Happy as nobody else ever made him. Even my own mother!"

"And yet I did something for which he would have expelled me, had he known."

Neither Matilda nor her husband was ever able to extract from their son another syllable as to what this act had been. They concluded that it must have been a prank that his natural grief for the old man had blown out of all proportion.

7

CHIP

CHIP AT YALE began to believe that it might be possible to become the master of his own destiny. In the larger view of life that emancipation from boarding school opened to him, he was able at last to fit his parents into his background in such a way as not wholly to obliterate it. He even thought that he was learning to understand them, and with this prospect there came a kind of compassion. After all, they certainly meant well, at least according to their own lights, and if they were unable to see the beauty in all the pleasures of life, the beauty in what they called sin, it might be sage to remember that they, too, had had parents.

The great thing for him to accept, as he now saw it, was himself. His heart, his mind, his body, composed the donnée of his life. If these should not be adequate for the role of Charles Benedict as Elihu and Matilda conceived it, then that might simply be too bad. If people found him attractive, if people wanted to fuss over him, where was the harm? They were probably making a mistake, but that was their lookout. "Chip loves Chip; that is, 'I am I,'" he paraphrased Richard III. Was he good? Was he bad? He had first to find out *what* he was. Free will, if it existed at all, would have to wait.

He declined to confine himself to his classmates at Saint Luke's and those of its long-time athletic rival, Chelton; these were too cliquish for his taste; and he found the men from Hotchkiss, Andover and Choate more interested in the college as a whole than in the common denominator of their own social backgrounds. It was perfectly true, as he pointed out to his roommate, Lars Alversen, that their group was entirely prep school, but so long as it included the men who ran the *News*, the Political Union and the fraternities, might it not be an adequate cross section? Would it not be artificial to go about canvassing men from high schools or on scholarships? Or would it? Chip was not sure. He still worried about being a snob.

Lars cited the man across the hall who, in his determination to know every member of their class, had posted a list on his wall and checked off each name as he met its owner. Lars, leery of anything in excess, dubbed him an egregious ass.

"But don't those people get results?" Chip asked earnestly. "Can you really accomplish anything in life if you're not willing to make a bit of an ass of yourself?"

Yale, at any rate, kept filling his life with pleasant things. He was on the *News*; he sang with the Wiffenpoofs; he rode on the Berkeley crew; he joined Zeta Xi; and his grades promised him Phi Beta Kappa. He was majoring in English, which everybody seemed to agree was the best preparation for law, and he enjoyed Chauncey Tinker's emotional disquisitions on the British Romantic poets and Johnny Berdan's more trenchant analysis of Pope. His friends confidently predicted that in the spring of junior year he would be tapped for Bulldog, the most coveted of the senior societies.

There was one member of his class, however, whose company he never sought. Chessy Bogart and he nodded to each other when they passed on campus or met in class, but that was all. Chessy, since Saint Luke's, had turned into something of an intellectual as well as a dandy; he was an editor of the *Lit* and wore black suits that fitted him too tightly. He let it be known that a maternal uncle had made a shady fortune in the Argentine and, being childless, had conceived the fancy of taking the dentist's son under his wing. Chessy had boldness and wit; he knew how and when to make up to people. He never thrust himself on Chip, but neither did he avoid him. There was always a touch of derision, a bit of a sneer, in his casual greeting.

Chip did not resent this. There was even a small, bizarre relief at the reappearance of the little devil with the prodding pitchfork; once he knew where he was, he didn't have to keep looking around for him. It might almost be a game to see whether this imp, whose function it presumably was to know his victim's secrets, would discover what none of Chip's friends had found out: that he paid a monthly visit to an expensive private brothel maintained by a group of businessmen in a brownstone on West Seventieth Street in Manhattan.

Chip had been introduced to this "club" by an older first cousin, Peter Duvinock, a nephew of his father and the son of the critical aunt who had spoken so sneeringly of Chip's mother's "great match." Peter, who bitterly resented that Uncle Elihu had found him too slow for the family business and had placed him in the Wall Street bank that handled the Benedict trusts, had conceived of the idea of revenging himself by corrupting the family's Galahad. He had been taken aback, however, by Chip's ripeness for debauchery. His younger and richer cousin had promptly become a regular customer of the establishment and had demonstrated his gratitude by offering to help his initiator with the very stiff dues. Peter had to concede that his mother's beautiful nephew was a lot less naïve than he appeared and treated him thereafter with a noticeable increase of respect.

Chip was never tempted to boast of these visits, as would have so many of his contemporaries at Yale. He knew that his need of the girls with whom he had intercourse was a deeper thing in his psyche than in his classmates'. If he kept it from all but the equally damned Peter, might he not create a dichotomy in his life in which at least one aspect, the Yale aspect, the home aspect, would be saved? As the girls on West Seventieth Street were part of his Venusberg, he could dissociate them entirely from love. Love was the great hall in *Tannhäuser* and Elizabeth's prayer; he would never make the mistake of wronging that august presence with a scandalous song. Even when one of the girls at the bar of the brownstone, intrigued by a customer so much younger and more shapely than the broad-bellied brokers, would whisper in his ear that she was available without charge on her day off, he would respond only with a smile and a joke about union rules. He wanted to pay.

Not that it was always so easy to find the money. West Seventieth Street was indeed for the rich. Chip received a large allowance from his father, more than that of even the richest undergraduate from New York, but it was part of Elihu Benedict's parental policy to teach his son to handle obligations as well as privileges by hooking on to the bestowed income the duty to support some poor relations, of whom, as the family fortune was not old, there were a goodly number.

"You are at liberty to blow your income on fast cars and race-horses," Elihu would tell his son with that amiable smile which belied the implied suspicion. "But if you do, Cousin Cora and Cousin Louise may have to go into a state home. Who knows? Maybe they'd be just as happy there. But *I* am certainly not going to pay their mortgage."

Chip, of course, was fairly confident that his father would pay the old girls' mortgage if he defaulted, but it was unthinkable that he should ever do so. He found, however, that with a large income, regularly paid, it was not difficult to borrow, and he thrust into the future the ultimate solution of paying for both the demands of his body and the upkeep of his old maid cousins.

As junior year drew to a close, Chip began to think more about the future. He had lived so long and so intensely amid the emotional trauma of the present that he had tended to leave the future to itself. Besides, had it not been arranged for him? He knew that his father expected him to go to law school and then practice for a time in the Wall Street firm that represented the family company. Ultimately he would be president of the company, unless he chose to remain in the law, putting in a brother-in-law as president (if one of his sisters married the right man) and moving himself up to chairman of the board. Surely it behooved him now to consider whether this was what he really wanted. And if he were to discover that he did want it — as well he might — should he not do something first to convince himself that he was not simply drifting into it? That he was Chip as well as Charles Benedict?

Lars Alversen also had doubts as to his own future, and they had long talks at night over many beers in the study that connected their two bedrooms with windows open to the clamor of College Street below.

Lars was not a large and brawny Norseman, as his name might have suggested, but was rather on the diminutive side, with features of a remarkable delicacy and with long, soft, brown hair. His skin was very pale, his cheekbones high, his nose short yet Roman, and his eyes, the color of his hair, bespoke humor and sympathy. For all the fineness of his constitution, there was yet a distinct masculinity to the whole, as if some ancestral Norse warrior had not been left altogether in the past, but would reappear on occasion in his descendant's half-humorous aggressiveness and oddly braying laugh. Lars had considerable charm, of which he appeared to be half-ashamed. He alternated between the pose of being one of the crowd and that of holding himself above it and, finally, he would laugh at both attitudes.

The son of a rich, self-made Boston importer, he had gone to Andover, like many of the leaders of the class, and it was he who had been primarily responsible for detaching Chip from his Saint Luke's group and launching him into the heart of undergraduate affairs. It had taken Chip a little while to figure out his new friend's inconsistencies. Lars would pretend to be a feckless epicurean at afternoon tea at the Elizabethan Club and then stay up all night working at the *News*. It was generally recognized in their group that Chip and Lars's friendship was special.

"You know what they're saying, don't you?" Lars put it to Chip one night. "That you're going to be the last man tapped for Bulldog."

It was the custom at Yale for the members of the junior

class on Tap Day to assemble in the center of the Branford College quadrangle and wait silently until members of the six senior societies, approaching their candidates from behind, would strike them smartly on the shoulder and cry, "Go to your room!" The tappee, glancing around to be sure that he had been bid by a society that he wanted, unless, like most, he was delighted to be tapped for any of the six, would then take off on the double, followed closely by his tapper. In his room he presumably would be sworn into the secret rites of the society behind the windowless walls of which he would spend every Thursday and Saturday evening of his senior year, in the company of the fourteen other members. As Bulldog was the most esteemed of these societies, the last man it tapped was generally conceded to be the foremost man of the class.

"Don't you get sick of all the chatter?" Chip asked impatiently. "Who'll get what? Who'll turn down what, hoping for what? It's all deals and counterdeals. Anyway, I wouldn't want to be in any of them without you. Shall we hold out for Keys?"

"But your old man would expire if you turned down Bulldog!"

"Maybe that's a risk I'll have to take."

"Of course, it's easier for me, with a father who didn't even go to college. All I have to do is tell him that Keys is better than Bulldog, and he'll swallow it whole. And Mummie doesn't know if they're football teams or New Haven bars."

Chip had a vision of life as a kind of fluid pudding, with a mother as inane as Lars's. No trumpets, no Last Judgments. Peace. Death. Yet probably better than his own, after all. "But if you were born without burdens, you've been quick to acquire them," he observed dryly.

"It's true. I'm constantly uneasy that more isn't expected of me. I suppose I really envy you that look in your parents' eyes when they're fixed on you. Of course, one can see through all that misty love to the long line of hurdles they expect you to take."

"But I'm always aware of the anxiety behind their expectations," Chip returned, half-surprised at his own sudden illumination. "They don't really think I'll make it. They think I'm going to trip and break my stupid neck!"

"Which would really mean breaking theirs?"

"Ah, you see it too!" cried Chip, striking the arm of his chair. "It's true of their whole damn generation, teachers as well as parents. When Tinker slobbers about the drowning of Shelley, don't you know that he's keeping his good eye on you? He's always afraid you might think he's a ghastly ham and that Percy Bysshe was an ass to go sailing in a storm."

Lars warmed to the theme. "Because they're all on the defensive. They crawl with paranoia. We must heal the *News*, win the games, sing boola boola and enjoy the golden years. And we must laugh at it all, too, at the same time, because that's the true spirit of Yale. Not snotty detachment like Harvard. The true Eli must tread the delicate line between sophisticated spoofing and maudlin sentimentality. Why? Because anything else is chaos! I think I prefer my old man's attitude. He made his dough and wants to keep it. As long as I don't become a red, he's content. But he's scared shitless that I may become a red."

"If he only knew how safe he was!"

"Don't be vile. I have my liberal days."

"Yes, I noticed last summer that you looked rather pained when your father referred to President Roosevelt as a kike and a cripple."

"All right, Benedict, when did you last ring a tocsin?"

"You know I never have." Chip sighed bitterly. "But does that have to mean I never will? Suppose I make a stand about Bulldog? Suppose I write a column for the *News* attacking the whole shoddy system of senior societies?" And he suddenly knew that this was exactly what he had to do. Of course! It fitted his need like an inspiration.

Lars whistled; he always caught on when his friend was serious. "That *would* kill your old man. What would you say about the big six?"

"That they enshrine an archaic form of social snobbery."

"But it will be argued that they're based on merit, on campus accomplishment."

"Only accomplishment in the Yale tradition. And what is that but a list of the fetishes of the upper middle class? Oh, there's a lot of sentiment and phony idealism mixed up in it. Sure. But when the smoke clears, after Tap Day, you find you have ninety sheep in a safe green pasture and a big rocky field full of goats!"

Lars laughed in his strident way. "We might call it 'The Sheep and the Goats.'"

"You mean you'll write it with me?"

"Do you think I'll let you have all the glory?"

"We'll be spat upon! We'll be Shylocks."

"I wonder. There are an awful lot of goats. I have some of my old man's flare for the stock market. I think I'm going to buy Benedict!"

They stayed up the whole night writing the column, and it appeared in the *News* the following Monday. It created wide interest, but Chip was disappointed to find that very little of the anticipated saliva found its way to him. Lars was right.

The climate of the day was receptive to criticism, even of the most sacred calves. A good many letters came to the *News*, saying that this was an issue that should have been aired long ago, and there was evidence of considerable support among the faculty for the roommates' position. The attacked societies, of course, like royalty, remained serenely aloof, disdainfully silent, although Chip wondered whether the rumor, acutely disagreeable to him, that he had started the whole rumpus to ensure being tapped by Bulldog — posing as an enemy in order to be subdued by incorporation — had not emanated from the society itself.

The only quarter from which he expected a reaction with which he'd seriously have to cope was soon heard from. He and Lars were summoned to drive north to Benedict the following Saturday to lunch with his parents.

"There you are, Lars," he said, tossing the telegram on his friend's lap. "We're in for it. You can't desert me now."

Lars had met Chip's parents, but only in New Haven and in Maine; he had never been to Benedict, because, as Chip candidly confessed to him on their drive north that Saturday, he, Chip, had been embarrassed to ask his friends there.

"It's such a company town," he explained. "Almost every house is occupied by an employee. The hospital and the library were built by Daddy. Everything has that peculiar sanitized neatness of a community ruled by a benevolent despot."

"Let's be thankful for the benevolent, anyway."

"Oh, sure. Daddy's reign is just, and his subjects are happy. That's why he never has to raise his voice. But it wasn't always so. Grandpa Benedict, who started the business, and whom I never knew, ran a ruthless sweatshop."

"How do you know that? Not from your old man, surely?"

"No, Daddy speaks of him as of someone sanctified. Even though I believe he's spent his life consciously rectifying the terrible things his father did. No, it was my cousin Peter Duvinock who told me. He remembers the old boy. A holy terror! He actually fired one of his gardeners for buying a Ford, and when Peter's mother protested that it was the new American thing for every man to own his own car, he called her a Bolshevik!"

They were now in Benedict, and Chip turned off the main road to the steep hill east of the glassworks, where the stylish residences of the company officers, Tudor, Georgian, "Mission Moorish," rose to the summit in order of the rank of their occupants. At the peak was the big square stone Colonial mansion of Elihu and Matilda.

The beaming butler who opened the front door, a former bank thief, seemed to have no notice of any possible chill in the atmosphere, and his air of unclouded welcome was repeated by Chip's parents in the parlor. They must have agreed at least to start on a conciliatory note.

Elihu Benedict's light blue, kindly eyes gave a dignity and composure to a tall figure and small head that would have been otherwise almost undistinguished.

"Well, you two boys have certainly created a stir," he told them at the lunch table, with a headshake and a grin. "And maybe it's not such a bad thing at that. You probably regard me as Methuselah, but in my day I caused a good deal of talk by putting up a Jewish friend for my fraternity and keeping at it until he was elected. Once he was in, of course, everyone liked him and realized that they had been the victims of a foolish prejudice. Look at Germany today, and you'll see what kind of thing that can lead to. And as to the senior societies, I'm not sure it isn't a good idea, every now and then, to take a long hard look at even the most basic principles. Should these societies exist at all? Do they pull their weight in the academic community? Well, maybe they do, and maybe they don't."

"But of course we must remember that the senior societies can't defend themselves," Chip's mother warned them. "I don't know whether you boys are planning a second piece, but mightn't it be a clever idea to play the devil's advocate and give some of the arguments *for* such institutions?"

Matilda Benedict could never bring herself to take as many chances as her husband. Her innate conservatism made her fear that Chip and his friend might take Elihu too literally. She never trusted a world in which she had had to fight for all the advantages she had so signally achieved. She was as tall and rangy as her husband and so plain that she used to say, in relation to her four beautiful children, that nature had reached a limit with her and had had to turn around.

"No, Ma. I'm not going to write another column. I've stated my position, and that's that."

Chip saw his mother try to catch his father's eye. She made no attempt to conceal what she was doing, but his father, always subtler, avoided the appeal. It was obvious that both were relieved by Chip's answer, believing, as they must have, that a single column, in an era of widening latitudes, would not disqualify him from the ritual tap.

"Well, I think that's about all we should expect of a young man, isn't it, Mother?"

When Elihu called his wife "Mother," it was to hint that the matter was closed. But today Matilda seemed not to be taking hints.

"I still think it would be nice if Chip and Lars wrote a column on the other side. That would show their impartiality — their concern, above all, for the good of Yale."

"But we're not impartial, are we, Lars? And how can we be sure what's good for Yale? We're plugging for the abolition of the senior societies."

"Lars, tell me it's not true!" Matilda cried in distress. "Tell me you're not going that far."

"Oh, I guess Chip's exaggerating a bit," Lars conceded. "I think that basically all we want is for people to feel more at liberty to reject their bids. The whole thing has become too much of a fetish."

"And fetishes should go!" Chip insisted.

"You know how sons are with mothers," Lars said to Matilda, with a conciliatory smile. "They always exaggerate. I do the same thing with my ma."

Chip looked darkly from his mother to his roommate. He knew that Lars could never be counted on, not because he was weak or unfaithful by nature, but because his sunny acceptance of the world of privilege was bound to predominate over his occasional, genuine moods of rebellion. Rebellion with Lars was all in the intellect; conformity, in the heart. And Matilda, sensing this, was using him against her son just as hard as she could.

Elihu, seeing that the discussion was heading into trouble, intervened.

"I think all we can ask of Chip is that he keep an open mind — right up to Tap Day itself."

"Do you mean, Dad, an open mind about the societies or an open mind about joining one?"

"Both."

"In other words, you expect me to stand in the Branford Court with the others?"

"If it's not asking too much of you. How do we know that you won't have a sudden conversion?"

"Like Saul on the road to Damascus!" Lars exclaimed, with his loud laugh. Elihu smiled, but Matilda did not.

"Why do you care so, Dad?"

"Because he was a member of Bulldog himself!" Matilda answered impulsively for her husband. "And because he knows all the fine things it stands for! Because he doesn't want his son to repudiate all of his values and spit at an institution that represents a spark of idealism in a dangerously cynical world!"

"Oh, Ma, can't you let anyone make up his own mind? Must you always butt into everything?"

"Chip! I must ask you not to take that tone with your mother. It is unkind to her, offensive to me and embarrassing to your friend and guest."

Only Elihu could say such things without in the least raising his voice.

"I'm sorry, Dad."

"Really, Chip," Lars intervened, "is it asking so much of you to stand in the courtyard? It isn't as if you were committing yourself to anything."

There was a considerable silence before Chip replied.

"Very well, I agree to stand in the courtyard. If you, Dad, and you, Ma, agree to say nothing more about it. And do nothing more about it!"

Elihu now gave his wife his steeliest look. It was brief but effective, and a silent compact was reached. The conversation was turned to Hitler and the Rhineland, and after lunch Chip and Lars drove back to New Haven.

· · ·

Only two weeks later, however, Lars reported a new development to his roommate. The society that was flirting with Lars wanted Chip as well, and Lars had been put on notice, with the greatest discretion, that Elihu Benedict had been in touch with some of his old Bulldog friends to reassure them about Chip. Elihu was evidently endeavoring to convince them that the column in the *News* had been no more than "a violet in the youth of primy nature, forward, not permanent, sweet, not lasting," and that Chip, as his name implied, was something off the old block.

"That does it then," Chip said grimly. "I shall not stand in Branford Court on Tap Day."

"Shall I stay away with you?"

"You know you want Keys. Don't be an ass."

It took him some time to persuade Lars that he was not irretrievably committed to his roommate's cause. And why was Chip so committed? Why did he regard the matter as concerning only him and not Lars, nor indeed any other of his classmates?

He went to West Seventieth Street in New York that night, but, in an uncharacteristic visit to the bar, he drank so much that he lost the capacity to do anything more. Flora, his favorite of the girls, who was in love with him, sat by him most of the night and listened uncomprehendingly to his rambling.

"I'm not what they think I am," he told her, again and again. "I never have been. I never will be. But I can't convince them. 'Look at him!' they cry. 'Can't you see he's an angel?' Even you, Flora, my love. Even you."

In the end she put him to bed and lay quietly beside him. The next morning he departed while she was still asleep. He did not even have a hangover.

Two days later there was a knock at their study door in

Berkeley, and Lars opened it and let out a little bark of surprise.

"Why, Mrs. Benedict! What a happy surprise!"

"Be a good boy, Lars, and leave me alone with Chip."

"Mother, it's his room, too!"

But Lars was already out the door, and Chip stood up stiffly when he saw that his mother was looking graver than he had ever remembered her. He saw, too, that it was more than gravity. He could sense the full extent of her desperation in the length of her preparatory pause. It was not like her, indignant, to delay the flood tide of her reproaches. Chip had been deep in Shakespearean tragedy that whole term, and he likened her now to Volumnia, preparing her warrior-son for battle.

"I think you must have found out that your father went to Chicago to attend his annual Bulldog dinner especially on your account."

"I certainly never asked him to. And I believe he committed himself to do nothing for me in the matter."

"Anyway, he went. Nothing else matters to him where your future and happiness are concerned."

"My happiness? Am I not to judge that for myself? It is my life, isn't it? Or is it?"

"I was waiting for you to say that. Of course it's your life. And I can perfectly understand that your father may have gone too far. It may be that the whole matter should have been left to you. But what I believe is not debatable — what I believe even you would not argue — is that your father was motivated by anything but his great love for you."

Chip saw at once how the issue had been drawn. If he let this pass . . . ! "Unless I were to argue that a son may be part of a father. And in that respect a paternal love may be tinted with ego. That even . . ."

"Do you dare to argue that?" his mother interrupted in a harsh tone. "Do you dare to argue that you have not been the very apple of his eye? Oh, take it out on me as much as you like. Call me a monster of selfishness, of possessiveness. Say that I don't mind using every murderous weapon in a mother's arsenal! I don't care! It's true, if you like. But at least admit that your father has adored you unselfishly from the moment you were born. Why, your sisters and I don't even exist for him on the same plane that you occupy."

Chip quailed, fearing that he was already lost. He made no answer, and she pounced on his silence.

"Very well. Then let that be settled. And now let us come to what you propose to do. You propose to reject a bid from Bulldog that is entirely your due and that your father has simply tried to make doubly sure would come your way. Why? Out of some kind of moral principle? What principle? You can hardly seriously argue that Bulldog is immoral or pernicious. Is it to be consistent? But you have said yourself that you need not be ruled by a single article in the *News*. So what is it?"

Chip stared at that frozen face, fascinated by its unusual rigidity. She hardly seemed his mother now; she was more like a jealous and abandoned mistress. "What is it?" he repeated, half in a whisper.

"It's your desire to wound your father!" she almost shouted. "Your desire to hurt him as deeply as you can. To humiliate him, debase him, roll him in the mire!"

"Mother! What are you saying? When have I been anything in my life but his son?"

"I don't know, I don't know." She was moaning now, closing her eyes and shaking her head back and forth as if to repel some horrible supposition. "I've never understood you. Ever since you were a little boy you seem to have been watching us as if we were — I don't know — freaks. My father used to say the same thing. That you were judging us. For what? For loving you so much? For loving you more than your sisters? For we did, God help us! Why could you never tell us what was wrong? It isn't as if we wouldn't have listened! All we ever wanted was for you to be happy and well!"

At this, appallingly, she cracked. Like some great galleon in a violent storm, she swayed to and fro and then half-fell to the couch, as under the crashing wreck of masts and sails, to give way to a fury of sobbing. When she seemed to be losing her breath in gasps, he hurried to her side and tried to clasp her in his arms. But even in his anxiety, even as she attempted vehemently to push him away from her, a part of his mind was still able to see that this was the Volumnia who forced Coriolanus to spare Rome at the cost of his life and soul.

"I'll take Bulldog if I'm tapped!" he cried in desperation. "I promise!"

Her only answer was to stop sobbing and sit up on the couch to repair some of the damage of her emotion with the aid of a handkerchief and a bit of powder, clumsily applied.

"I don't care what you do," she said shortly. "I'm going home. You needn't come down. The car is right below."

Chip took her at her word; one always did. When she had left the room, he went to the window and saw that, sure enough, her chauffeur, an ex-forger, had parked the old green Cadillac directly by the Berkeley gate. He saw his mother emerge on the street accompanied by Lars, who must have been lurking in the corridor. And who must have been the one who had warned her of his resolution not to be tapped! They were engaged in a conversation that continued for a few minutes after she had got into the car, Lars leaning in the window.

Then she drove off, and Lars, waving up to Chip, re-entered the college.

"Your mother wants me to be sure to remind you of your promise. I gather her arguments have prevailed. A good thing, too. You've been making a mountain out of a molehill."

Chip was rent between the impulse to laugh wildly and a bitterness that threatened hot tears. So it had all been a scene, after all! And he had worried about having thoughts of Shakespeare while she suffered! She, who was no longer Volumnia, magnificent in her obsession, but Hamlet's mother, Gertrude, doing her vulgar maternal duty as she vulgarly conceived it. When he spoke at last to his roommate, his voice, very cool, was yet tremulous.

"You may take the same message to my dear mother, Lars-Osric, that Hamlet sent to the King. 'Sir, I will walk here in the hall; if it please his majesty, it is the breathing time of day with me; let the foils be brought, the gentleman willing, and the king hold his purpose, I will win for him if I can; if not, I will gain nothing but my shame and the odd hits.'"

"Which means, I take it, that you will walk in Branford Court on Tap Day and win at the odds?"

"I fear I shall gain my shame even so."

Lars's smile gave way to an expression of guarded concern. "I'm afraid you're still taking it all a bit tragically, my friend. Consider, like Dr. Johnson, how insignificant this will appear a twelvemonth hence."

"Osrics are not expected to know when they are acting in tragedies."

Lars let out one of his whoops of laughter. "Are you trying to insult me, Chip? I verily believe you are!"

.   .   .

Chip was the last man tapped for Bulldog, and he jogged off obediently to his room, where he was duly initiated into the rites of that arcane institution. But later that night, when he and Lars, who had accepted his bid from Scroll and Key, were sitting up over a brandy, they discussed an unexpected development of the day.

Chessy Bogart had also been tapped for Bulldog! The seniors had evidently felt that it was time to give recognition to the new editor-in-chief of the *Lit*. Of course, Lars knew the story of his expulsion from Saint Luke's and the attempted implication of Chip. He was concerned that Bogart's election might ruin his roommate's pleasure in his own. But Chip did not think so.

"In a way I'm almost glad. I like to have him where I can keep an eye on him. I've always been conscious of him skulking in the background."

"Now what on earth do you mean by that? Or must I go back to Hamlet to find out?"

"It's hard to explain. Have you never felt that a person has been endowed with the special mission of punishing you?"

Lars stared. "Is there something about you and Bogart that I don't know?"

"Nothing that would strike you as having any importance. It's only a question of what happened to whom when."

"Do you enjoy trying to baffle me?"

"Isn't it obvious that I don't want to talk about it? Don't worry, my friend. I have it all under control. When I told my ma I would do as she asked, a change came in my life."

The term was almost over; a premature summer seemed to be crowding into the last days of Academe. Chip invited Chessy to go to New York with him for a night. He took his old Saint

Luke's acquaintance to the finest of French restaurants, and the two young men got fairly high on cocktails and wine.

"You know, Chip," his guest observed at last, "I was a shit, four years ago, to betray you to your grandfather. But I didn't imagine he'd even mention it to you. I thought he'd just quietly quash the whole scandal."

Chip had been waiting for this; he was entirely at his ease. "Oh, I saw all that. I think you even owed it to the guy who was caught with you. You didn't know Grandpa, that's all. I had to let you down. But if I owe you something, I can make a payment tonight. Drink up and I'll take you to a place I know."

At West Seventieth Street, Chessy, dazzled for all his would-be sophistication, was introduced to the beautiful Flora, who took care of him for the whole night.

On the train going back to New Haven, Chessy was silent. He dozed most of the journey. But when they got to their station, he smiled almost sheepishly and gripped Chip's elbow.

"Jesus, that was a night! Thanks, Tarzan."

Chip said nothing, but in the taxi on their way to the college, Chessy, wider awake now, remarked with a smirk, "And I always thought you were such a good boy."

"Was I so good at boarding school?"

"Are you referring to that one little slip? But I assume I was irresistible! Why did it torture you so, Chip? Everyone did it."

"I guess I liked to imagine myself as the one wicked person in a virtuous world."

"You couldn't have thought I was virtuous!"

"But you see, that was just the conceit of it. You existed only as one of my tempting devils."

"Thanks!"

"You asked for it. Anyway, I have belatedly discovered that I was wrong. The rest of the world is quite as bad as I am."

"Or as good?"

"Either way. Does it matter?"

"And is it better for you, now, having made this great discovery?"

Chip thought for a moment. "I really don't know. Certainly it makes me less dramatic."

"To yourself?"

"To whom else?"

"Ah, you *are* an egotist."

For the remainder of the term Chip and Chessy were constantly together. It was a bit of a trial to the little group at Berkeley, particularly to Lars. Chessy's social standing in the class might have soared with his election to Bulldog, but his appearance and manner were hard for Chip's friends to accept. Chessy, with his uncle's allowance, was a far more dapper character than he had been at prep school; he now affected brilliant vests, bow ties and striking cuff links, and he had managed to get himself put on a New York debutante party guest list and had met a number of the girls whom Chip's friends knew. Yet his cockiness, his sarcasm and biting wit did not endear him to the campus leaders. He was obviously a social climber — indeed he made no effort to conceal it — yet once he had penetrated a circle that one might have deemed the ultima Thule of his worldly ambition, it seemed to have been only for the purpose of making fun of the men he found there.

"It may sound hypocritical to you, but I find it in my heart to be almost sorry for the guy," Lars confided, a bit disingenuously, to Chip. "The moment he achieves a goal, it loses all its taste for him. If he ever gets to heaven he'll be looking over God's shoulder to see if there isn't someone more important he ought to be talking to."

"He'll never get to heaven."

Lars looked at him curiously. "Is that another of your conundrums? What do you see in him, Chip?"

"Don't you suppose the Benedicts and Alversens were like that a generation back?"

"No, I'm damned if they were! Everyone in the top drawer didn't have to social-climb to get there."

"Maybe it's just my own vulgarity. I recognize a fellow sufferer."

"But you haven't a vulgar bone in your body!"

"How do you know what I am — deep down?"

Lars shrugged. "What did you two do in New York the other night?"

"Oh, we took in a show."

"What show?"

"I don't remember."

Lars sighed and gave it up. "All right, pal, have it your way. But I'd like to be a fly on the wall at one of your sessions in Bulldog when that guy gets going on his plans for the future!"

"There's more to Chessy than is dreamed of in your philosophy, Horatio."

"Can it, Hamlet!"

Chip said no more, but he had to admit privately that Lars's apostrophe was just. For had not Hamlet awakened from the dream of his own guilt to confront a guilty world? Gertrude and Claudius were shabby folk, but were they any shabbier than the court over which they presided? At any rate, he would do things his way from now on.

8

⤞⤜

ALIDA

CHESSY BOGART called me early on the morning after the Swimming Club dance where I had met his friend Chip Benedict. He seemed to have taken it for granted not only that I should be up, but that I should be expecting his call, for when Mummie rapped on my door she called in, "I told him you were asleep, but he insisted you weren't!" As I picked up the telephone, I looked out the window and saw that it was once again one of those perfect Bar Harbor days.

"If you want to come sailing with Chip and me, you'd better get down here."

"Where's here?"

"I'm at Max's, getting things for the boat. It's only a step from the pier."

I hurried out of the house, without bothering to answer Mummie's anxious inquiry. She was clad in a pink wrapper with coffee stains, and she was holding a half-eaten piece of toast. What had I to do with such a dowdy?

After parking my car behind the Star Theatre, I walked down the hill on Main Street, my heart aglow. The gulls wheeled and squawked above, and in a restaurant window even the doomed lobsters, cruelly piled one on top of another, failed to arouse my usual repulsion.

Chessy, immaculate in a white T-shirt and ducks, was waiting for me outside the store, holding the brown bag that contained his purchases. His smile was frankly insinuating.

"So you liked my friend," he said as we started down to the pier.

"He seems very sure of himself."

"He has a lot to be sure of."

"As much as all that?"

"Well, he has all the things I want, anyway. The obvious things. It's why people hate him."

"Do they hate him?"

"They envy him. It's the same thing."

"Then you must hate him, too."

"Ah, but you see I'm different. He and I are part of each other. You might put it that we've made a kind of blood compact."

"Just you and he?"

"And the devil. Isn't he always the third?"

"You mean you've sold your souls?"

"Dear no. He didn't have to buy us. We were born his. Chip even aspires to be his first lieutenant."

"To lead the armies of Satan against the citadel of God?"

"And don't kid yourself. We may yet prevail."

It seemed to me that we were getting pretty silly, even for Bar Harbor. "What's so great about being wicked?"

"Wicked is a term of abuse used by Jehovah. The damned are no more wicked than the saved are good."

"Meaning that yours is really a noble rebellion?"

"Against the tyranny of whatever is."

"You speak of your friend as if he were your commanding officer. I always thought of you as independent, Chessy. Whatever happened to that Argentinian uncle?"

"He went bankrupt and blew his brains out."

I glanced to see if he was kidding. "And left you nothing?"

Chessy formed a naught with his forefinger and thumb. "I depend entirely now upon my generous friend."

"Then you really have sold your soul?"

"Oh, I think he'll get his money's worth."

Before us now was Chip's gleaming white boat. Its master, dressed like his friend, was busy with the sails. He paused only briefly to wave at me. Chessy leaned over to place his brown bag on the deck and then handed me into the boat.

"Have a nice sail, you two."

"Aren't you coming?" I asked in astonishment.

"And make a crowd? I know better." And he walked down the pier, whistling, without once turning back.

Chip did not ask me to help him with the sails. He was too competent even to pretend that he could be assisted. He offered me a newspaper and a beer, both of which I declined. I simply sat on the fantail and watched him. It was amazing. He was even better-looking than I remembered. And his ignoring my presence helped to keep alive my heady sense of unreality.

At last we got under way. I took the tiller as he pulled up the sails. We did not exchange a word until we were clear of the harbor. Once we were settled on a course along the shoreline, with a mild breeze behind us, he slipped into the seat beside me and relieved me of my task.

"What do you want? You know I'm engaged."

"Do you like Browning? 'Your leave for one more last ride with me.'"

"You mean you're going to take me for a ride?"

"You accept?"

"What else can I do now? Swim ashore?"

He laughed and quoted mockingly:

> "'The blood replenished me again;
> My last thought was at least not vain:
> I and my mistress, side by side,
> Shall be together, breathe and ride,
> So, one day more am I deified.
>   Who knows but the world may end tonight?'"

"Except that I'm not your mistress."

"Neither was the lady in the poem. In that sense of the word. I only wanted to get you away for a bit. Out here on the ocean there's just us."

"What are you going to do to me?"

"Nothing. Except look at you."

"Well, I guess that's safe enough. A cat can look at an engaged girl."

"You keep coming back to your engagement."

"Isn't it natural?"

"Not if you don't believe in it. And you don't."

"What makes you say that?"

"Isn't it obvious? You wouldn't have come out with me if you did."

"I didn't mean to come out with you. I meant to come out with Chessy."

"You only came because you knew I'd be here."

"You have a nerve!"

"Don't be vulgar, Alida. It doesn't become you."

I found that I was willing to accept this, shaming as it was. "Very well. I did come because I wanted to see you. But I don't understand where it is going to get either of us. I have no idea of giving up Jonathan. And I certainly have no idea of having an affair with you before I marry him. That would be vulgar."

"Agreed. But you say you have no idea of giving up Askew. Is there really anything to give up? Isn't he just a fantasy?"

"Of yours or mine?"

"Of both. Insofar as we let him stand between us."

As at the dance, I felt his extraordinary effect on me. It was not simply sex appeal — unless that was what it simply was. No, it was more the intriguing sense of having no further decisions to make, of being folded up and packed into what I somehow imagined as the smart snakeskin traveling case of this grave and beautiful young man.

"Who are you?" I asked. "Tell me about yourself."

"There's not much to tell. Except that my life began last spring. When I decided, belatedly, that I was going to live. I mean live my own life, not anyone else's."

"And what made you come to this great decision?"

"I looked at my parents and suddenly saw them. That was all."

"I gather you didn't much like what you saw." I sighed in sympathy. "I saw mine at a somewhat earlier date."

"What I really saw was that there was no point trying to oblige them."

"Because you never could?"

"Exactly. Because I never could."

"Is that what Chessy means when he says you're damned?"

"How like Chessy to put it that way." But he did not answer the question.

"And what about me?" I went on. "Is there any point trying to oblige me?"

"I only want you to oblige yourself. We know we're attracted. I see no obstacle. I certainly don't consider Askew one."

"Even though he's my fiancé?"

"You don't care for him! You couldn't. He doesn't even exist where it's a question of you and me."

"I think I want to go back now." He did not reply and made no move to change course. After a few minutes of silence I asked sharply, "What are you going to do? Drown me?" When he still failed to respond, or even look at me, I said in a different tone, the sudden gravity of which surprised me, "All right. Go ahead!"

"Coming about," he said gruffly, and we turned our bow back to Bar Harbor.

At the pier, when he had taken down the sails as I watched — expertly and speedily, of course — he said: "Chessy and I will be leaving tomorrow for Dark Harbor. After that I go back to Yale. I'll call you in New York in September. If you'll agree to have dinner with me, I'll take you to a place where no one will know you."

And that was all. Feeling at once very flat and oddly exhilarated, I drove home alone. I found Jonathan on the porch, waiting for me. He asked sulkily where I had been.

"I've been for a sail."

"With that callow blond fellow you were dancing with last night?"

"The same."

"Alida, how could you?"

His tone was high and shrill. He ranted on about my obligations to him. Ultimately he burst into tears. I watched him coldly. He seemed a part of my life, even an undetachable part, but he was in the past — like Mummie and Daddy. He was me. He was awful.

"You needn't worry, Jonathan," I said wearily. "Nothing is going to happen between me and that young man."

"And how, pray, can I be sure of that?"

"Because he's damned."

"He certainly will be if he doesn't let you alone!"

"I don't think I want to discuss him with you. If you insist, I shall have to break our engagement."

"Alida, please!" And he went down on his knees just as Mummie appeared in the doorway. It was a thoroughly ridiculous scene.

9

~~~~

ALIDA

CHIP WAS GOOD to his word; I did not hear again from him or from Chessy during the short balance of the Bar Harbor season, or even for two weeks after our return to town. I began to wonder whether the whole episode, dreamlike from its beginning, might not have been indeed a dream. And yet, for some deep and probably neurotic reason, I did not suffer from as much emotional turmoil as I anticipated. I was aware of an unringing telephone and a fruitless mail delivery, yet I was not constantly hovering by the machine or rushing down to the front hall at the postman's ring. The contrast between my new friend and my betrothed was so vivid that they could not, it seemed to me, very well exist in the same world, let alone in the same restless female heart. I had created in myself a dichotomy between the reality of my proposed marriage and the reality of Chip Benedict.

Lady Lennox had returned to England, and Jonathan had opened up his father's old town house on East Eighty-ninth

Street, a gloomy French Renaissance mansion, full of dusty bad paintings and nicked gilded furniture, in which he dwelled sulkily with an old family butler, very deaf, and two crones of maids. He had still not recovered from his jealous fit in Maine, but as I refused to discuss it, he had no alternative but to follow my bright, artificial conversational leads into other subjects, any other subjects. We went out together two or three times a week and went over the details of the large spring wedding that my parents had agreed to give us — entirely at Jonathan's expense, as I later found out.

It may sound heartless that I should have gone into such detail with him over a wedding the reality of which I no longer believed in. All I can say in my defense is that I seemed to be living increasingly in illusions and was terrified of what might happen if I emerged from them.

Chip broke his silence in late September with a letter suggesting that I meet him at a restaurant in the upper West Side. He did not ask me to respond; he simply wrote that he would be there on a particular night. And so, of course, was I. It was certainly not a place where anyone would have expected to see the fiancée of Jonathan Askew. It was dark and leathery and had large reproductions of Remington paintings of cowboys and Indians. The booths were private and the food good. Only much later did I discover why Chip was so familiar with the area.

We were soon meeting weekly. Chip seemed to have no difficulty leaving New Haven. He did not even mind missing a meeting of his senior society, which I did not then understand was a serious matter. We would talk with great animation and congeniality about the obtuseness of our families and the ineptitude of our friends. I was fascinated by his picture of the family rule at Benedict, and he, for some reason, by mine of my crazy home. We never mentioned Jonathan or my engagement. After dinner and many brandies he would take a taxi to Grand Central, dropping me home on the way. In the taxi we would neck violently. He handled me in a way that left me sleepless, frustrated and aching with desire for the rest of the night. Little did I then know that his own nocturnal hours were bothered by no such restlessness. The taxi would take him on, actually not to Grand Central, but to a lush private brothel that this blue-eyed angel had been frequenting for years.

I have said we both talked a lot at dinner, and we did, but Chip talked the most. He was very serious about both of us, but he was particularly serious about himself. He was a great admirer of Thorstein Veblen, and what he most deplored in his family was their efforts to negate in their own lives the principle of "conspicuous consumption."

"It's perfectly possible for a man to free himself of material concerns," Chip argued. "I don't deny such saints as Francis of Assisi. But what I abominate is people who live for the world and yet make a religion of denying it. My parents' whole life is dedicated to the making and preservation of wealth. Yet in their false simplicity, their splendid isolation up there in Connecticut, they would have you think they're as pure as the early desert fathers!"

"What about your grandfather? The headmaster, I mean, not the tycoon. Didn't you consider him a saint?"

"And perhaps he was, poor dear man. He may have dimly suspected that his school was only a front for the most rabid form of economic laissez-faire, but what could he do about it? Basically, he was a canary warbling in a gilded cage. Oh, yes, the Benedicts like canaries."

"But surely you don't imagine that my family are any less worldly? Even though they don't have much to be worldly about." I coughed at the very idea. "To put it mildly!"

"But that's just the point. There's no nauseous hypocrisy about them. They're straight out of Veblen. Bar Harbor could be a footnote to illustrate his thesis. Your ma under the umbrella table at the Swimming Club corresponds to an Indian squaw decked out in beads to show the prowess of her chief."

I tried to imagine Daddy with a feathered headdress doing a war dance. "Is it so great a thing to be frank about being worldly?" I asked dubiously. "Suppose one is really poor? Isn't it rather a fraud?"

I doubt that he got the point. "So long as people are what they seem, I can deal with them," he emphasized. "With you, for example, I know that I'm living in the real world. You made no bones about trying to be the most famous debutante in order to catch the richest stag."

"*Merci du compliment!*"

"Seriously, it puts you way ahead of the Benedicts and all their gang. Because if you can deal with the world as it is, you can handle truth, and if you can handle truth, you're free!"

I stared into those shining blue eyes and marveled at what he believed. For a minute I debated the pros and cons of seeing whether *he* could handle the truth. Should I try to persuade him that his parents were a dozen times superior to my poor shabby progenitors? For I perfectly understood that he was making an Alp out of the molehill of Mr. and Mrs. Benedict's merely human fatuity. They were probably an admirable couple, suffering only from the common need to dress up their underlying motivations. But what was there and then to change my life was that I suddenly saw — in a flash of mental illumination — that to point this out would be to dish myself forever with this fanatic. Truth had been fascinating to Jonathan; with Chip it would have cost me all my glamour. And I wanted Chip — oh, yes, I wanted him as a desert monk wanted salvation!

"Are you richer than Jonathan?" I asked boldly.

"Very likely."

That was the night, when I came home, that I found Jonathan waiting up with my parents. He had finally put a detective on me and knew all about my dinners with Chip. There was a very noisy scene, which I witnessed as coolly as if I had been at a play. Mummie screamed at me as violently as Jonathan, and even Daddy made throaty noises of protest. I did not know at the time how deeply they were both financially in Jonathan's debt. At last I went up to my bedroom and locked the door. The last words I heard were Daddy's as he tried to persuade Jonathan to go home, promising him that he would talk me around in the "cold, clear light" of morning.

When I came down to breakfast in that cold, clear light after a heavy sleep induced by three Seconals, I found Deborah in the dining room. Mummie was still in her room, and Daddy had gone to his club, as one might, in despair, go to church.

"I think you're behaving very badly," Deborah said, and I knew at once that her averted eyes and controlled tone masked the deepest resentment.

I have not written much about my younger sister. I am afraid she has never really interested me. She was always just making it; that is, her grades at school were just respectable, her looks, bland and suggestive of future puffiness (alas, now confirmed) were just short of pretty, and her temper just missed being amiable. If Deborah (to use a current term) had been a jogger, she would have been one of those wide-bottomed waddlers you see panting slowly and painfully around the reservoir in Central Park. Everything came hard to her, but she tried to make up for this in the smugness of her assurance that in any race with her older sister the tortoise was bound to come out ahead. She may yet.

"If engagements can't be broken," I retorted to her implication, "what on earth is the point of them?"

"The point is to find out if two people really love each other. But that wasn't the point of *your* engagement. You never had any idea of loving Jonathan. You've just found somebody richer, that's all."

"That's not true!" I cried, stung.

"That he's not richer?"

"No, that I'm being mercenary. I didn't love Jonathan, and I do love Chip. Do you still think I ought to marry Jonathan?"

"Yes! Because you led him on. You owe it to him. You made a bargain in cold blood. Now you're welching. I think it's vile!"

"Deborah! Your tone!"

"I mean it, Alida. All your life things have come easily to you, so you sneer at them. You sneer at all the things I haven't had. And now you sneer at Jonathan and kick him over because something prettier has caught your fancy. What do you care if he's broken-hearted? What do you care about the scandal and what it may do to *my* chances of ever getting married?"

"Scandal? What scandal? Why should it be a scandal for a girl to break her engagement?"

"Because Jonathan wants money back from Daddy he can't repay! You should have heard what went on after you went to bed. They woke me up with their shouting. Oh, why do I waste my breath? What do you care?" And Deborah, bursting into angry tears, rushed from the room.

When I had swallowed two cups of black coffee, I took a taxi to the Metropolitan Club and sent my name up to Gus Leighton. He met me in the visitors' lounge, which at that early hour was empty. Typically, he showed no reaction as I related what had happened; he simply waited, expressionless, until I had finished.

"And just what is it that you expect me to do?"

"I hoped you would take care of breaking it to the press."

"There will be no need of that. By noon everyone will know."

"Shouldn't I have a statement ready?"

"What for? To try to explain it to the Benedicts?"

"Oh, you know their name." I had not mentioned it, simply referring to Chip as a new friend.

"Do you think I don't know that you met Charles Benedict last summer and went sailing with him? There are no secrets on our northern island."

"Or on this one either, apparently."

"Let me ask you just one thing. I believe that our former association justifies it."

"Certainly."

"Has Benedict committed himself?"

"To marrying me? In no way."

"That's what I was afraid of. Do you know that he is the heir of the Benedict Company and the very apple of his parents' eyes?"

"I have surmised it."

"And have you any idea what Mr. and Mrs. Benedict are like?"

"I understand they are virtuous folk. Very high-minded. No doubt they will disapprove of me."

"Alida, they will fight you tooth and nail!" Gus was very grave now. "They will use every weapon in their arsenal, and they have plenty. For God's sake, don't give up Jonathan before you're sure of Benedict. You may have been a famous debutante, but think of your family and the fragility of your position. One false step, and the world will have it in for you!"

"But don't you see, Gus, that this may be my one chance for decency? To do it this way? *Before* anyone's committed?"

Gus gave me a long look. Then he nodded.

"I'll see what I can do about the press. I'm afraid it won't be much."

It wasn't. The publicity that accompanied my "broken troth," as the headlines called it, exceeded my worst expectations. But on the whole I was not displeased. It was a kind of punishment, perhaps a merited one. The papers did not pick up Chip's trail, for even in his fury Jonathan did not wish to be shamed by such an exposure, but they picked up everything else, including the ugly fact that Mummie and Daddy had received large loans from Jonathan, which they now refused to pay back, claiming that they had been gifts. It appeared that there might be litigation. I could imagine the long faces at the Benedict breakfast table when they learned that this was their darling's new girl!

But would he continue to be interested? Would the sordid row be Veblenesque enough for him? If I loved Chip before, it may be imagined how I adored him when I heard his firm, calm voice on the telephone.

"I want you to come to Benedict for lunch on Sunday, Alida." It was not until we were engaged that he used even such mild terms as "my dear" or "dearest." "It's high time you met my parents."

"What must they think of all this!"

"I guess that's got to be their problem. I know what I think.

I don't give a damn about the papers! There's a train that gets in at 12:05. If you can make it, I'll meet you."

Oh, that lunch! In that expensive, antiseptic dining room with the blue walls, the primitives, the Duncan Phyfe chairs! We were eight; I suppose the Benedicts couldn't face me alone. The others, I believe, were neighbors. Chip's only ally, unless he was a parental spy, was his former roommate, Lars Alversen. I gathered that the family disapproved of Chessy. Why not? Look at the trouble he had caused!

Mr. Benedict, on whose right I was placed, was very gentle, very polite. He couldn't have been rude to Lady Macbeth; it wasn't in his nature. But his homely wife, with whom I had exchanged a few remarks about the weather — or, rather, to whom I had addressed a few such remarks before the meal — could hardly bring herself to speak to me or to anyone else. She kept glancing at me with eyes full of apprehension and almost undisguised dismay. She could no more have pretended that she was giving a pleasant lunch party than had she just been told that her son was stricken with a fatal disease. I almost felt sorry for her.

But I decided that nothing I said was going to be right. Talk fell upon the usual crisis in Europe. The Benedicts were solidly opposed to Neville Chamberlain and ready to take up arms with England against Hitler. So I proclaimed myself an isolationist and expressed the opinion that Europe was none of our business. When the conversation was abruptly changed, I threw caution, even discretion, to the wind. I became pro–New Deal, pro–high taxation, pro-labor; I think I even managed to come out for companionate marriage! Mrs. Benedict's anguished eyes drove me to it. I wanted to *cost* Chip something!

After lunch Chip retired to his father's study, where I was

sure his mother would join them. Lars, whom I had at first rather liked, walked with me in the garden. It was early spring.

"Why do you want them to dislike you quite so much?" he asked.

"Isn't it only kind? They're going to, anyway. Now they have an excuse."

"I suppose with Mrs. Benedict you may be right." He laughed, and I was surprised at the heartiness of the sound. Lars had a delicacy of appearance that his spirits denied. "The American ma and her son's girl friend — yes, it's almost hopeless. But Mr. Benedict could be won over. Oh, yes, he could! And look you, he is not the typical American dad. He rules the roost up here."

"He doesn't rule Chip."

"Except by indirection. Chip has changed a lot in the past six months. I think you may be just what he needs."

"Thank you! And what about me? What do I need? I suppose we needn't go into that. It's too obvious, isn't it? A penniless, rather phony debutante with a shabby family who made the headlines in every evening paper when she failed to nail Jonathan Askew!"

"Ah, but you had nailed him. And you gave him up."

"Let him go, rather. Opened the door of his cage, poor fellow, let him fly away. And why did I do even that good deed? Out of the kindness of my heart? Never! Because I had my eye on something even richer!"

"Alida, you belie yourself. I could see that all during lunch. You're obviously in love with Chip."

"Is it that obvious?"

"Well, not to his family. No doubt they still regard you as a designing woman. But I know you're just what Chip needs.

· 112 ·

And I haven't said he's what you need because I doubt that you need anything. I've followed your career in the papers. Originally it was because Chessy Bogart talked so much about you. But then I became fascinated on my own. I deduced (a) that you have a strong character and (b) that you believe in nothing."

I stopped to stare at him. "Is that why Chip needs me? Because he hasn't a strong character? And believes in too many things?"

Lars laughed. "No, no. He has a very strong character. And he believes passionately in Chip Benedict. He needs you because you will give him the air of being a successful rebel."

"Which he isn't?"

"Not in the least. The only people Chip wishes to defeat in hewing his way to the top of the family company and then of the world are his parents themselves."

Had I gone through what I had gone through to have this little man pull everything to pieces? "I see your game, Alversen! At least Mrs. Benedict is direct. Why in God's name are women supposed to be subtle? But you! You want to get rid of me by persuading me that I'm too good for Chip!"

He simply laughed again, even louder than before. It was a remarkably cheerful laugh. "You *are* in love with him, aren't you? Well, he's all yours. And now we'd better go back. There he is on the terrace. And I believe he's actually glowering at me!"

Chip insisted on driving me back to New York. His countenance was grim; he must have had a first-class row with his parents. He had come, he told me in a voice that admitted of no dispute, to an important decision. He and I must marry as soon as possible, privately, without our parents and without a reception. Chessy would be his only witness; he hoped that I would have as few as possible.

"Only Gus," I heard myself say, and I added, "Gus Leighton," when he seemed not to recognize the name.

Then I suppose it must have struck him that he had never formally asked me to be his wife. "You *will* marry me?" he asked, looking away from the wheel at me.

"Of course I will!" I exclaimed hurriedly, for he was driving much too fast. "Now watch the road, please. Won't your parents cut you off without a cent?"

"They can't. I have my own money."

There were no problems! And suddenly my heart was so full of happiness that I thought I shouldn't be able to contain it. I needed a vent through which some of it could escape; I searched my mind, now as fluffy as a baby's crib, for the silliest thing I could say.

"Where shall we live? Do I move into your rooms at Berkeley?"

"I'm afraid that's not allowed. No matter how accommodating Chessy may be. No, we'll take a flat off campus. And next year we'll get a house in Charlottesville. I'm going to Virginia Law School."

"Oh, that's all decided?"

"Yes. Whether or not I go into the company, law will always be useful."

I remembered what Lars had said, but what did I care now? "I suppose I can go to the movies on Thursday and Saturday nights."

"Why so, dearest?"

It was the first time he had called me that, and my heart seemed to lose a beat. "Well, don't you have your Bulldog sessions?"

"I'm going to resign from Bulldog."

"Chip! Has anyone ever?"

"There's a first time for everything."

"You don't have to do it for me, you know."

"I'm doing it for myself."

It had started to rain, and I shivered a bit as I closed my window. I wondered whether I had not discovered the real cause for his break with his parents.

IO

⨯⨯⨯⨯

ALIDA

THE FIRST three years of my married life constituted a kind of Nirvana. After Yale, when we moved to Charlottesville, we had a charming little red brick house, octagon-shaped and supposed by a persistent few to be the handiwork of Jefferson, with a view over the rolling lawn of a country club towards the Blue Ridge range. I had a black couple who did everything that had to be done, including most of the care of little Ellie, born nine months after our wedding. Chip drove the five miles to law school in his Lincoln Continental, leaving me a scarlet Ford coupé to run about the countryside as I chose. In the immediate neighborhood there resided some dozen other "Yankee" couples, all affluent, amiable and handsome, the husbands, like Chip, law students, and the wives, like me, young mothers and idle housewives. It made a pleasant center for a social life that expanded easily to take in occasional faculty members from the university and the owners, some Virginians, of the local estates and horse farms.

The war started in Europe, but it seemed very far away. When I rode, occasionally with one of the other wives but more often alone, I reveled in the long blue vistas and the rich red clay. At home I read novels and poetry to my heart's content and purported to justify my romantic escapism by writing an occasional sonnet, fussing idly for whole mornings over a single rhyme. At night Chip worked in his study at home, unless he had to use the law library, but he tried to keep regular hours and usually quit by ten or eleven, in time for a Scotch with me before bed, and Saturday nights were sacred to the dinner parties that we either gave or attended. The life, for the men at least, was a curious combination of revelry and industry. Chip's friends had certainly not overtaxed themselves at college, but in law school they tended to be more serious. Chip himself was almost a grind.

Young women today will wonder why I did not do more: take courses or work for a cause. But I thought I had everything a woman could want: a handsome husband who rarely lost his temper and made regular love, a healthy infant, plenty of money and friends. Indeed, there were times when my good luck almost frightened me. It was as if some beneficent fairy godmother had waved her wand and removed at a clap my tiresome parents, my clinging fiancé, my ludicrous social career, and changed the scene to this romantic university, where youth and beauty seemed to gambol before the white paint, red brick and shimmering greens of Mr. Jefferson's inspired vision.

I had no feeling that I owed myself a career. Being Chip's wife, it seemed to me, was going to be quite enough. And I could always write, couldn't I? Chip was ambitious, organized, efficient. He did not confine himself socially to the New Yorkers and Philadelphians in his class; he made a point of meeting everyone. He was duly elected to the Law Review, and in the spring of his second year elevated to editor-in-chief. He ultimately became a member of the Honor Court, the Raven Society and the Order of the Coif; in short, he developed into a personage on campus. In an afterlife that would presumably follow the pattern of his academic one, he would need a social partner, and I was perfectly content to be that. In Charlottesville he merely expected me to be charming to his friends, which I was, and to run the house smoothly, which I essentially did, though I left most of that to the couple. Only in this latter area did Chip, who had a housekeeper's eye, occasionally criticize me. Yet even here he was mild enough.

So what was wrong? For my readers will have flared by now that something *was* wrong. Was it only the Eve in me that could not resist the temptation to find fault with Eden? Was I looking about for an apple to bite? Sometimes I feared that my experience would be that of Psyche, who, forbidden to view the lover who gave her such nightly bliss, was abandoned by the most beautiful of the gods when curiosity at last won out and she lit her lamp. I needed no lamp, obviously, to see my husband's body; the parallel, if one existed, had to be his soul. What sort of a man had I married? But surely I knew. He was direct, forceful, coordinated, scrupulously fair, political in that he liked to manipulate people, high-minded, a bit impersonal, perhaps even a touch hard. There! I had brought out the word at last. But was I being fair? Didn't he listen conscientiously to every problem I brought to him when he was not abstracted by a legal one? Didn't he gratify my every desire and need? Didn't he include me in all the things he did? Did he ever look at another woman? Ah, but did he mind if anyone looked at *me*? There was the time I told him of the pass a drunken Law Review editor had made at me at a party, and he had merely laughed! Obviously there was not a bone of jealousy in Chip's make-up. But could love exist without jealousy?

Or was I just another nervous female, with too much time on her hands, moaning like an unmilked cow for true love?

No, no, it had to be more than that. I never complained to Chip that we were not truly intimate, because I was afraid that I might only reveal to him — and to myself — a gap that he was incapable of bridging. I allowed him to dominate me, because I had no idea what I should do with myself if he didn't. My real worry was more likely that Chip had deliberately selected me as just the companion he believed he needed for the particular role in life he had chosen to play. I might have been measured, so to speak, beside a list of specifications and found to fit. I had had to have looks and health and intelligence; I had had at least to "seem" a great sexual catch; and I had had to represent a dramatic and decisive break with his own domestic past. But what would happen to me if the drama with Chip's chosen role were to be changed? What if some new script required a different leading lady? The mere idea was anguish to me, for my whole life was possessed now by this strange, unyielding man against whom I had no complaints except in fantasy.

And for what was he so industriously preparing himself? Did he want to be a great lawyer, a great glass manufacturer, a judge, a governor, a President? He never specified. When I asked him, he would simply shrug and say, "We'll cross that bridge when we get to it." Yet he was certainly not bent on fulfilling the aspirations of his parents, whom he had more or less rejected, or obeying the dictates of God, from whom he seemed also to have turned. Chip, like myself, had no religion, but unlike me I think he had had. He had swept the lares and penates from his household shelf and was intent on standing on his own feet. Today I suppose one would call him an existentialist.

Which did not for a minute mean that he was amoral. He was, on the contrary, most scrupulous in all daily matters of right and wrong. He was truthful to the point of being sometimes rather blunt and, in my opinion, overconscientious in cases of personal obligation. He would be highly critical, for example, if I kept a library book overdue or neglected to correct the smallest error in my favor in a bill or bank balance. Whatever the image in his mind of the man he wished to become, it was certainly that of a totally honest one.

All of which observations settled gradually in my mind but were fully in place by the fourth year of our marriage and the final one of Chip's law school course. In the fall of that year Gus Leighton paid us a visit that was to have a significant bearing on my relations with Chip's family, and, indirectly, on my relations with Chip himself.

The breach caused by our having married without either his parents' blessing or their presence had been closed — at least formally. Mr. and Mrs. Benedict had come twice to Charlottesville in our first two years there, but they had stayed at the Farmington Country Club. On each occasion we had fêted them with a dinner party that had helped to spare my mother-in-law and me the embarrassment of any pretended intimacy. And in each of the two intervening summers we had spent one weekend at the family home in Maine. But that was all. Chip spoke of his parents as little as possible and seemed perfectly content to live apart from them. Mr. Benedict accepted the situation with the ease of one who counts on time to take care of everything, and his wife, who was obviously miserable about it, could still not bring herself to be more than decently civil to me. As for the three girls, they were enchanted to forget the past in favor of a new available base close to a men's college, and they visited us rather more than I wanted. Yet they were pleasant enough and pretty enough, if not very brainy. Chip seemed to have a monopoly on the family intellect.

Gus Leighton had known Chip's mother since his schooldays at Saint Luke's. He had been a passionate admirer of Mr. B, then only the chaplain, and had met Mrs. Benedict on one of her weekend visits to her father. Gus as a boy had apparently bubbled over with Christian fervor, a not unusual first chapter to a maturity of polished worldliness, and in his youthful enthusiasm for the chaplain he had won the friendship of the latter's formidable but very filial daughter. I could understand how even the severe Mrs. Benedict might have yielded to Gus's sincere gushing. As a matter of fact, it is not uncommon for doughty, moralistic older women to be pushovers for younger, glibber, effervescent males. It may be the attraction of opposites.

"Matilda has a great heart," Gus explained to me. "She piles boulders around it in the constant fear of assault. But in those days a concern for her wonderful little father was her vulnerable point. I think she always felt a bit guilty about marrying and leaving his humble abode for the splendors of Benedict. So when she discovered a boy who appreciated her old man for the saint he was, she warmed to him at once. And when Matilda comes over to you, it's for life. I might have been one of those delinquents she hires as houseboys."

We were sitting on the terrace after breakfast, drinking coffee. Chip had gone to school, and Gus and I had nothing to do on that fine October morning but breathe in the golden air and gaze across the rolling greens and reds to the glory of the Blue Ridge. It was delightful enough, to be sure, yet something in Gus's presence made me apprehensive. So large and soft, black haired and black garbed, with those big eyes that saw too much, he might have been an envoy from the great metropolis in the north sent to convince me that my little paradise was the illusion I had all the while suspected it was.

"Was it common for boys in Saint Luke's in your day to be so religious?" I asked.

"It was not uncommon. There was always a little group of the 'inspired.' Chip's grandfather had a great effect on us. We used to think of him as an early apostle. The kind of simple person who had learned from Christ directly and was not bothered by the theology of later Christians."

"A Saint Francis?"

"Or a Saint Luke. I wanted to be a missionary then."

"Why didn't you?"

Gus's shrug was mildly regretful. "I lost my faith. Sophomore year at Harvard."

"And the others?"

"Some did. Some didn't. A few became ardent Catholics, oddly enough, for Mr. B was not in the least doctrinal. One even became a Trappist monk."

"Was it like that in Chip's day?"

"Much less so. Mr. B, you see, had become headmaster by then. He was more absorbed in administrative details. Saint John, if you like, had become Saint Paul."

"Chip is full of Christian rules," I observed pensively. "But if he has any faith, he keeps it to himself."

"Then he probably doesn't have any. That's something that worries me about the Saint Luke's boys of Chip's time. The serious ones, I mean. They seem to have the rules without the faith."

"What's the harm in that?"

"There's nothing to moderate the rigidity of their logic."

"But surely the real danger comes from people with too much faith!" I protested, disliking the direction of our talk. "Fanatics and bigots. People who want to burn Jews and heretics."

"Well, of course, too much faith may be as bad as too little. What I suppose I'm trying to say is that if you scrap Christ, you'd better scrap the whole business of religion and take your chances with reason."

I stared. "I think Chip is perfectly reasonable. Don't you?"

"Is he reasonable with his mother? Is it reasonable to let the poor woman languish in his neglect and disesteem? Surely, if Chip were governed by his reason he would see that it is wanton cruelty to treat his mother as he does."

"Couldn't Mrs. Benedict make the first move? After all, it was she who started it."

"She doesn't dare! I've seen the poor woman. She's eating her heart out over Chip, and she hasn't the least idea what to do about it. Why don't you go up there and see what you can do?"

"But Chip would be furious!"

"Are you going to spend the rest of your life being scared of that young man? Where's the girl who gave Jonathan Askew his walking papers?"

"But I don't want to be that kind of girl! I'm perfectly happy being the kind of girl Chip wants."

"And how do you know he's always going to want such a milk toast?"

"I knew you were going to make trouble! I knew things were too good to last."

"Well, is he going to kill you for making peace in his family?" Gus demanded. "Do you want *me* to speak to him?"

"Oh, no, no."

"Then let me tell you something. A lot of the so-called ethics of the *jeunesse dorée* is simple snobbery. When God goes, Emily Post takes His place. It's bad form to lie or cheat. I suggest you convince your husband that it's lower middle class to be unkind to one's old ma."

"You don't know him, Gus," I said with a shiver.

"Maybe not, but do you?"

The more I thought about what Gus had said, the more I began to think he was right. Was there not perhaps in the very persistence of Chip's silence about his parents a concealed guilt? Might he not actually be relieved to admit it? And little by little the idea of playing the role of dove of peace began to appeal to me. Two weeks later, when I went to New York for the announcement of Deborah's engagement to Tom Ayers (Chip could not leave his Law Review work), I telephoned Mrs. Benedict to ask whether I could drive out for lunch. After a distinct pause of surprise she responded in a firm voice: "Of course, my dear. I'll be glad to see you. I'm sorry your father-in-law is away."

When I arrived at the house, an hour before lunch time, I was told that Mrs. Benedict was in the greenhouse, and I joined her there. I saw at once that talk would be easier for me if she was doing something with her hands, and I sat on an iron bench while she repotted her begonias.

"You're wondering why I came up."

She was standing with her back to me, but she now stopped handling the flowers. "Isn't it natural for a son's wife to call on his mother?"

"Not in our case. But does it have to go on this way? Can't we ever be friends?"

That long back, garbed in a gardening smock, was still un-turned. "Do you really want us to be?"

"Very much."

"Why?"

This almost daunted me, but I pressed on. "Because I need you."

Mrs. Benedict turned at this, and there was at last a hint of sympathy in her haggard, watery eyes. She sat down abruptly on the bench beside me. "Tell me why you need me, Alida."

"Because I'm married to the most wonderful man in the world. So wonderful that *he* doesn't need me!"

"Does he need anyone?"

"Oh, he must! Deep down. You, maybe. His father. I'm so worried!" I hadn't realized until that moment how much I was.

"But haven't you got just about everything you wanted?"

"Oh, I know you think I went after Chip. It's not true. He chased me wildly!"

Mrs. Benedict was at once severe again. "But that is a thing young men do. You were engaged. You had no business see-ing him."

I saw now that my only chance lay in tears. And when they came, they were not artificial. Far from it. I wanted to be loved by this gaunt, implacable creature! It was as if she were some grim guardian about to close forever the golden gate of salvation. "Please, Mrs. Benedict," I gasped with a sob, "can't you help me? I love Chip so, and I want to help him, and I don't see how I can do it without you and your husband!"

Well, that did it. Those long bony arms were around me, and I was clasped to the Roman matron's breast. I was aware of her faintly malodorous breath. But I didn't care. I hugged her as I had never dreamed of hugging my own mother!

"Bless you, my child, you and I are going to turn over a clean new page! And we're going to write wonderful things on it, too. You see if we don't. I think for a long time I've been wanting to love you. And that's not just a way of getting back into Chip's heart, either." Then she released me and sat back to contemplate me with a small sad smile. "If Chip has a heart, that is."

"Oh, Mrs. Benedict, don't even think that he hasn't!"

"Very well, dear, I shan't."

When I departed, after a long emotional lunch in which I learned a hundred things about Chip's boyhood that I hadn't known before, it was agreed that she and Mr. Benedict would come to Charlottesville for Thanksgiving.

But it was small thanks that I received from their son. I did not tell him about my talk with his mother until our cocktail time of six o'clock and then only after he had finished his drink. But he reverted at once to his soberest demeanor.

"Now what induced you to get into that?" he demanded in a sharp tone. "Didn't you know I had that situation under control?"

"I guess I didn't know it was that much of a 'situation.' "

"Of course you did! And you knew I didn't want you in their camp. Isn't that true?"

"I don't understand you!" I exclaimed, flushing. "I don't see why there have to be camps. Why can't I get on with your mother? Why can't we all be a happy family together?"

"Because I've broken away from them. And they're not going to get me back. And I don't want you mixed up with them. Is that understood, Alida? Is that clear?"

I almost rebelled then and there. But I checked myself at the last minute. I was still too afraid of him, afraid of what might happen to our marriage if I really crossed him.

"Very well. I'll tell them not to come on Thanksgiving."

"No, no!" he retorted impatiently. "That would be making too much of it. Let them come, but be sure you're on my side."

What was his side, and how could I not be on it? At any rate, the Benedicts came for Thanksgiving and stayed, not in the Farmington Country Club, but with us, and everything went off smoothly enough, thanks to my father-in-law's wonderful talent for appearing to take for granted that nothing was in the least way out of the ordinary. Mrs. Benedict wisely made no effort to communicate with me privately; she seemed to sense that any observed understanding between herself and me would be resented by Chip. But when she left, she gave me a warm embrace and murmured in my ear, "Don't worry, darling. We're getting there."

But were we? And where was "there"?

. . .

A greater crisis for Chip and me came shortly after this, just before Christmas in his last year at law school.

I have not spoken of Chessy Bogart, though he continued to play a considerable role in our lives. He had come to Virginia Law School with Chip, and he was very much a part of the weekend group that met every Saturday night for dinner and bridge or poker, sometimes at our house, sometimes at the house of one of the other law school couples who lived in the Farmington area. He had received a settlement from his uncle's supposedly bankrupt estate, and he had just enough, as a single man, to keep up with his richer friends, but at the end of our second year in Charlottesville, to everybody's surprise, he had married a New York girl, Suzanne Derby, whom I had known in my turbulent debutante year and who was sweet and pretty but had no money. Somehow it was not the match that we had expected of Chessy, but we thought the more of him for it.

"I know what you all were thinking," he told me, when he and I first discussed his engagement. "You thought I was going to marry some girl for her money. Now look what's happened. Some girl's marrying me for mine!"

"I'm sure that's not true. I remember Suzy. She's a darling."

"You mean she's dumb."

"I mean no such thing!"

"It's all right. I have no wish to marry a bright girl. *You're* bright. You're brighter than Chip, for that matter, but much good that may do him, once you've ceased to be his odalisque and become his consort."

"And just what do you mean by that?"

"I'm not going to tell you, because you know perfectly well what I mean. Anyway, we're talking about me and my engagement. All I expect of Suzy is that she be a good bedmate, have an amiable disposition and not let me down at the bridge table. And I have every reason to be assured of all three."

"Even the first?" I asked. It was long before the sexual revolution.

"Do I shock you?"

Chessy and Suzy found a tiny house right by the university and furnished it largely with wedding presents. Suzy seemed to adapt herself easily to her husband and his friends, and although she was uninteresting, she made a pleasant addition to our group. How they made ends meet, I don't know; I suspect that Chessy borrowed money, and probably from Chip. But Chip never talked to me about his finances. He gave me all the money I needed, though I never knew how much of his income it represented. When I asked him once, he simply replied, "Do you really want to get into that?" And I decided that I didn't.

Chessy, anyway, seemed assured of a good future. He was too much of a party-goer, even by Virginia standards, and he did the minimum homework, but he listened to the lectures, and his remarkable memory taped, as it were, every spoken word of his professors.

"They're all peacocks," he explained to me, "in love with their own tails. Spell it *t-a-l-e-s*. So long as you have the wit to toss back their own garbage on an exam, you have it made. Actually, you don't have to crack a book, except just enough to be able to answer occasionally in class."

His brilliance won him an editorship in the contest for the Law Review, but it proved a poor substitute for industry in the writing of articles, and his failure to pull his oar soon became a bone of bitter contention between him and Chip. When the final rift between them came, however, it was over something much graver than Chessy's omissions. It was not nonfeasance but actual malfeasance that now confronted us. You see, I had picked up some legal terms from Chip.

When I saw one morning from the living room window Chessy's blue Chevrolet pull up by our door, I thought at first it was Suzy. Chip had gone to school, as I assumed his friend had. But then I recognized Chessy at the front door alone, looking graver than I had ever seen him.

"I've got to talk to you, Alida."

"You look as if you could do with a cup of coffee."

"I'd rather have a whiskey, thank you."

"At ten o'clock in the morning? Well, you know where it is."

When we were settled by the fire, which I had lit, for it was a cold day, he began.

"Do you remember Bob Reardon?"

I did. He had been a classmate of Chip and Chessy's, a Virginian, from Norfolk, an agreeable but silent young man, an editor of the Review, who had shot himself in the cellar of his fraternity house the spring before for no reason that anyone had ever been able to determine. But Virginia men could be like that, I had learned — inscrutable, mysterious.

"Of course. Chip asked him out here a couple of times. He didn't say much, but his silences were better than our yacking. Have they ever found out . . . ?"

"Why he did it? No. But that's not why I bring him up. His mother recently sent Chip a folder of his Law Review notes. She thought they might be of some use."

"How considerate. And were they?"

"Wait. You will be the judge of that. Do you recall how hotly Chip has been after me to write a note for the February issue?"

"Oh, yes. I really don't see why, Chessy, you make it so hard for him."

"Well, I wrote the damn note. It was on what constitutes a failure to bargain collectively under the Labor Relations Act. It was a subject that I had assigned last year to Bob Reardon and on which he had submitted an outline. I decided to use the poor fellow's outline, and I wrote the note. Chip accepted it and scheduled it for the February issue."

I looked at him blankly. "Is there some question of plagiarism? Surely an outline's nothing."

"A mere outline is nothing, I agree. But there's more to come. In Reardon's portfolio there was an almost completed note that bore a curious resemblance to mine. Enough so for Chip to accuse me of plagiarism."

My little world, bounded by the Blue Ridge and Mr. Jefferson's rotunda, tottered. "But if you didn't have Bob's draft . . . ?"

"Ah, but Chip says I must have. He has removed my note from the galleys of the February issue. He has replaced it with an old one of his own that he brought up to date."

"So that's why he worked till dawn the last two nights! I wondered what had happened."

"Yes. He said he had to fill the space somehow."

"But how do you explain it, Chessy? A fantastic coincidence?"

"A coincidence. They happen, you know. Possibly Reardon and I had discussed his note in more detail than I remember. But I promise you, Alida, I did not have a copy of that draft."

"Why couldn't Chip have published the note with both yours and Reardon's initials on it?"

"I suggested that. He turned it down flat. He said it would be compounding a crime. That he could not do such a thing under the university's honor system. Or, he added, under his own."

I looked hard at Chessy's oddly constricted countenance. Was he, who laughed at everything, restraining a laugh at this? I groped for a spar amid the swish of sinking vessels.

"Anyway, it's over."

"But it's not. Chip says if I don't resign from law school, he'll report the matter to the Honor Court."

"You're not serious!"

"Would even I be guilty of that joke? You must talk to Chip, Alida. You must make him see some kind of sense. I verily believe the man's gone mad!"

"Then what can I do?" I moaned.

Chessy and I discussed the matter passionately for another forty minutes, but we added nothing to what I have already described. It was an hour after he left before Chip came home for lunch, and I had had two stiff drinks out of the bottle Chessy had opened. Chip picked up the glass by my chair, sniffed it and said tersely, "Chessy, of course, has been here."

"Darling, let me get *you* a drink before we discuss it."

"I have no need of one. You know how I feel about drinking before six."

"But this is a crisis."

"I don't know that it's a crisis. It's a tragedy. For Chessy, anyway. And, to a lesser extent, for me. Because our friendship will hardly survive it. It's certainly not a crisis in the sense that there's anything to do about it. It's done."

"You mean the note's withdrawn."

"Well, that of course. I was referring to my ultimatum to Chessy."

"Surely you won't stick to it!"

"What are you talking about, Alida? Of course I'll stick to it."

"You mean you'll deliberately ruin Chessy's law career? Maybe his whole life as well?"

Oh, how tightly Chip set his lips! He was silent for a few minutes while he controlled his impatience. When he spoke, his tone was clipped, almost condescending. "You are being dramatic. Chessy's career will not be ruined unless he chooses to go before the Honor Court. If he does that and is convicted — as I have little doubt he would be — he will be expelled from the university without credit. If on the other hand he resigns, on any grounds he chooses — health, lack of funds, ailing parents — he will be able to transfer to another law school. The

Wall Street firm that has already offered him a job will probably not be too concerned. Actually, I am doing him a great favor. For I'm not at all sure that my failing to report him isn't in itself a violation of the honor code."

"But, darling, how can you be so sure that he copied that note? Couldn't the resemblance be a coincidence? Chessy swears it was!"

"You can judge for yourself. I've got both notes in my briefcase."

"But what do I know about collective bargaining?"

"You don't have to know anything about it. The similarities are obvious. A child could see that Chessy was a plagiarist. And I don't think any more of him for coming weeping to you and lying in his teeth."

In his now handsome indignation, so much more appealing than his cold contempt, he might have been Sir Galahad. I shook my head to dispel a reluctant admiration.

"But this is you and Chessy, Chip!" I cried, as the full grotesqueness of the situation suddenly struck me. "You and Chessy and a cribbed note, if you like. It's been taken out of the Review. There's nothing left of it! Chessy isn't going to do anything like that again. He only did it, anyway, because you put so much heat on him. Can't you forgive him?"

"It's not a question of forgiveness. We took the pledge to observe the honor code when we came down here. One of the principal duties is to report a violation. And there is no question in my mind that Chessy violated the code when he submitted a paper that was not his."

"But you caught it in time, darling!"

"Fortunately for Chessy, yes. If it had already been published, I should have had no alternative but to report him."

"Isn't that what we used to call snitching?"

Chip did not flinch. "That's what we should have called it at Saint Luke's or Yale. But in Virginia they think differently about these matters. The university is full of stories of men turning in their closest friends. I didn't have to come down here, but having come, I certainly intend to abide by their rules."

I stamped my foot. "I can't see it! Here we are, you and I and Chessy. In a few more months we'll be out of this place. How can you let some crazy code designed by ancient slaveholders control what *we* three do in a matter known only to us?"

"That is your way of looking at it. I've told you mine."

"But doesn't it kill you, Chip?"

"Kill me?"

"To hurt Chessy this way? Your dearest friend? Who introduced us?"

Chip could quote Shakespeare at the damndest times! He actually smiled now. " 'What? Michael Cassio, that came a-wooing with you?' "

I saw then that it was hopeless. "You'll be smothering me next," I muttered. "Like Desdemona."

I don't know what I might not have done had he not stepped forward just then to take me in his arms. "I know this is hard on you, dearest. And after all, you didn't take the oath. But I did, and you must try to let me live with my conscience."

I hugged him, sobbing. "But it's such a monster for me to share you with!"

I said no more, because I was a coward. If Chessy threatened to stand between me and my love, I was going to throw Chessy, innocent or guilty, to the dogs. That was simply the way things were. I am afraid that Chip's very ruthlessness, his hard bright honor, as shining as his blue eyes and pale skin, had a strong sexual attraction for me. In life, as in fantasy, I wanted to be held tightly, dominated, suffocated. Yes, like Desdemona!

I did not see Chessy before he left school. He explained to people that he had to move back to Brooklyn to be closer to his mother, who had had a stroke. He transferred without difficulty to New York University Law School. I believe that Mr. Benedict, who was a trustee of that university, provided some assistance at Chip's request. I doubt that Chessy told the true story to anyone, including his wife, though I suppose he must have squared his mother in some fashion to make her feign a temporary ailment. But from what little I knew of Mrs. Bogart, she was putty in her clever son's hands. Certainly Chip never told anyone, so the secret is revealed for the first time on this page.

No, that is not true. I have just remembered that I *did* tell somebody: my mother-in-law. When Chip graduated, she and Mr. Benedict came down to Charlottesville for several days, and she and I took a couple of long walks in the spring countryside. On one of these I told her the story of Chessy and confessed my doubts as to the rectitude of what Chip had done. Mrs. Benedict stopped short and looked at me in surprise.

"But, Alida, what else could he possibly have done? I think he behaved admirably! And with the greatest kindness and consideration, too. I suppose you will not want me to speak to him about it, but otherwise I should offer him my heartiest congratulations!"

"Well, please don't" was all I could murmur. These Benedicts!

11

CHIP

AFTER CHIP married Alida, and before he went down to Charlottesville, he visited the Bank of Commerce on Wall Street to determine exactly what family property had been put in his name and under what conditions. The officer who received him, though polite, was reluctant to impart the whole truth, but under persistent questioning he had no choice but to do so. Chip was not only the absolute owner of a considerable number of securities; he was entitled to the income of a sizable trust fund. These properties had been handled by his father under a power of attorney signed by Chip on his twenty-first birthday. This he now promptly revoked, directing that the income henceforth be remitted to him directly and sending formal notice to his father that he would no longer be responsible for any poor relatives. He would not be rich, he concluded, by Benedict standards, but when he moved to Charlottesville, he would probably be one of the richest students at Virginia Law.

His father invited him to lunch at the Yale Club the very next day. Chip could hardly decline.

"Of course I'll take over the cousins," Elihu told him with his usual cryptic smile. "But are you sure, my boy, that you're acting in your own best interests? I thought you and I had agreed that I should handle any money settled on you for tax reasons while you were busy being educated."

"I've changed my mind. That is, if I ever really made it up. From now on, I'll be my own boss."

"You don't consider that you may hold money that your mother and I gave you in a kind of moral trust?"

"I don't see how a money trust can be moral. But of course I understand what you're driving at. You'd be entirely justified in disinheriting me. Go ahead."

Elihu, as usual, betrayed no indignation. He simply raised his eyebrows as if he had just received an interesting proposition. "I know that some young people today despise what they consider the ill-gotten gains of their progenitors. But I never heard of an idealist who chose to live off those gains while he reviled the generation that earned them."

"I'm not reviling anybody, Dad. Nor am I in the least a radical or revolutionary. I simply consider that the money you and Mother settled on me is a fair price for the moral domination you have chosen to exercise over me. I shall probably need every penny of it to pay for the operation of severing that umbilical cord!"

Looking into his father's widened eyes and at his now shriveling smile, he knew that the shaft had gone home. Was the dark pleasure, which was bound to turn into a pain as acute, if not more so, for himself, really worth it? And yet he could not help himself; he knew that he was doomed to strike and strike again.

"I don't care what you say, Chip. I refuse to cut you off. I shan't give you that satisfaction. Now go on down to law school, do one hell of a job there and forget all about your mother and me!"

As if Chip could! The family affection, the family expectations, seemed to permeate the atmosphere around the temporary oases of New Haven and Charlottesville like a coiling miasma. He had cut himself free for the moment, it was true; he was standing on his own two feet. He would have regarded as a sentimental weakness any refusal on his part to use money that had been legally settled on him. But the maintenance of that liberty was still going to be a long and arduous endeavor. It would have been easier had he been allowed to effect, at least during his law school years, a total breach with his parents, but how could he do that in the face of their refusal to take formal offense? He would have seemed shockingly brutal to his whole family, to his friends, to Alida. He had not even been able to prohibit his parents' rare but regular visits. Alida, on whom he had counted for total cooperation, on whose dislike of his mother he had built his hope of alliance, had insisted on inviting them.

He suspected that his attitude towards women might bear a relation to that of the ancient Greeks: that the satisfaction which they offered was largely physical. But Alida was obviously not going to be contented with any such limited role in his life. She seemed determined, on the contrary, to explore every aspect of his personality for the possible existence of hidden doors and rooms. The beautiful worldly debutante, who had happily resigned her tiara to be Mrs. Charles Benedict, was showing definite signs of using her leisure time — of which, it seemed, she had decidedly too much — to study her lord and master. Why could she not find a better occupation?

For unlike his Greek predecessors, Chip was not opposed to careers for women, nor did he deem women intellectually inferior to men. He had the greatest respect for his mother's intellectual capacities, and if he recognized that his father's were greater, he did not think that sex was the reason for it. But he did believe, where mere companionship was concerned, that men had more to give men, and women, presumably, more to give women, than either sex had to give to the other. He would not have begrudged Alida a job; he did begrudge her a life hobby of himself.

"Why don't you write a novel?" he would ask her. "These sonnets are all very well, but I think it's time you took on something more challenging."

It was a pity for her, he supposed, that he had a mind that could take in only one field at a time. At Yale he had been preoccupied with literature, Alida's favorite subject, but now it was law, and there was no way that she could join him in the subtleties of interpreting the commerce clause or in the intricacies of corporate reorganizations. Besides, she wouldn't have liked it even had she understood it. It wasn't her kind of thing. She could never have shared his delight in legal categories or in the relief that his imagination found at the "reasonable" borderlines where legal thinking called a halt to speculation. She would not have admired, as he did, the practical solutions of the common law to the chaotic problems raised by human perversity. Alida's enthusiasm and romanticism, indeed, had begun to seem messy to him.

And yet if she would only stay, so to speak, on her side of the bed, how charming she could be! Chip did not believe in making love except when he was actually so engaged; in fact, he was disgusted by couples who were always exchanging amorous ogles. He had been most attracted to Alida when she had most resisted him; he wondered, wistfully at times, what had happened to the mocking girl who had been so rude to his parents on their first meeting.

His restlessness at her aimlessness, however, turned into something more like disapproval when she at last seemed to have developed a purpose in life: that of bringing about a reconciliation with his parents. It was as if she had scented the renewal of "normalcy" that must inevitably follow his graduation, the return to the "real world" of Benedict that would end the golden fantasy of Charlottesville, and that she wanted to break in her husband to the life that there had never been any serious doubt (except in his own daydreams) that they were going eventually to lead. Was Alida any different, really, from his own mother in her fixed female adherence to the here and now, her refusal to accept any real nobility of concept as aught but a male fantasy? Oh, women could be revolutionaries, yes, and then they threw bombs, but short of that they took their chances, all too happily, with the status quo.

But the worst thing that happened to him in Virginia was not of Alida's making. It was of Chessy's. That Chessy should have shown himself rotten to the core, putrid beyond any chance of redemption, had been a blow from which Chip did not immediately see how he was going to recover. For it had been Chessy with whom he had first allied himself, soul to soul, in the crisis that had shown him his parents for the shallow materialists they were. And if Chessy had to be cast into the outer darkness to which all along Elihu and Matilda Benedict had gladly consigned him, if Alida, the bright and beautiful, was converted to an obsequious daughter-in-law, if all the privileged youth of the Farmington Country Club brayed mockingly like donkeys at the very idea of Chip Benedict ever being anything that they had not taken entirely for granted (did he not subsist on Benedict dividends?), what had become of his resolution to be a free soul? Did he even have a clear idea of what he wanted to do with the shining sword of his new professional capacity?

. . .

For all of these reasons the advent of war came as an actual relief to Chip. All decisions were now indefinitely or — who knew? — perhaps permanently postponed. Right after graduation he enrolled in midshipmen's school on the USS *Prairie State,* docked in New York, and received his commission as an ensign just before Pearl Harbor.

He was ordered immediately to sea and spent a year on an old destroyer escorting convoys in the Caribbean between Guantánamo and Colón. It was dull duty, punctured by a very occasional submarine attack, for the Germans were more occupied with the supply route to England than with stopping the shipment of cigarettes and magazines to the armed forces in the Canal Zone. To Chip, the long night watches and the never-changing tasks constituted a not altogether unpleasant vacuum, a kind of drugged routine, a suspension of life.

He did not feel so much parted in space from Alida and their baby girl as in time. His wife and child seemed to belong to Charlottesville, to the Blue Ridge, to the golden haze into which his law school days had retreated. He did not really miss them, because in an odd way they had ceased to exist for him. When he thought of them, he thought of them with affection, and his letters to Alida were conscientious and detailed. But he did not think of them very much. And when, during his ship's dry dock period in Colón, he moved into the apartment of a famous stripper, who filled the biggest cabaret in town nightly by a dance in which she simulated her own rape by a gorilla, her torso divided longitudinally between a hairy ape skin and shining nudity, he felt no remorse. The stripper corresponded to war as Alida did to peace.

Alida wrote him long, lonely, nostalgic, uncharacteristic letters from Benedict, where she was living with his parents.

"It seems so wrong that I should be sitting up here with every comfort while you toss about the ocean, a prey to hungry gray Nazi sharks. And yet I would gladly change with you, darling, for the mere bliss of knowing you were safe. Yet imagine you here, with the baby and me on the bridge of a destroyer! How you would loathe me if I were able, by a miracle, to effect such a transfer! War seems to bring out the elementary difference between the sexes. But is it not time that you applied for a little home leave? Might you not even be entitled to a spell of shore duty? Oh, dearest, please! Your mother refuses to join me in this plea, which I have just read aloud to her. She says that a man must make up his own mind in these matters. Didn't you once compare her with Volumnia in *Coriolanus*? You were so right! And yet she and your father have been more loving to me than my parents ever dreamed of being. They are beyond praise."

Chip did not at all like this rather crawling submission to what he deemed the suffocating affections of Elihu and Matilda. And he certainly had no idea of applying for shore duty. Instead, when his destroyer was scheduled for decommissioning, and the officers were asked to submit their applications for new duty, he put his in for amphibious training.

The skipper raised his eyebrows when he read it. "Here's

one application that's sure to be granted. What the hell are you doing this for?"

He was granted two weeks' leave before reporting for duty at an amphibious training camp on the Chesapeake, and he elected to spend it in a suite in the St. Regis in New York. Alida joined him there, with the baby, but he dispatched the little girl and her nurse back to Benedict after only a day that they might not interfere with musicals and night clubs. Chip planned the maximum distraction to help him and Alida with the difficulty that so many couples found in wartime reunions, and he was relieved when it was time to go to Virginia. He hoped that he would be able to cope with this too adoring, rather sticky war wife when peace returned, but in the meantime he could not seem to be both a naval officer and a husband. He was able to do something for the poor girl, at any rate, for, as they soon found out, she was pregnant when he left.

It would have been possible for Alida to stay in a hotel near Camp Crawford, but he would not allow this. He told her, honestly enough, that her presence would distract him, and she meekly assented. He had no wish further to confuse his time zones.

At Camp Crawford, where the long brown barracks descended a long brown bank to the flat gray of the Chesapeake, Chip found himself the designated commanding officer of an LST, or landing ship tanks, a three-hundred-and-thirty-foot amphibious vessel then nearing completion at the Boston Navy Yard. In Virginia, for indoctrination with him on training LSTs in the Chesapeake, were his eleven junior officers. Chip soon realized that his new elevation was a hardly dazzling one. None of his fellow officers had ever been to sea, even in a sailboat; they were fresh out of college and ready enough to take orders from a man who had not only spent a year on a destroyer in a war zone, but had graduated from law school. The courses were easy, and he spent most of his time coaching them.

The only person at Camp Crawford who interested him at all was his future flotilla commander. Gerald Hastings, Commander, USN, thirty-seven years of age, was a stocky man, a bit on the short side, with thick, long blond hair that came down low over his forehead, a hooked nose and eyes of an expressionless white-gray. He looked out of the latter at a world of conscripted civilians as if he were doing all that he could to control his impatience, and before he spoke he would pause, as if to get his natural exasperation under rein. It was obvious that he considered his amphibious command as one totally unfitting an officer trained in the "real" navy. Rumor had it that as navigator of the newly commissioned battleship *Florida*, he had been held responsible for the grazing of the sacred hull against a rock on the Maine coastline during her shakedown cruise. Disgrace had been followed by amphibious assignment. Rumor also had it that the captain of the *Florida* had disregarded his navigator's warning but that a doctored log had covered the true culprit at a board of investigation. This was enough to make Hastings a Byronic hero to Chip, and he forgave his aloofness, his driving discipline, his occasional savage sarcasms. For Hastings was a relentless taskmaster, who never saw fit to praise or even encourage. Reserve officers to him were so many gnomes who had to be drilled; one could not expect excellence, and it would be idle to deplore incompetence.

One autumn afternoon some twenty officers were on board one of the training ships to practice beaching. Under way to the area of operations, Chip watched Hastings standing alone on the starboard wing of the bridge, facing the brisk wind, his eyes watching the old battleship *New York*, also on a training cruise, as she approached the slowly moving line of LSTs. He saw the chief quartermaster, sleek, fat, mustachioed, approach the commander with the oily insinuation that some basic understanding had to exist between a regular officer and a regular NCO exiled in a motley mob of reserves. Chip could not hear what the chief was saying, but he could hear the commander's reply.

"I don't have to talk to you, Chief."

Chip almost laughed aloud. There was no reproach in the commander's tone, no reprimand, hardly even a rebuff. It was the simple statement that he did not choose to speak to anyone to whom he was not duty bound. And the chief took it so! He carried his rejected gossip back to the wheelhouse, where he was soon enough busy taking down a flashed message from the *New York*. But when he emerged to show the message to the commander, he would not have been human had he not revealed a glint of malicious satisfaction. Later, Chip learned that the message had read, "Get that junk out of my way."

So did the commanding officer of a battlewagon deign to address an order to an amphibious flotilla! Chip noted the tightened lips of the commander as he silently handed the message back to the chief. The line of LSTs changed course.

Later, during the beaching exercises, Chip watched the commander's face each time their vessel approached the shore at her flank speed of eleven knots. Just before the impact the commander would abruptly avert his gaze. He could not bear to witness the contact of the bottom of a naval ship to soil! Was it not the nightmare of every regular officer to find himself heading at full speed to an imminent collision? And did that nightmare not have to be a living hell to the former navigator of the *Florida*?

On their way back to the camp after the exercises, Hastings walked suddenly over to Chip and lit a cigarette.

"I understand you served a year on the *Seward*, Benedict. Whatever made you put in for this duty?"

"It's a new kind of warfare, sir."

"But you might have had a spot on a cruiser."

"I suppose it seems odd to you, sir. But as this may be the only war I'll ever be in, I wanted to see more than one side of it."

Hastings grunted. "You sound like a dilettante."

Chip stiffened. "Will that be all, sir?"

"No. How would you like to be skipper of my flagship?"

Chip was pleased but hardly surprised. He had seen the commander's eye on him; he was obviously better than the others. "Very much, sir."

"I'd like to talk to you." It was difficult for Hastings to show even passable manners to a junior. "Shall we go out tonight for a few drinks?"

"I'm at your disposal, sir."

"I'll pick you up in my jeep at eight. At your BOQ."

They drove that night to a bar in a town ten miles from the camp. Clearly the commander wanted to get away from everything that suggested the amphibious navy. In their dark little booth he drank Scotch after Scotch. To Chip's surprise, he did not seem to wish to discuss flotilla business. He told him instead about the insulting message from the *New York*.

"If I had been told as a middy that I would ever live to experience such a humiliation . . . !"

Then he broke off abruptly and asked Chip some questions

about his life and background. It appeared that he had done his homework on his flagship skipper, for he knew about the Benedicts and Benedict. But he had no objection, he observed curtly, to wealth.

"Annapolis men are supposed to be snobs. Or didn't you know? We have to marry dough if we want our children to grow up to be little ladies and gentlemen. I've never been in the swing. Like a poor sap, I married for love."

"I didn't take you for a snob, sir."

"Just for an SOB? You dropped the *n*?"

"I don't care if my boss is an SOB so long as he's a competent flotilla commander."

"And I'm that?"

"So far, anyway."

"Are you trying to flatter me, Benedict?"

Chip suppressed a smile. "By agreeing that you're an SOB? Maybe. Are you so proud of it?"

Hastings snorted. "Okay. We're quits. I *am* a good flotilla commander. And what's more, you're going to be a good LST skipper. Though that's not saying much. I never saw such a sorry lot of supposed naval officers as I have down here. Does it matter, though? What is an LST but a sea truck? Anyone can drive one. But I'm damned if my flagship isn't going to have at least a vague resemblance to a naval vessel. If it kills me! And that's why my flag is going up on your LST."

"I am honored, sir."

"Oh, no, you're not, Benedict! Don't give me that. You're pissed off. Every officer and man on your tub is going to hate your guts. They'll know they can't be ragamuffins under my eye. And, by God, it'll be your job to see they're not!"

Chip glanced at his almost empty glass. "Will that be all, sir? Perhaps I should be getting back to the base."

As he had anticipated, Hastings looked disappointed. "Is it so pressing?"

"Not, of course, if you want me to stay."

"Well, God damn it all, I do want you to stay!" Hastings was beginning to show the effect of the whiskey. "Can't you imagine that even a flotilla commander might want a little human company?"

But Chip was unyielding. "Human company or naval company? Does the commander want to drink with the lieutenant? Or does Gerry Hastings want to drink with Chip Benedict?"

"Drink with me, Chip."

"With pleasure, sir. And we'll have a bottle on me. Waiter!" Chip proceeded to order a quart of the best Scotch that was available.

Hastings nodded to approve. "I like the way you did that. For you know, Chip, even if I married a poor girl, I'm still a snob. I like aristocrats. I'm a bit of one myself. My great-grandfather was a captain under Farragut. And my old man served with Dewey in Manila."

"That's better than making glassware, isn't it?"

"Oh, I think so," Hastings candidly agreed. "I never meant that your family was aristocratic. I meant that you were. You're too good for a grubby trade like that, my lad. Though I suppose once this war is over, your old man will expect you back in the shop."

Chip had never before heard the idea expressed that *he* might be too good for Benedict. He found it decidedly agreeable. "I'd love to know why you went into the navy."

"There was never any idea I wouldn't. From the time I was a small kid. We have a family tradition of service. It's as if we had been chosen by God to guard America. Seriously! We look at all you capitalists as so many children romping in the fields, blissfully unaware, as you pick one another's pockets, of the wolves watching hungrily from the forest. And every couple of decades we have to take charge of things until the wolves have been beaten back. But then you can always go back to your little fun and games."

"I see. You really feel superior to us."

"Of course we do! Because whatever else we may be, we're men. And the only way you can tell a man from a dog is if he can kill and skin a wolf. We don't set much store on the art of pickpocketing."

"You belong to the Middle Ages, don't you?" Chip surmised. "When a man could live by his sword and leave moneymaking to Jews and usurers."

"Just so. The Industrial Revolution did away with gentlemen. You find them today only in the armed services."

"And it takes gentlemen to win a war?"

"You bet it does. MacArthur, Patton, Marshall — where will you find their types on Wall Street?"

"Then I am fortunate indeed to go into battle under the flag of Gerald Hastings!" Chip raised his glass.

"But what the hell can I do with a fleet of barges?" Hastings demanded, gloomy again. He hung his head as if struck by a sudden blow of depression. "When I think of the opportunity I had! Navigator of a battlewagon! You know, Chip, we wait all our lives for the blessed chance of war — it's what we live for, don't kid yourself it isn't, whatever the other regulars may say — and when the gods give me the one thing I begged and prayed for, what do I do but blow it? And condemn myself to this!"

"Where you will make your name," Chip insisted, with an air of confidence that he did not quite feel. It was almost awesome to him that even under the influence of the liquor Hastings would not attack the commanding officer who had foisted off his error on a junior. "How do you know the gods didn't plan it all for your benefit? Amphibious warfare is the coming thing. What can you do with battleships but fight other battleships?"

. . .

Chip and Hastings worked well together from then on. They went to Boston for the commissioning of the ships of the flotilla and the assembling and training of their crews, and Hastings moved his flag and small staff aboard Chip's LST. They sailed on a shakedown cruise to Providence, and the flotilla then crossed the Atlantic to London to await the anticipated invasion of France.

All hands chafed under the commander's relentless drive. But Chip noted that it worked. Hastings would board one of his vessels without warning at two in the morning, rouse up the captain, bring the crew to battle stations, put them through all the drills, including fire, collision and even man overboard, and then inspect the ship from bow to stern. He was always impassive and deliberate; he addressed his criticisms to the commanding officer and none other. He never offered the smallest commendation; a thing done wrong had to be corrected, that was all. And it was corrected, too. For the commander's dreaded nocturnal visitations would continue unabated until it had been.

One thing that surprised Chip was the degree of Hastings's animus against the enemy. He had surmised that a man with so small a regard for civilians might have a natural admiration for the spirit of Japan and Germany, which could create such splendid war machines. But this was not the case. Hastings took his role of protector of his nation so deeply to heart that he seemed to feel an actual obligation to hate and despise all that threatened it. There was no evidence that his universe contained a god, but it certainly contained a number of devils. Sometimes Chip wondered whether his friend was not more concerned with killing than saving.

"Why are we worth defending?" he asked him once.

"We?"

"All us wretched capitalists. All the people you sneer at: movie moguls, slick brokers, purveyors of porno rags and mags, shyster lawyers, quack doctors — all those that fail to recognize the supremacy of the navy blue. Why not let them burn up in the cleansing fire of a fascist victory?"

Hastings seemed shocked. "But don't you see I've got to have hope?" he cried. "What in God's name is the point of keeping America free if America won't someday produce something? And isn't that, damn it all, precisely what smart, trained bright guys like you were made for? Jesus, there must have been some reason for you!"

Only with Chip did he relax, and Chip, to deserve his confidence, had to run the tightest ship of all. He had become totally identified with his unpopular but respected superior, and the skippers of the other vessels always came to him when they needed something from the flag. It was not unlike his sixth-form year at Saint Luke's, when the masters used to ask him to intervene in their favor with Mr. B. He had as much faith, too, in the commander as he had had in his grandfather. Gerald Hastings was undeniably a great administrator.

12

✕✕✕✕

CHIP

THE INVASION went off easily, without damage to any of Hastings's flotilla, because they landed in Gold Beach, where the German opposition was not as strong as in the others. But on their second trip to Normandy, while they were waiting offshore at anchor for the tide to go out before disembarking their ammunition trucks, the ship was struck by a bomb from a low-flying Stuka. As there was no detonation, Chip, on the bridge, at first assumed that the bomb must have passed through a bulkhead and plunged into the sea. But the report of a search party soon revealed otherwise. It was on the tank deck in an ammunition truck. His first thought was that Hastings must at once transfer his flag.

He found the commander in the wardroom, drinking coffee, waiting for him.

"The bomb's in one of the trucks. It must have pierced two bulkheads. You can see it. It's sticking out."

Hastings was expressionless. "How near the bow doors?"

"Close. Second row."

"Good. Open them and lower the ramp. I know about demolition. I'll handle it. I'll need just one man, a volunteer, and a stretcher to carry the bomb. Get the crew aft as far as you can except for the men on the guns."

"Why? If it blows, it'll take the whole ship."

"Don't argue with me. You never know with bombs." Hastings was on his feet, putting his cap on. "Get that man, will you."

"I'm your man."

"Don't be an ass. You're the CO."

"The exec can run this tub. You've said yourself anyone can do it. You need a cool hand. I'm it."

Hastings paused, but only for a second. "Okay. You get the stretcher and turn things over to the exec. I'll be looking at that bomb."

Chip remembered afterwards that his mind seemed to have room only for action. He went to the bridge, told his white-faced executive officer to open the bow doors and assume command. All personnel not on guns were ordered to the fantail. He then went to the tank deck via sick bay, where he picked up a stretcher. He found the commander outlined against the dawn light filtering through the opening bow doors, intently studying the round black end of a cube protruding through the hole it had made in the truck side.

"It's all right," Hastings muttered. "If it's been through two bulkheads without going off, it's probably a dud. Put the stretcher down right here and do exactly as I tell you."

Chip felt an instant shock of relief. A dud. We're going to be heroes over a dud! But as he watched the commander's fingers begin to manipulate that cube, he realized with a second shock that Hastings was not treating it as a dud. His fingers moved so slowly that they seemed only to be grasping it.

The minutes ceased to be time; this was a void in space. So this is how it will end, Chip thought curiously. I won't even know it. Suddenly it will be over. Did I ever really exist? And if so, how can I end? But I will. And the problems will be over, too. Benedict. Mummie. The right and the wrong.

Out of nowhere came the commander's voice.

"You'll have to get the nose when it comes out. Handle it as if it were your sore prick. When I say 'Lift,' we place it on the stretcher."

Unbelievably, these things happened. Chip was surprised by the hard touch of the metal. Then he and the commander were lying on their stomachs on the ramp, lowering the stretcher, by its leather thongs, inch by inch to the water.

"Slowly, oh so slowly," Hastings whispered. Not till it was totally submerged did he say, "Okay. Let go."

Chip stared at the black water surface, hypnotized.

"Let's get the hell away from here! It may still blow."

Chip, walking down the tank deck after the quickly striding shape of his superior, realized that his shirt was a soggy, heavy lump of sweat.

Topside, in officers' quarters, Hastings said tersely: "Return the men to battle stations. And then report to my cabin."

When Chip pulled aside the curtain of the commander's compartment, a bottle was thrust suddenly in his hand. It was brandy. He took a long swig.

"Do you realize, Lieutenant Benedict, that you're drinking while your ship's at general quarters?"

"I'm following the flag, sir."

He felt Hastings's tight grip on his shoulder. They were the same hard fingers that had gripped the shell.

"Okay, pal. Now get your ass back to the bridge."

And Chip, standing up in the fresh early morning, looking out at the vast, now peaceful flat sea, felt a happiness such as he had never known before.

.   .   .

When the flotilla was next in London, Chip paid a visit to his friend Lars Alversen, at Navy Headquarters in Grosvenor Square. Lars was on Admiral Stark's staff, in a position of responsibility beyond his rank of mere senior lieutenant, as one could at once see from his large office and bare desk. He jumped up as Chip came in, his eyes alight with enthusiastic affection.

"Chip, by God! I knew you were in, and I was just going to your ship. I have news for you."

"Can it wait? Till I tell you something first?"

Lars looked at him, dumfounded. Then he laughed, as if this was Chip all over, and returned to his seat. "It will keep, I guess. What's on your mind?"

As Chip told the story of Gerald Hastings and the bomb, he could not but be impressed by how sympathetically Lars listened. Lars was that rarest of men, the perfect staff officer. It was obvious from the trim fit of his unwrinkled blue uniform, from the relaxed attention of his demeanor, that he had not been recently in any areas of bloody action, but he managed to imply that he knew you had been and to seem to deprecate, with just the right emphasis, his own immunity. Chip knew that Lars could not have escaped that immunity, no matter how much he had tried. He was too evidently indispensable to an efficient headquarters.

"He sounds like a great guy, but then you didn't do so badly yourself," Lars commented when Chip had finished his tale.

"Oh, I just stood by and did what I was told," Chip retorted, embarrassed at the idea that he might be seen as seeking credit for himself. "As a matter of fact, I think my duty as skipper was to have stayed on the bridge."

"Under the circumstances, that might be overlooked."

"Seriously, Lars, do you think you could put in a word for Hastings? He would give his soul to get back to what he calls the real navy."

"I'll certainly watch my chance. I happen to know there's a very important person in this building who considers that he got a raw deal on the *Florida*. The subject came up in personnel when we were going over the list of the LST group and flotilla commanders."

"Oh, Lars, if you only could!"

"I'll do my best. And if he gets a battleship or cruiser assignment in the Pacific, I suppose you'd like to go with him?"

"Would I? I certainly would!"

Lars looked at him curiously. "And now are you ready for my news?"

Chip stared. He had forgotten it! Suddenly he gasped. "Alida? It's come?"

"A fine eight-pound boy. Both doing well. Your ma sent word through the Third Naval District." As Chip simply gaped, Lars continued, "I'd have told you straight off, but you wouldn't let me."

"It must be the war. It gets you." Chip felt again the void that he had sensed on that early morning off the Normandy coast. Why in the name of God did he not feel more?

"Let me ask you something, Chip. You've been on sea duty now for over two years. You've had hardly any leave. I think

I could arrange for you to do a spell of shore duty in New York or Washington. Wouldn't you like to catch up with Alida and the new baby?"

Chip twisted his brown cap and then folded it smoothly again on his knee. "I suppose I sound like a monster to you, Lars, but I want to see this thing through first."

"You don't sound at all like a monster to me. But I fail to see why you must do quite so much more than your share."

"Maybe you could spare an evening and go out with me and Hastings. I think you might see what I mean. With him, everything seems to make a kind of sense. Even if it's a pretty ghastly sense. All you have to think about is getting the Hun's bloody paws off the Continent. The more krauts we kill, the better."

"Better? You mean it would be best if we killed them all?"

"I guess the bad ones would be enough. Most of the prisoners I've seen at the beaches are tickled pink to be out of it."

"And do you and the commander feel the same way about the Japs?"

"What's the difference?"

"So you'd be just as happy on duty in the Pacific?"

"Happy isn't the word. Satisfied, if you like."

Lars whistled. "Who'd have thought you'd become such a fire-eater, Chip?"

"It isn't that. It's the simplicity of it. Of course, it's probably artificial, but everything's been artificial since we donned the fig leaf. The point is, I don't have to be concerned with Mummie and Daddy and Benedict and God and love, love, love. All I have to do is kill rats. They're out there, in the sky, the sea, the air. And maybe in killing them I can get rid of some of the rottenness in myself."

"I see," Lars mused. "It's a kind of exorcism. Of the devil in you. The excuse to kill."

"Call me a nut and have done with it."

"Ah, but it's nuts like you who win wars! Time enough to muzzle you when we have an armistice. Yes, I'd like to meet your commander. You wouldn't be free tonight, would you? I can usually get out of here by ten or eleven."

Somewhat to Chip's surprise, Hastings appeared to like Lars. The latter took them to his club, Roters, which Hastings obviously loved, and where through some dispensation (Lars always obtained one) they were able to sit in the bar until two in the morning.

As Chip drank, deeply for him, he felt a surge of the same euphoric happiness creep through his body as he had felt on the bridge of his ship after the disposal of the bomb. What was it? He looked about the long narrow room, of which they were the only occupants, with its low leather chairs and dark prints of dead statesmen, and saw nothing to elate him. Was it the arrival of the little boy across the Atlantic and the relief that Alida was well? But he had been convinced all along that the child would be a boy and that Alida would bear him easily. That pleasure had been discounted in advance. No, it had more to do with his pleasure in the sudden congeniality between his two friends as they discussed the war in the Pacific.

"Lars here knows the navy as well as a regular," Hastings observed to Chip.

"I never thought I'd live to hear Gerry Hastings say that of a reserve!"

"Chip thinks I'm prejudiced because of what I've said about amphibious officers. But they're hardly a fair sample of the reserve."

"Come now, Commander. Surely some of ours have done very well."

"But look whom they've had to train them!" Hastings exclaimed with a laugh of unabashed conceit as he finished his drink and rose to refill it at the now unattended bar. "You don't have to have been to Annapolis if you've been trained by an Annapolis man."

"Like me!" Chip agreed, not minding at all that the whiskey made him fatuous.

"Chip seems to think he's learned a lot from you, Commander," Lars observed. "It makes me wonder if I haven't missed an essential part of my education by being stuck at a desk."

"Well, London's not so far from the front, and it's going to be right on it when these new flying bombs start your way." Chip noted that Hastings seemed eager to put Lars at his ease. Was it simple deference to headquarters? Or an immediate awareness of the essential gentleman in Lars?

"What is your opinion of the real lesson of war?" Lars continued. "I mean to basic civilians, like Chip and me."

"Chip may not be as basic a civilian as you think," Hastings replied with a wink. "Though I suspect you are, Lars. And in your case, anyway, I mean that as a compliment. But to answer your question in the simplest terms, the real lesson of war, in my opinion, is that we need one every so often to keep us from getting soft and mean."

"That was Justice Holmes's theory," Lars commented, turning to Chip. "Do you remember how we all deplored it at Yale? 'The Soldier's Faith'? The sword-slashed faces of the students at Heidelberg that inspired Holmes with such respect? It was the price, he maintained, of breeding a race fit for leadership." He swung back now to Hastings with a disarming smile. "Why isn't that Hitlerism, sir?"

"It's part of Hitlerism, I grant," the latter conceded equably. "But only a part. There's no law that compels me to buy the rest of the bag. Look. I don't care how much you squirm and twist at the idea, the fact remains that every male knows, deep down in his heart, that what I say is true. Oh, of course you do everything you can to avoid so distasteful a conclusion. You point out that it takes as much guts to be truly independent and humane and reasonable as it does to fight a war. And maybe that's so — if a man is truly independent and humane and reasonable. But how many of the breed are? No, you can't get away from it, Lars. There's a horrid basic connection between the male leader and the warrior."

"What about a female leader?"

"Women are different. They don't have to be able to fight to preserve their character. That's why it's so often said that they're wiser than men. That in a world run by women there wouldn't be any wars. And maybe there wouldn't be. But it would have to be a world inhabited *only* by women. Don't blame me for this. Blame the Creator."

"Then there must always be wars?"

"It will be a sad thing for our sex when there aren't any. Unless we can invent some sort of substitute. Which we may have to, if wars get much more destructive."

"And by like token," Lars pursued, "we should be grateful to the Nazis and Japs?"

"Only in the sense that we're grateful to a vaccine that immunizes us from a dread disease. Gratitude doesn't alter the fact that it's full of foul germs."

Chip had been listening intently as he drank. In his rising

elation, he wondered whether anyone could seriously prefer a twentieth-century glass manufacturer to a medieval knight. History was all at once delightfully simplified.

"Suppose I were to stay in the navy after the war?" he asked suddenly. "Would I get ahead? Or would I always be branded as a reserve?"

"What would become of the sacred family business?" Lars demanded.

"It can look after itself. Anyway, Dad will live forever. No, I might seriously think of it. If Gerry here thinks I'd have a chance."

Hastings became even more serious; he shook his head. "Don't think of it, Chip. Not that you wouldn't get ahead. You would. We're going to need a huge navy after the war to police the world. England's shot; she won't be able to do it. And we'll have to use our reserves, yes. But that's not the point. The point is that you'd hate the peacetime navy. Red tape, bureaucracy, long duty at dull bases where your wife would have to say pretty-please to some admiral's horsy consort. No, Chip; you were born for the great world. You like the look of the armed forces in wartime, because now we're top dog. But just wait. Chip Benedict, president of Benedict Glass, will be a much hotter shot than Captain Benedict having one too many at the officers' bar in the Brooklyn Navy Yard after a dull day of signing forms."

"He's right, Chip."

"Will you form a law firm with me then, Lars?"

"I'll certainly think about it."

"He was my best friend," Chip said to Hastings, waving an unsteady arm towards Lars. "My best friend at Yale. But then a man called Bogart came between us. A cheat and a louse. Did you know he was that, Lars?"

Lars rose, smiling. "I didn't know *you* knew it, Chip. I'm glad you found out. I heard he left Virginia Law School. I wondered why. But now, if you both don't mind, I'm afraid I must turn in. I have to be at the office at seven."

"You think I'm drunk!"

"Well, you ought to be, Daddy."

And Hastings and Lars solemnly raised their glasses in a final toast to the newborn heir of the Benedicts.

. . .

In the six months before Chip received the anticipated transfer to the battleship *Maryland* in the Pacific, to which vessel Commander Hastings had preceded him, his LST crossed and recrossed the Channel some dozen times, but nothing of real note occurred. The personnel he transported to France, as the fighting front receded farther and farther from the beach, were increasingly auxiliary: supply corps, engineers, Red Cross and ultimately United Service Organization actors and singers to entertain the troops. Returning were paratroopers, the wounded and ultimately German prisoners. The last of these came aboard in orderly fashion and voiced no objection to the filthy condition of the tank deck into which they would be crowded, two or three thousand at a time, for as much as three days. One group, ordered to disembark at Southampton, actually complained that they needed more time to clean up the ship.

One night, at sea, Chip heard hundreds of voices from the tank deck below raised in a Brahms lullaby.

"It is as if they had left the devil behind them in Germany," he wrote Hastings. "You will call me a sloshy capitalist, wanting to have my soul and eat it, too, but I impenitently wonder if I didn't send something evil in myself to the bottom with that stretcher that we dropped over the side in Normandy."

Hastings, characteristically, did not comment on this passage in his answer. But when Chip was standing by his side, an assistant gunnery officer on the deck of the *Maryland*, their ears wadded as the gray leviathan shuddered and rocked with each detonation of her eighteen-inch guns aimed at the visible and defenseless coast of a now almost defeated Japan, he seemed to refer to it.

"There!" he exclaimed after the last roar. "That's for Pearl Harbor! And the next will be for Bataan and the death march! Do you know, Chip, it is almost worth having lived on this dreary globe to see our little yellow brothers get it for what they've done."

Chip marveled at the gleam in his friend's eyes. Impregnable on a battleship in a sea stripped of the enemy's fleet, he was the same relentless Hastings who had been within a second of being blown to bits by a German obus. But was there any reason that there should *not* be a light in his eye at the destruction of the forces of Satan?

"It won't be long now, Chip."

"Long before what?"

"Before this is over, and you capitalists can go back to your little games of picking pockets. Do you remember our talk the first night we went out to that bar at Camp Crawford?"

"Oh, yes. And you can go back to your little game of watching the wolves. Well, maybe we're both ready for it." He raised his binoculars to scan the distant, dull coastline. Then he shrugged. "After all, is this any more a man's job? To me it's like shooting cows."

13

CHIP

CHIP, however, was to allow himself one moment of euphoria before the reaction to four years of war fever set in. The terrible two A-bombs had been dropped and the great surrender made, and the long, gray engine of nemesis on which he served was entering the harbor of Sasebo to play its part in the occupation of the enemy. It was a cold autumnal day, slightly, perhaps ominously, overcast, and the dirty dark waters were faintly rippled by the chilly sea breeze. Chip, standing just below the bridge, had a broad view of the silent harbor and the masts, sticking up above the surface like broken or bent bollards, of sunken warships. Ahead of him, and soon all around him, were the anchored vessels of the conquering flotilla. Had Octavius Caesar entering the port of Alexandria, or Scipio Africanus descending upon Carthage, enjoyed a headier sight?

He tried briefly to put down the elation that was flooding

over him. He supposed it was giddy and immature to identify the power of industrial America that had brought to its knees a nation whose principal fault, in the opinion of many, had been simply to have come too late to the imperialist free-for-all, with the triumph of God's army in *Paradise Lost*. But wasn't it only human? he asked himself impatiently aloud, to the astonishment of the gunner's mate standing beside him. Wasn't it a point that these people had sown death and destruction, torture and mayhem, throughout Southeast Asia, and now were struck down? For one gorgeous, glorious hour at least, could the victor not allow his heart to pound to the thundering chorus of the Dies Irae? Even if he were succumbing to the forces of fantasy, could he not, for that little hour, have the pleasure of identifying himself with the good souls awakening on the terrible Day of Judgment, as shown in the old triptychs and tympanums that his mother had made him look at as a boy, and contemplating smugly the writhings and twistings of the damned? Sanity would come back soon enough.

It came in less than an hour. When the great ship had dropped her hook, he joined Gerry in the officers' mess for lunch. Most of the others were still on deck, and they had an end of a table to themselves. Gerry turned at once to business.

"We've got to see that our gunners get the word about proper behavior on shore. The old man's preparing a bulletin already. Apparently only yesterday four marines on liberty off the *Rochester* got drunk and held up a bank. It was kind of a lark, I suppose, but the admiral is livid. He says it's just the kind of thing that confirms what the Japs have always thought: that we're a nation of gangsters."

"They should know about that."

"Not at all. They're the most law-abiding country in the world. They have almost no lawyers, relatively speaking."

Chip grinned. "Is that your criterion of civilization? What about the prison camps and the death marches?"

"That was what they did *outside* Japan. They've paid for that. That's over."

"So now we can be the best of friends?"

"I don't know about friends. We can be allies. And we're going to need allies, too, in a reddening world."

"Can you really turn around that fast, Gerry? When I think of how you went on about the Germans and Japs! I thought you'd be as unforgiving as Clemenceau at Versailles!"

"I'm a military man, Chip. You keep forgetting that."

"It's precisely what I can never forget."

"Then you still don't know what a military man is. Well, how could you, with all these reserves around? Let me explain. A military man doesn't identify the enemy with any particular nation. The enemy is a state of mind that develops *in* another nation and has to be extirpated. Once it's extirpated, there's nothing left to hate. Clemenceau, may I remind you, was a civilian."

"I guess, then, I must learn not to think like a civilian," Chip said with a sigh. "Particularly as I shall so soon be finding myself one again."

"I'll send you a card every Christmas, saying, 'Who's the enemy now? Think!'"

Chip knew better than to ask Gerry about geisha girls; there were regular officers who had been to Japan before the war who were far better equipped to inform him, and in two days' time he managed to have, all to himself in a rented villa, one of the loveliest and most expensive girls in Sasebo. Her charm, her tact, her beautiful manners and quiet, muscular competence made her a new and enchanting experience. And her demonstrative pleasure at a bauble was the same that she showed if he gave her a diamond; he knew, for he did both. She carried artificiality to an art so high that it seemed even morally superior to naturalness.

Gerry had more to say to him about the nature of their conquered foe on a train journey they took to inspect the ruins of Nagasaki. Chip had tried to organize cultural expeditions in Sasebo for the men of their division — there were some beautiful shrines, a monastery and a palace — but he had had few takers. What the crew wanted to view was Nagasaki, an hour's trip away, which required a pass.

"What does it tell you about our countrymen," he asked Gerry, "that the only thing they want to see is something that has been totally destroyed?"

"A gaping hole instead of a lovely shrine? What do you expect? Isn't there something quintessentially negative in a culture based on the sale of antidotes to bad breath and body odor?"

"With an occasional breakfast food thrown in," Chip retorted. "No doubt it's the civilian in us."

He organized a party of some forty men, obtained the passes and took them to the train. Gerry and he, boarding only a minute before departure, mistook the last car for the more luxurious one reserved for American officers. When the conductor pointed this out, they assured him they were happy where they were and wouldn't bother to move. But the man shook his head emphatically and barked his answer like a drill sergeant.

"No, no! This not officers' car! You go officers' car!"

And he insisted on holding the train until they had taken their seats where they belonged.

"Why does he care so about our being comfortable?" Chip asked.

"He doesn't give a damn about our comfort. He wants to see that we go where we are *told* to go. Orders are orders — for us as well as him. That's why the Japs are going to win this occupation. They accept the fact that they have to obey MacArthur. But what they also see — and what preserves their national dignity — is that we have to obey MacArthur, too. So instead of being drowned in self-pity, like the occupied French, they stick their chests out. Americans and Japs are equally subject to the new Mikado, who just happens to be an American general."

"You really admire them, don't you? These men who, a month ago, you referred to as little yellow brothers?"

"Ah, but they were enemy then."

Nagasaki, ell-shaped, had lost the whole of one ell. Because most of the houses had been of wood, the destruction by fire was almost total, and as the rubbish had been assiduously cleaned away, Chip and Gerry drove their jeep almost unimpeded over the vast red-brown wasteland, punctuated here and there by the twisted steel structures of burned factories looking like the skeletons of fallen dirigibles. Stopping before one of these to take photographs, they saw a group of boys staring at them. For the first time in Japan Chip recognized hate in native eyes.

"Could anything justify it?" he asked as they drove on.

"The bomb? How about saving a million American lives?"

Chip felt too bleak to want more of his friend's remorseless realism. He had been about to ask whether the bomb could not have been demonstrated on some less populated area, but then the whole stark horror of it silenced him. They completed their tour almost in silence and then returned to the station.

"I think I know something that I mind more even than the loss of life," Chip said, ten minutes after the train back had started.

"The life lost wasn't so much more than what was caused by our incendiary bombs," Gerry muttered. "And nobody gripes about them."

Chip ignored this. "It's the loss of valor. Valor won't count for anything now. If your enemy can annihilate you, you have to give in to him. Churchill could have talked all day about fighting in the streets and in the fields, but if Hitler had had the bomb, 'We will never surrender' would have been an idle threat."

"Well, we'd better make damn sure no one else gets that bomb" was Gerry's only comment.

But Chip, as he pondered his new deduction for the rest of the ride, began to wonder whether there might not be an actual relief in the very core of this new horror. If men could exterminate each other, was it not possible — or at least conceivable — that they would not resort to war? And if they could no longer resort to war against an oppressor, they would have to come to terms with that oppressor. And presumably, in such a case, they would cease to dub him an oppressor. For what would such a dubbing be, after all, but simple bad manners? And without the nomenclature, perhaps some of the quality so denominated would disappear. If right could no longer beat down wrong, might right and wrong, having to live together, fusing perhaps, not become the same thing?

Chip could even speculate that a lifelong burden might be about to fall from his back, like Christian's in Bunyan's tale. It had always been his religion — or his obsession — or his superstition — that the world was made of evil, which had to be endlessly destroyed. Now perhaps it had become true that the process of destruction was futile. If so, was there anything to do but get on with one's life? Surely it was just as well that he would soon be going home.

14

ALIDA

ONE'S LIFE seems to divide itself into chapters of much varying length. In the beginning we need a new one for each school that we attend, sometimes each vacation, certainly each love affair. But then there come periods when whole years, maybe even decades, can be lumped into a single division, when our existence resembles nothing so much as a long western train trip over prairies that stretch uniformly to a constantly receding horizon. Such periods, however, need not be unhappy or even boring. Indeed, they can be the best of one's lifetime.

Such a period for me was the one that began with Chip's return from the war, early in 1946, and ended fifteen years later with our departure from Benedict to New York. During much of this time I experienced a happiness and peace of mind that I had not believed obtainable by a person of my nervous temperament.

Chip, released from the navy, practiced law briefly in New York in the Wall Street firm that represented the Benedict

Company. He and Lars Alversen were soon put in charge of the not inconsiderable section of that firm that took care of the company's law business. Chip was afterwards moved to Benedict, where he became his father's principal assistant. In due course Elihu's master plan was implemented, under which Chip became the managing chairman of the company while retaining a more or less nominal partnership in the law firm, and Lars, remaining in New York, was placed in full charge of the company's legal affairs. Chip's father's lifetime ambition was thus achieved; he was able to look forward to a benign old age in which his brilliant son would take over all of his business and civic responsibilities. As evidence of our commitment, Chip and I built a wonderful modern house, all craggy gray brick where it was not all gleaming, view-filled glass, on the level of the residential hill immediately below his parents'.

But the great thing was what happened to Chip's personality. He had returned from the war with what I can only describe as a bursting appetite for peace. Never shall I forget his flushed countenance on the first night he arrived back from the Pacific and took me out to a night club. Never before had he spoken so openly of himself. And, to be truthful, almost never since.

"It's hard to describe what I'm feeling," he kept telling me, making it less difficult, however, by constant replenishments of whiskey. His drinking that night seemed almost medicinal. He must have wanted to tell me something that would have seemed incredible in sobriety. "It's hard to describe an internal state that doesn't make any sense. And in which I don't intellectually even believe! But all my life I've been dogged with a sense that I was . . . wicked."

"But we were taught that in Sunday school. Isn't it original sin?"

"Yes, but mine was somehow worse. Perhaps because I had such a swelled head. I had to be more damned. I couldn't be just like the others. I was Charles Benedict of Benedict! And then, in college, it seemed as if the whole world had suddenly blown apart in a veritable orgy of sin. The Japs started slaughtering everyone in China and Manchuria and down the coast, and the Germans tried to exterminate the Jews. In Russia, Stalin killed peasants by the million, and in Spain . . . well, why go on with it? Mankind was damned, and this time there would be no ark. But then, Alida . . . well, laugh at me if you want. . . ."

"I'm not laughing at you, dearest. I'm not laughing at all."

"No, you're not, it's true. You're a good girl. You're putting up with me." He took another drink. "Well, anyway, it seemed to me that there might, after all, be some kind of redemption. I remembered what my grandfather had said about God loving the Germans but still wanting the Allies to win. I guess it was something like that I felt when Gerry Hastings and I lowered that dud shell from the bow of the LST. As if we were dumping with that grim black object the core of all the wickedness in the world. Or perhaps not really dumping it but planting it where it would take a long time to grow. And in that time was a chance for . . . well, why not for redemption?"

"You believe in God, then?" I asked hesitantly. "It's funny, but I've never asked you."

"I know. In our world that's considered bad form. Mr. B— my grandfather, I mean — belonged to a simpler time. But no, I don't think I believe in a personal god. And I'm not at all sure about divine mercy or even an afterlife. But I don't care about those things. What I've always been sure of is evil — evil in me and in other men. I've always believed that man was basically rotten, putrid, mean, that the universe was made out of bad things. But now it seems to me that wickedness is some-how temporarily in abeyance. Oh, very temporarily! But we have a period, a few years maybe — I don't know — in which we can *do* things! Live! I think now I can be a good husband and a good father and a good son."

Well, the astonishing thing about all this was that it turned out so. Chip did become all of those things. He did not again discuss himself with me so personally, but he lived up to his three resolutions. Perhaps he was best in his third. Neither of his parents had aught but praise for him from then on.

As a father Chip left more to be desired, although I believe he did his best according to his own lights. Eleanor never quite recovered from the four years of having no father, and as she grew up her increasingly critical and sometimes surly dispo-sition spurred her on to the political left, where she took stands inimical to all that the Benedicts regarded as gospel. Yet even when she was at her worst, Chip tried to be patient with her, and I used to tire of their endless arguments, in which he tried, with exasperating equanimity, to win her back to a more capitalist way of thinking. With Dana he was more successful, because his son admired him intensely and dreaded disap-pointing him. It was touching to see the boy walking behind his father on a fishing expedition, carrying his rod and cocking his hat exactly as Chip did. But it was obviously unhealthful that he was so afraid of Chip, and I knew that one day we should have trouble. But why should I have borrowed it?

I cannot say that my understanding of my husband was much more profound than it had been in New Haven and Charlottesville, but I decided — I think on the whole wisely — that a profound understanding between spouses was not essen-tial to a happy marriage. What at least then seemed much more important to me was that I was now an integral part of his active life. I had had little to do with his law career, and nothing with his naval, but the position of the wife of the chairman of the board in a company town is not unlike that of an ambassadress. I was a true partner in my husband's work.

There were not only the many office parties that had to be given and the visiting businessmen who had to be entertained; there were the board meetings of the hospital, the settlement house, the library, even the country club, that had to be attended. If Chip was expected to take over his father's responsibilities, I was no less expected to take over, or at least to share, his mother's. Mrs. Benedict showed no jealousy at my forced inclusion; she seemed ignorant of the very knowledge that most women in her position would have clung to their prerogatives. Her remarkable aptitude and the fact that I welcomed her assistance at all times no doubt eased the situation. I had no ambition to be queen of Benedict; I was sincerely contented to be one of the court.

So much is written about people who can realize their full personalities only by breaking out of an oppressive family or social hierarchy that one is not always aware of how many there are who can accomplish the same thing only by breaking in. The joys of eschewing multiplicity for unity, the thrills of belonging as opposed to escaping, are less celebrated, yet I believe that a sense of being an outsider is at the core of most people's misery. Sometimes their exclusion is obvious, as that of Jews by anti-Semites, or blacks by rednecks, or the untutored and unwashed by the perfumed and cultivated. But actually the sense of not being a true part of a dominant group is almost universal, because it is a state of mind not necessarily reflected in the external facts. A superficial observer, for example, might have thought that Alida Struthers in 1937 was not justified in her acute sense of social inferiority. Had she not been of old Knickerbocker stock, a graduate of Miss Herron's Classes, a nationally known debutante? Perhaps — but what did those things mean to her? To me the important facts were that my father couldn't pay his bills, that my mother was dowdy and pretentious and that both were sneered at by the people who really knew what was what. I could read gossip columns about "lovely blue-blooded Alida Struthers" till the cows came home without altering this.

Now the delightful thing about my social position in Benedict was that it was assured against even the murkiest doubts of my id. There was no questioning the fact that Alida Benedict was looked up to by all. Oh, of course I assumed they made all kinds of cracks behind my back about "gold-digging tramps from the big city," but neither my origins nor my small deserts could dim my present glory in their envious eyes. Everyone was charming to me — that was the real point — and if Macbeth had been brought up as I had been, he would never have disdained "mouth honor, breath." But I shouldn't be too cynical. Some of my new friends were no doubt sincere. Everything at the top of the heap isn't necessarily hypocrisy. To tell the truth, there's probably no more of it there than at the bottom.

The happiest thing about my occupations in town and company was that they took some of the heat off my earlier compulsion to know what my husband was doing and thinking. We were embarked on the same journey with presumably the same goals, and I found myself increasingly inclined to accept the evaluation of Chip by his associates as it was continually expressed to me. "What a wonderful man your husband is" was the kind of laudation to which I became pleasantly accustomed. And it was true. He was a wonderful man — to live with, anyway — considerate, neat, punctual, efficient, shrewd and surprisingly patient. I say "surprisingly," because one was always aware of how much better *he* would have done the thing, the mishandling of which had given cause for his patience. And if our parties, our summers, our very home life, were all part of the Benedict operation, that did not mean that we had no fun. We had plenty of fun.

And love? Oh, there I go again. Do women who aren't passionately loved ever deserve to be? Chip would probably not have chosen me for his wife had he had it to do over, but how many husbands would? He was as affectionate, as interested, as most spouses. Half the wives in Benedict would have swapped their husbands for him, and not just because he was chairman of the board, either. Even if I was only an appendage to Chip Benedict, wasn't it something to be an appendage? I discovered that there could be an actual satisfaction in putting a collar around my ego, a pretty collar, to be sure, and allow it, like a sleek and manicured poodle, to trot docilely down the avenue after the stately Doberman of Chip's personality. Perhaps I went a bit far in mentally condoning the infidelities that, I suspected, occurred on his business trips. Had I reached the point of abjection where such conduct in my lord and master made him seem even more my lord and master?

I have said that Chip was widely admired in Benedict. He was not universally so. Many of the old-timers felt that he had cheapened the quality of the glass, particularly in tableware, and many deplored his extension of the business into such affiliated lines as porcelain and kitchen products as a debasement of the founder's more concentrated ideal. Some of these also deplored his pro-union policies, suggesting that he was more interested in a political future in Connecticut than in the true welfare of the business. But Chip, at small gatherings of officers and directors where such objections could be discreetly voiced, always denied that there was any basic difference between his policy and that of his late paternal grandfather.

"In the old days it paid to fight the unions," he would point out. "It no longer does. Labor strife is too expensive, and half the time you lose. The public wants its unions; let it support them. Pay what you have to pay your workers, and add it to the price of your product. If you can — and Benedict still can."

"You may find a limit to what you can charge for cheap glass," someone responded.

"I have that in mind. But we haven't reached that point yet. The public is still willing to pay more for less. Welcome to the twentieth century!"

There was also some opposition to Chip in the family. Two of his sisters, Flossie and Elaine, were now married to men who worked for the company, and Margaret, the youngest, still unwed, acted as her father's secretary. All three had developed considerably from the boy-crazy, giggling sillies who had visited us in Charlottesville, but there were times when I almost wished they hadn't.

My two married sisters-in-law offered an interesting contrast in their ways of dealing with husbands who had no money. Flossie, the elder, a big, breathless, emotional, easily hurt woman, had decided that her cool, tight-lipped, rather condescendingly aesthetic spouse, Ted Millbank, was the spiritual superior of all the Benedicts and that the latter were indeed fortunate to be able to supply the money needed to promote his career. But there was a certain element of the Benedict push behind her noisily announced adoption of the Griselda role, and Ted Millbank had been pressured into giving up what might have been an adequate curatorial career in Williamsburg, Virginia, to take over the small glass museum of the Benedict company. Ted had taste and capability, but he had also many of the limitations of the scholar and tended to view the business community as so many Philistines. Regarding the museum as the primary purpose of the glass business, instead of, as it was, a small public relations agency, he and his too vociferously loyal spouse were on an early collision course with Chip.

Elaine, on the other hand, had married a Saint Luke's and Yale classmate of Chip's, Alvin Barnes, who, although his family, formerly rich, had lost all in the depression, had certainly not married for mercenary reasons. Indeed, it was a joke in Chip's family that Alvin had married Elaine to separate her from her money. He was a short square man with a deceptively boyish face and tousled hair, who combined a strong will power and a bad temper with toughness and integrity. He had taken a position at Benedict only at Chip's solicitation, and he insisted that his wife subsist entirely on his salary. Elaine, who had a sunny disposition and a pleasant ability to laugh at her husband without offending him, complied, but I always felt that had Alvin's income proved inadequate, she wouldn't have hesitated to defy him and make use of her own. Elaine, in her own way, was almost as strong as Chip.

The first serious friction between Ted Millbank and my husband occurred on a night when Ted and Flossie came to dinner with us to meet Chip's old commander, Gerald Hastings. The latter, now a rear admiral, and his rather subdued, but eager-to-please, tiny wife were spending the weekend with us. I don't remember just what year it was, but it was before the Soviet Union had attained full parity of nuclear power with the United States, as will be shortly made clear by what happened. I was rather in awe of Hastings because of the deep respect that Chip felt for him, though certainly the flatness of his discourse — at least when he talked to women — was not impressive. That evening, however, he made the whole table sit up when Chip asked him what action he would take, were he President, to counteract the Russian atomic threat.

"Oh, I'm quite clear about that," Hastings responded in the voice of easy authority that he always knew how to adopt if the conversation became military. "I should do the only sane thing a great nation can do. And which we will probably have only another year or so at most in which *to* do. I should present the Russian authorities with an ultimatum. Either they consent at once to a total dismantlement of all their nuclear plants, subject, of course, to our military supervision, or they take the consequences."

There was a tense silence around the table.

"And what would those consequences be?" demanded Ted Millbank, in a voice that trembled with anticipatory indignation.

"The consequences would be an atomic attack on their nuclear bases. I have little doubt that we could bring their production to a halt."

"And what about the people?" Flossie Millbank cried out. "What about the millions of people who would be killed?"

"I daresay it would not be millions. I should limit our strike, insofar as possible, to military targets. But yes, there would certainly be appalling casualties. However, the Russians have only to choose."

"I never heard anything so barbarous!" Ted exclaimed shrilly. "Of course no proud nation could cave in before so arbitrary an ultimatum. You would give them no choice. It would be genocide!"

"I beg your pardon, sir; it would be just the opposite. We would be saving the human race. For I should send the same ultimatum to any other nation, friendly or not, that was making nuclear arms. My position would be the simplest: that we Americans have brought this terrible weapon into being and that it is our responsibility to ensure that it should never be used. The nations of the world would henceforth have to settle their disputes without resort to nuclear arms."

"Except for us," Ted sneered. "Rather an exception, don't you think?"

"It is a high calling to live up to the challenge of civilization," Hastings continued imperturbably. It was obvious that he had faced such opposition before. "The fact that we alone have the bomb imposes on us the terrible duty of using it to save the world."

"I agree with Gerry," Chip put in flatly.

"And do you think for a minute," Flossie demanded angrily of her brother, "that anyone in our government would go along with this mad idea?"

"Unfortunately not."

"I agree with Chip that we may lack the guts to do it," Hastings continued. "But I also believe that in ten years' time everyone at this table will wish to hell we had!"

Chip and the Millbanks did not confine their differences of opinion to international affairs. They found even more explosive territory at home. The glass museum, which had been started as an additional attraction to the glass-blowing for the increasing number of summer tourists who passed through Benedict on their way north, had grown, thanks largely to Matilda Benedict's interest, from a couple of rooms of Colonial bowls and tumblers to a small but exquisite Palladian pavilion that was on its way to demonstrating the whole history of glass-making from Roman days through Venice right down to Tiffany and John La Farge. But now Ted had conceived a greater plan. He wanted to show the use of glass in architecture, in medicine, even in warfare. He wanted to suggest a world where glass was God!

Chip had asked me to be present when the museum committee, consisting of Ted Millbank, his wife and mother-in-law, were to present his master plan. We met in Chip's office, which occupied the whole of the blue dome on top of the administration building, with four great oval windows that commanded views of the town and the countryside. Chip's round desk stood in the middle of the chamber in the center of a round blue carpet. The tables and shelves along the walls were covered with specimens of glasswork, including some huge unshaped pieces of ruby red and emerald green. Ted had spread his plans out on the floor, and we walked about, perusing them.

Basically, the project called for the erection of four glass wings, radiating out from the four corners of the present pavilion. The wings would be dedicated to different functions of glass: glass in architecture, glass in science, glass in history, glass in art.

Chip studied the blueprints for some fifteen minutes before he spoke.

"It's a great plan, Ted," he said at last.

Ted could not forbear a look of premature triumph at his wife and mother-in-law. How quickly he anticipated victory! As if even such a materialist as Chip could hardly fail to succumb to his genius. But my heart seemed to lose a beat. I knew that forward thrust of my husband's chin.

"I thought you'd see it, Chip. You really couldn't not."

"Wait a second, Ted. I said it was a great plan. It is. But for whom? General Motors?"

Ted frowned. "Meaning?"

"Meaning that it's far too grand for the likes of us. Do you know what percentage of our annual gross this would cost?"

"That's hardly my concern, Mr. Chairman. My task is to determine quality. Whether or not it pays is your concern."

"Just so."

"Except that I happen to believe that one can never lose with the best."

"But that's not your responsibility, Ted, is it?"

"Of course, you know, Chip," Matilda Benedict now put in, "I might be able to contribute a part of the cost."

Chip turned at once to his mother. "I trust not by selling or pledging company stock."

"Would that be my only recourse?"

"For any significant contribution, yes." He turned abruptly back to his brother-in-law. "Let's not drag this out, Ted. The extensions that you propose are out of the question. The most that I'll consider is a small gallery devoted to glass in art."

I watched Ted's eyes congeal as he took in the finality of this response. "Is that really all, Chip?"

"It's all I have to say."

"Then I'll have to take it to the board."

"That is your privilege. It hardly seems likely that the board will go against the recommendation of the chairman in such a matter. Still, you can try."

As Ted now moved grimly to pick up his plans from the floor, Flossie turned furiously on her brother.

"You think you rule the roost, Chippy boy, but some of those chickens may have been counted before you know what! We'll see what Daddy has to say about this."

"We certainly will," Chip replied.

"You think you have Daddy sewn up, the way you do Mummie, don't you?"

"Please, Flossie!" Matilda Benedict remonstrated. "Don't be vulgar. Nobody's ever had me 'sewn up.'"

"Haven't they? You're as bad as Alida, in my books. All the man of the family has to do is crook his little finger, and you both come running."

"While you, of course, are totally independent of Ted," I retorted.

Flossie turned her big, red-shot eyes on me in bitter contempt. "You! What do you care what happens to a small-town company? What's it to you but a source of dough to spend on New York clothes and jewels? What do you care if we make the cheapest and ugliest glass in America so long as you get your share of the loot?"

"Oh, Flossie, go home," Chip snapped at her, and Ted, the plans now under his arm, propelled his wife silently from the room. Mrs. Benedict, in her usual stately way, tried to pick up the broken pieces of our dissension.

"I apologize, Alida, for my daughter's rudeness. It was quite uncalled for. Nobody cares more for the company than you, my dear, or has done more to help out. Florence gets so engrossed with Ted's projects and ideals that she forgets herself. All this will blow over."

"I'm afraid, Ma, it won't be as easy as you think."

"Well, seriously, Chip, doesn't she have a bit of a point? When you get right down to it, must we condemn ourselves to mediocrity?"

"The times condemn us. Look, Ma. For a hundred years now every forward-looking person has been working for better conditions for labor, for more pensions and welfare and so forth. Well, all those things have come. We're up to our ears in them. I'm not complaining. I'm adjusting to the facts. It should be obvious that paying the wages and taxes that we have to pay, we must forgo some of the quality in our products. The finest workmanship in the future will have to be left to nations with less developed welfare programs. If you don't believe me, you and Alida, look about and see what's happening in the areas you most care about, the cultural areas. Ask your publishing friends how they feel about bringing out the first novel of an unknown. Ask your producer friends how they feel about that interesting, intellectual new play. And it's all just beginning, too, mind you. Inflation will continue to rise until the only public entertainment will be on TV, and that will be trash. Opera and ballet will follow drama into the bottomless pit. Oh, philanthropy may put it off a couple of decades with productions of old chestnuts like *Aïda* and *Carmen*, but the end is clear."

"But you seem so enthusiastic about it!" I cried, appalled.

"I'm not enthusiastic about it," he retorted brusquely. "I see it, that's all. And I'm not going to have an ass like Ted, who can't see anything, look down his snotty nose at me!"

Ted Millbank, anyway, was ass enough to take his fight to nonfamily stockholders, and this proved a declaration of war, for the stock of Benedict was no longer solely owned by Benedicts. Chip, seeking greater capital for his business expansion, had "gone public," with the result that the family now owned less than half the outstanding shares, but as the Benedicts voted in a block, and as the other stockholders were numerous and unorganized, control of the company had not been lost. The risk of a combination against the Benedicts, however, was always a dread possibility, and it was for this reason that any dalliance by a Benedict with unrelated shareholders was regarded as the direst treason.

When Alvin Barnes, Elaine's husband, called on Chip and me one night after dinner to report what he had heard about Ted's activities, it was like the discovery of an enemy atomic plant within national borders. Alvin's young face and middle-aged eyes struck me as almost comically grave.

"There's no question about it, I'm afraid. He's been in correspondence with every holder of more than two hundred shares. It's a campaign!"

"Very well." Chip's features had frozen. "He must go. I'll see Dad and Ma tonight."

Chip did not take me with him when he called on his parents, but when he came home late that night he was able to tell me that he had prevailed.

"It was pretty grim," he said. "Flossie came storming over, without Ted, and made the most fearsome scene. Really, I've never seen such a Valkyrie! She howled and stormed. She said she'd leave Benedict and never come back. Ma wavered all over the place, but Dad was a rock. When I made it clear that it was Ted or me, he had no choice."

"Oh, darling, couldn't you just give Ted a warning? One last chance?"

"With a guy like Ted that never works. He hates my guts, and he's determined to get me. Talk to Alvin. He agrees."

"Oh, Alvin will do anything you say!"

"Alida, my dear, you're a wonderful wife, but you don't understand business. You must leave this decision to me."

Well, what else could I do? Ted Millbank, after all, had dug his own grave. When he loomed the next morning, gray and somber, like some resurrected John the Baptist, at our breakfast table, I wanted to push him out of the house, get him out of my sight, anything to avoid the contemplation of his misery. I was hurrying from the room when Chip bade me stay.

"Yes, I too would just as soon you were a witness, Alida," Ted volunteered. "All I really have to say to your husband is that I regard him as a man without vision in business affairs, without sensitivity in matters of art and without heart in his dealings with his fellow men. Flossie echoes my sentiments. We hope never to have to see him again."

"How can you be so horrible, Ted?" I cried. "You know you were trying to stab Chip in the back!"

"If trying to bring a little beauty into the dull grays and browns of life in Benedict is stabbing Chip in the back, then indeed I have stabbed him."

"Why don't you go now, Ted?" Chip asked in his coldest, most patient tone. "Now that you've made your little speech."

"That's all you have to say?"

"There isn't any point saying anything more to a man like you. I have no wish to hurt you, and I know that your mind is unchangeable. You are determined to separate Flossie from her family. You are making a big mistake."

"Why?" Ted demanded in surprise, almost in spite of himself.

"Because when she doesn't have us to turn on, she'll turn on you."

Which in fact was just what happened. Flossie left Ted within two years. But the poor man, unconscious of the second

Benedict doom hanging over his head, now presented us with his back.

I wondered why Mrs. Benedict had given up so easily, but it was not long before the reason was clear. Like me, she was dominated by her husband. Not only did Mr. Benedict confirm the dismissal of his son-in-law; he arranged that Chip should have voting control over all the family stock, which placed the management of the company now squarely in his hands. Chip reigned as supremely over Benedict as the Sun King over Versailles.

When I tried to discuss the situation frankly with my mother-in-law, she presented her entire acceptance of it like a wall between us.

"I think we're on the path to a new job for Ted," she told me blandly. "There may be an opening at the Boston Fine Arts. He'll be better off away from Benedict. Of course, Flossie may never forgive Chip, but as old age comes on, I'm learning that I have to face the fact that I can't control the affections or animosities between my children."

"It surprises me that Mr. Benedict doesn't have more concern about Flossie."

"Oh, he does. But shall I tell you something, Alida? My husband is basically what your daughter Ellie calls a male despot. The rack wouldn't get it out of him, but he believes in a male-dominated world. I've always known that he cared more for Chip than for all his three daughters. And when Chip came home to take over the company, Elihu was ready to chant his Nunc Dimittis. Ted and Flossie have been the victims. Let us hope they'll be the last. I wouldn't even bet on my humble self if I crossed swords with your glorious husband!"

I think it was at that moment that I became just the tiniest

bit afraid of Chip. I wondered whether I could not detect a
slight hardening in his features. Chip was almost as handsome
as he had been when I first met him; he had lost no hair and
gained no more than ten pounds. But there was something
about his eyes . . . how shall I put it? Well, I kept thinking
of an idiotic cinematic trick in a film about King Arthur's
Round Table, where the sapphire light in Lancelot's eyes had
gone out after he had slept with Guinevere. Something not too
unlike that seemed to have happened to Chip. And it wasn't
just because of a woman, either.

15

※※※

CHIP

WHILE CHIP was in the process of establishing himself in Benedict, he had to come to grips with the proposition that the development of his personality there was going to be a lonely process. He had chosen a life and a site that were barren of the deepest kind of human companionship, at least as he conceived it. That this was partly due to aspects of his own character he entirely accepted. After all, Benedict was made up not only of his family and their business; it was also made up of Charles Benedict.

The most important emotional result of his decision to settle in his home town had been the assimilation of Alida by her family-in-law. This had obviously been a needed step for her happiness, and he had even encouraged it, but it had nonetheless had the effect of uniting her with a group that, however loving, however admiring of their bright new leader, had still a watchful, and sometimes a faintly apprehensive eye fixed on his activities. Alida, together with his parents and sisters, constituted a kind of board of trustees who, if they quite properly left the management of affairs to their brilliant executive director, were still aware that they had placed all their eggs in a single basket, which this sometimes too innovative carrier might dangerously shake.

Yes, they were all a bit afraid of him, or afraid for him, if there was a difference. When he and Alida had been alone together, there might have been a kind of sex appeal to her in the very enigma of his personality, and one that it was easy and even agreeable for him occasionally to exploit, but now that she was allied with his parents and siblings and approaching the plain of middle years, she was less allured by mystery and more alerted to fact. Alida had begun to show an interest in his business trips and in his hobbies, but it was a suspicious interest; she was inclined to resent rather than to respect the areas of his life in which she had little or no part. He had hoped, when she at last discovered that his parents did not — as she had once jealously suspected they did — own a part of him not available to herself, that she would be content with what she had, as all that a wife could reasonably expect. But it had not turned out that way. When Alida discovered that he was with his family very much what he was with her, it seemed only to indicate to her that she, rather than he, had all along been right; that she, not he, was the one in step. She would urge him now, for example, to spend more time with the children, or to go more often to see his mother, or to be more available to the officers of the company, or to dance more with the Benedict wives on Saturday nights at the country club. He would demur, usually with a laugh, but at times there was a dryness in his mirth.

"When you married me you wanted Lancelot," he told her,

"and now you'll settle for George Babbitt. I suppose that's the story of the American wife."

"When you married *me*, you wanted Cleopatra," she retorted, "and now you'll settle for Dumb Dora. I suppose that's the story of the American husband."

His parents were less articulate, but it was obvious that they were increasingly on Alida's "side." There was something in the way Matilda always brought Alida into any conversation and consulted her ahead of Chip that implied there was some neglect to be made up for. Hints were dropped, like: "Why don't you take Alida to France this summer?" or: "Do you think Alida would enjoy a surprise party on her birthday?" But it was a small penalty, he supposed, to pay for the avoidance of the mother-in-law–daughter-in-law rivalry that characterized so many of the company families. Peace was always at a price, and peace he most of the time had.

His father was the person who gave him the greatest uneasiness. Since the stroke that had partly paralyzed him without affecting his mentality, Elihu had become somewhat withdrawn from affairs. He still, however, came every morning in his wheelchair to his office, which was directly below Chip's, and spent a couple of hours reading company reports and looking out his window at the glassworks below. He kept abreast of all Chip's plans and modifications, and he limited the articulation of his obvious disapproval to a minimum of comments.

"We live in a different era," he would repeat. "The fact that I don't happen to like it doesn't mean that I can't adapt to it. The one thing I am determined never to be is the retired skipper haunting the bridge and whispering unsought navigational advice to his successor. You have the con, Chip. It's up to you to steer the course."

Chip got on well enough with the other officers of the company, but he had no intimates among them. They were, by and large, able and pleasant men, dedicated to their work, but on the whole he found them dull, and he abominated their endless discussion of sports and politics. He also declined to discuss sex with the few who enjoyed that subject — the majority were inhibited by the fear that one man might tell his wife, who would tell theirs — because he felt that the subject was of deeper concern to him than to them. For he had resumed his old habit of visits to private brothels on trips to New York. The place that he had frequented in his Yale days was long gone, but there were plenty of others, and he was willing to pay the highest price. He could not abide an atmosphere of leers and dirty jokes. The sexual act with a beautiful partner was to him a most serious business and had to be conducted, with all its preliminaries and aftermaths, in a comfortable, even luxurious privacy. When he found the right partner, he would go back to her for months at a time, but his heart was never involved; that was not so much a rule as a condition to ecstasy. When Chip read in books that purchased love was a drab and hollow affair, he would simply reflect that the author did not know how to buy.

He was, in fact, a constant reader. He sought in books the knowledge, almost the companionship, that he did not find in the people of Benedict. He rarely discussed his reading with others, for he wished to avoid the fatuous picture of the ambitious corporate executive seeking culture in selected readings from the Harvard Classics. He did not even much relish bookish talk with Alida, because he suspected that literature to her, despite her own pretensions to be a writer, was more of a decoration to life than an inner necessity. Poetry, fiction and, to a lesser extent, painting had begun to play a role for him not unlike that of the girls he met in New York. It was beauty — the beauty he did not find in Benedict.

When he read *Madame Bovary*, he would piece together every parallel to Alida's life in their factory town, as at Yale he had traced his own mother in Hamlet's or Coriolanus'. When he read *The Ambassadors*, he saw Matilda in Mrs. Newsome and himself in Chad. When he read *Moby-Dick*, his favorite of all novels, he saw his late grandfather, Mr. B, as Ahab in a lifelong and ultimately suicidal pursuit of the devil. The white whale! Had any poet more splendidly conceived the intrinsic evil of the universe?

On trips to Manhattan, more frequent than his business required, he was a constant visitor at the Whitney and Modern Art Museums. He would not read books on art, any more than he would read criticism of literature; appreciation to him was entirely a matter between the artifact and the beholder. He would stand before a painting in motionless contemplation for ten minutes at a stretch, picking times when he would encounter the minimum of other observers. So disgusted would he become at the least hint of "gushing" or "expertise" that he would leave the gallery or, at a party, abruptly change the conversation. It was not surprising that he gained the reputation of being rather a Philistine among the ladies of Benedict who went to New York every two weeks for courses in art appreciation and raised money for the Metropolitan Opera.

One friend with whom he still enjoyed some intimacy was Lars, whom he always saw on a New York visit and who frequently came to Benedict, but there was always in Lars, beneath his smiling, tolerant benignity, beneath the faint shrug that implied that he accepted the possibility of a purposeless universe, a side of his nature that seemed to endorse the attitude "But so long as we know nothing, why not conform to a norm that at least pays the rent and the butcher?" Karen, his wife, was different. She was a Boston girl, of Boston's best, a Hooper, blue-eyed, bright, tall and strong, with a skin of shining, unblemished alabaster and ideals that would yield to nothing. She was also very intelligent, and Chip had found that he could talk to her as to nobody else. It didn't even matter that she would repeat what he said to her husband.

On one of his Manhattan trips, when he had been persuaded to fill in as an extra man at a dinner party the Alversens were giving, he had an unusual conversation with Karen. He had been bored at dinner between the wives of two lawyers who seemed interested only in schools and offspring, and he sought his hostess as soon as Lars allowed the gentlemen to leave their brandy and cigars.

The living room was very Boston, at least as Chip imagined it, long and narrow with rather uncomfortable Colonial chairs and settees, their backs to the wall, and a few perfect things: a Whistler etching of Venice, a Chinese scroll painting of herons, a Japanese screen. It was like Karen, who in her shining rectitude seemed to repudiate New England buccaneer forebears who had forced opium on the Orient, to have preserved a handful of artifacts, reverenced almost with an air of apology. She pointed cheerfully now, when she saw him, to the empty chair beside her, and he slipped into it with relief. After he had told her about the ladies at dinner, with the freedom of the perennial guest to whom much is allowed, he drew her attention to a Japanese lady across the room, a businesswoman from Tokyo, whose company was a client of Lars's.

"One thing I learned in Japan, Karen, is that everything we heard of those people was the direct opposite of the truth.

People used to say they would fight to the last Nipponese soldier. And what did they do? Laid down their arms very
sensibly the moment it became apparent the game was up. We
also used to say they lived in the past. Now we see that they're
the most modern people on the globe. Look at your guest of
honor. A generation ago in Tokyo, women, like children, were
meant to be seen and not heard. But that lady could take the
sharpest trader in our garment district to the cleaner's!"

"Do I detect in your tone a hint that the change has not been
altogether for the better?"

"You mean that I don't approve of women in business? No,
I have no such prejudice. So long as they don't get too mannish."

"Is efficiency mannish?"

"Not necessarily. What I hate to see happening is Japanese
women losing their essential seductiveness. The geisha girl, for
example, carried the art of pleasing to a degree unequaled in
the annals of eroticism."

Karen stared. "That is one business, I take it, you believe that
women should always be in?"

"Most emphatically."

"And where did you learn of the art of the geisha?"

"In Japan. During the occupation."

"I suppose as a naval officer you had to read all the reports
of that kind of thing."

"No, Karen. I learned it at first hand. I had a wonderful girl
in Sasebo."

She seemed a bit breathless at his candor. Her lips formed a
frozen half-smile as she sought the right note. "You mean a
kind of Madame Butterfly?"

"Except there was no dishonesty. No betrayal. She and I
understood each other perfectly."

"So that makes it all right!" Karen now allowed herself to flare. It pleased him that no consideration of his importance as a client would abate by a jot or a tittle the natural flow of her indignation. "Well, I'm certainly sorry for poor Alida!"

"Alida never knew about it. Do you think I'd be such a cad as to tell her?"

"You're telling me."

"That's because I trust you. I'm perfectly confident that you would never betray me to anyone in the world but your husband, and he knows about it."

"He does? Oh, you men. You're all thick as thieves."

"Lars, anyway, is my only thief."

"Suppose Alida had had herself a gigolo while you were away? How would you have felt about that?"

"I should certainly not have considered myself entitled to complain."

She seemed slightly taken aback by this. "Well, that's something, I suppose. Of course, I'm sure she didn't."

"I'm sure she didn't, also."

"Really?" Her eyebrows soared at his presumption. "Well, would you mind telling me why I am honored with these confidences? Wouldn't you do better to keep them to yourself?"

"Don't you have moments when you want to see yourself reflected in a mirror exactly as you are? Don't you ever want to talk to someone who will listen to what you say? Well, your eyes are that mirror, Karen. I am perfectly aware that you have all kinds of New England scruples and disapprobations. But I don't care. All I care about is that you're honest. And I don't know anyone but you who is."

"Not even Lars?"

"Well, he's honester since he's been married to you."

She burst out laughing, but stopped when he didn't join her. Then she suddenly seemed to fall in with his mood. "You're not happy, Chip, are you?"

"I don't know. I honestly don't know. I may be as happy as it's possible for a man like me to be. I have certainly supplemented my life in areas where I found it lacking. And I believe I have done so without causing undue pain to my primary obligations."

"Because those primary obligations don't know?"

"That's it."

"But they do know, Chip. It's not a question of telling. I'd know soon enough if Lars had a girl. No matter how discreet he was. You've been very frank with me. Shall I be equally frank with you?"

"That's what I want."

"If Alida doesn't satisfy you physically, tell her why and how. Maybe she can change. You'd be surprised what can be accomplished by directness."

It was his turn to be taken aback. "I don't think she could do that."

"You mean she couldn't be as cuddly and cozy as a geisha?"

"Now you're shocking *me*!"

"You asked for it, my friend! Why, anyway, should a woman have to turn herself into a kitten? Why should a man and a woman not make love freely and proudly, as if they were doing something of which the gods could be envious?"

"I don't think I'd be a customer at your bordello."

"I'm not going to start a bordello! What you're looking for, Chip, you may very well find at home. Isn't that where the bluebird was?"

He did not remember looking into eyes so clear since Mr.

B's. "It's hard on Alida, I suppose, that I was such a different man when I married her. Then I wanted to be clear of my family and my whole background."

"And what has she done but tried gallantly to be each different Alida that each different Chip wanted?"

"She'd have done far better to be herself."

"Do you know, Chip, that you're a bit of a heel?"

As he looked at her smiling lips and her unsmiling eyes, he had a vision of her making love in the high, frank manner that she had evoked. Perhaps indeed it would have been a noble experience. The bluebird, then, was not necessarily at home. "What a pity I didn't meet you earlier!" he exclaimed.

"Are you trying to make love to me?" She maintained her smile, but it was not altogether a pleasant one.

"No, I'm not that much of a heel," he said with a sigh. "Or that much of a fatuous ass."

Lars came up to them. "You two look pretty serious. Am I interrupting something? Or am I just in time? How about a drink?"

Chip went with his host to the sideboard in the dining room while Karen turned to her other guests. He put a hand on Lars's shoulder.

"It's like a cold shower," he said, "to be told home truths by a beautiful woman who is totally immune to one's charm."

"Oh, she's that, all right," Lars cheerfully agreed. "Sometimes I wonder if she isn't immune to mine!"

Chip reflected as he poured his drink that in all the years of his philandering he had never made love to another man's wife. And what was more, he knew now that he never would. Perhaps that kind of virtue was inconceivable to Karen. Or perhaps, more simply, she did not, in view of his confession, consider it very much of a virtue.

16

⪡⪡⪢⪢

CHIP

FOR MONTHS after Ted Millbank's departure from Benedict over the glass museum row, Chip had suffered from periodic attacks of acute resentment. He knew that all of his family, including Alida, felt that he had been hard on Ted, but it was impossible to defend himself so long as none of them openly accused him. What galled him most was Ted's notion that Chip, in common with other American business executives, either rejected, or was incapable of living up to, his responsibility of bringing art to the public. It was not, God knew, that Chip wished to seek refuge in the argument that there were magnates who covered their office walls with abstract painting or filled their plazas with nonrepresentational sculpture; he understood that Ted, quite rightly, would have flung such examples back in his teeth as banal types of "conspicuous consumption." No, what he objected to was the blindness, the asininity of Ted, common to so many of his kind, in failing to see that art could not be handed out like doughnuts and coffee. There were no Lorenzo de' Medicis in the Chamber of Commerce for the same reason that there were no Leonardos in SoHo and no Florentines in the public squares of Manhattan. Art in the twentieth century, for all the cant about public appreciation, was a lonely affair.

There was, Chip was beginning to admit to himself, an increasing dichotomy between the solitary reader and art lover and the vigorous, forward-looking Charles Benedict, who was lauded in *Forbes* and *Fortune* magazines for cutting costs, expanding sales and adapting his products to the need of a middle class increasing in size and affluence. If he had, however, to be nailed to the golden cross of progress with a card over his head proclaiming that to cease to grow was to decline, could he not at least keep a mind that had its own glimpses of divine equations whose truth was useless in business?

And now came Ted Millbank, sleek and comfortable, lolling in a hot bath of married money and preaching the false doctrine that Philistines might atone for their Philistinism by convincing the multitude that they could extract the redemptive juice of beauty out of the hard shell of art by anything but a lifetime of laborious cracking. How he despised Ted!

It seemed to him now that Alida tried to communicate with him seriously only when he was troubled. It was as if they had achieved a plateau in life where difficulties and incompatibilities of personality could be regarded as in abeyance, absent some crisis; as if life were a play that had no business not to run smoothly once both the principal actors had learned their lines. Alida was happy enough, he surmised, but it was not a happiness that was going to endure too many questions, and it had accordingly to be significant when she asked one morning at breakfast, regarding him silently with quizzical eyes over her raised coffee cup, "Chip, what is it?"

"What is what?"

"You've been totally preoccupied for days. You hardly know I'm here."

"Actually, we're faced with a rather nasty proxy battle. Something called Barnheim Industries has been picking up our stock. I've asked Lars to come up from New York to see what's what."

"With Karen?" Alida was very fond of Lars's wife. "Couldn't we ask them to stay with us?"

"Sure, if you'd like."

"But that isn't it, is it? I mean what you're really worried about. You rather like a battle, actually, don't you?"

"I guess I do." He was faintly surprised at this sudden perspicacity. Not often now did she show such interest in his enthusiasms. "Of course, ever since we went public, I've known we were in danger of a takeover. But I think we can give these boys at Barnheim a run for their money."

"And if we lose . . . ?"

"Well, that's the funny part of it. If you lose a proxy fight, you end up making even more money."

"Then that's not what you're really worried about."

"Oh, no? Can you imagine Daddy's face if we lost control of Benedict?"

"Ah, but you won't," she said confidently. "You never lose control of anything. Certainly not of me. So what is really wrong, dear?"

Studying her face, he marveled as always at the preservation of her pale skin. Except for a slight puffiness under the eyes and a small increase of weight around the hips, she might still be the Alida Struthers he had courted so desperately. "It's Ted Millbank," he said gruffly. "And his idiotic idea that there's something I can do about the state of the arts in Benedict."

"And you can't?"

"Not and still run the company."

"Couldn't you let the museum do it?"

"How?"

"By having shows and classes. By sponsoring lectures for the workers. By showing beautiful things to people starved for a little beauty!"

Was this the dark-eyed, raven-haired daughter of libertine Manhattan who had dreamed of being another Edna St. Vincent Millay? Who had once smiled at his mother as a puffed-up frog in an exiguous puddle? Surely she had now clambered up on that lily pad beside Matilda!

"You can't educate people to appreciate beauty by showing them beautiful things," he retorted. "That's the fallacy of museums. What good does it do to show people masterpieces if they've never seen anything *but* masterpieces? Go to New York and compare the zealots at the Museum of Modern Art with the lethargic zombies who crowd dutifully through the Metropolitan. The former are there because they've seen hundreds of pictures and want to see more. The latter think they can take in art by osmosis. They'd be better off at the movies."

"I think that's a very narrow and snobbish point of view."

"It comes from the heart, at least. From one who's learned the hard way. The only person who can teach you anything real is yourself. You don't get it from Acoustiguides drooling on about the influence of X on Y!"

"You could try."

"Oh, Alida, please, I don't want to go on with this!" he snapped in sudden exasperation. "I don't want to get testy and mad at you."

She looked at him for a moment. "Do you know something,

Chip? I wish to hell you would get mad at me. I wish you cared enough to!"

He had not been quite frank with her about the office threat. The proxy battle launched by Barnheim Industries to take control of Benedict was regarded with the greatest agitation by every officer of the target except its chairman. Barnheim was a syndicate that manufactured furniture, imported Asian carpets, ran a chain of hardware stores and was making its bid to become the foremost supplier of household equipment in New England. Benedict lay geographically across the path of its advance as Poland had lain before Germany's.

In public, of course, Chip bore himself as a stern and beleaguered leader should. Passing groups of cheering workers in the lunch hour, he would even raise the index and middle fingers of his right hand in the Churchillian V for Victory sign. But in the secret regions of his heart he had to confess to a rather shameful sense of relief at this interruption of a routine that had begun to pall.

For his doubts had been long growing as to the validity of what he was accomplishing with the company. He knew that his father was a silent disbeliever in his son's idea of "progress." Elihu had been a devoted believer in high-quality glassware — the perfect product for the perfect clientele. Yet the old man had said nothing. How could he? What alternative had he to offer? Everyone knew that if you didn't go forward in business, you were fated to drop behind. So there they were. They had to go forward. They had to go forward till they dropped in their tracks. But did that mean that it was wicked to welcome the diversion of a proxy war?

Surely, at least, it was permissible to find relief in battle. Chip had little difficulty in convincing himself that whatever the degradation of Benedict's product, it would be as lovely as the finest Venetian glass compared with what a victorious Barnheim would produce, and he lashed himself into a near frenzy of enthusiasm as the campaign was initiated. Suits against Barnheim were launched in five different states; the syndicate was accused of everything from antitrust violations to swindling its own shareholders. Private investigators were employed to examine the personal lives of its officers and directors; accountants were retained to pore over its books in search of fraud and tax violations.

"I haven't seen you so aroused since the war!" Lars exclaimed with a laugh when Chip read aloud to him the report of a Barnheim executive who had indecently assaulted an office boy in the washroom.

"But it *is* war! And these people are as bad as any we fought in the last one."

"Isn't that going a bit far? Why can't we just put it that they believe in cheap products? We're fighting for high manufacturing standards, not morals."

Chip did not like this, so he remained silent. Even if his standards were higher than those of the enemy, they were still not noble enough to be emblazoned on standards in a holy war.

"Does it ever strike you," he asked Lars in sudden gloom, "that everything we accomplish is negative? What's my job up here? Getting bugs out of the machinery. Fighting sloppiness and inefficiency or worse. And when the big crisis strikes, and we're up in arms, what's it all about? Keeping the bad guys from taking over the works. Negative, always negative."

"But isn't that true of everything? As a lawyer I spend my life saving people from taxes and lawsuits. If I were a doctor, I'd be saving my patients from diseases. Or as a minister, I'd be keeping my flock from wickedness. Ever since Eve bit that apple, we've had to keep weeding the Garden of Eden."

"You think there's no way, then, to be creative?"

"Well, artists always claim that they're that, don't they? Why don't you write a play or paint a picture?"

"Ah, but that's just it!" Chip pounced on it. "What do they create? I mean the best of them. They create pictures of nothingness, of violence and despair. Like Beckett in *Godot*. Or Gorky in his terrible last painting of the black monk. Or Picasso in *Guernica*. Or Sartre or Camus."

Lars assumed the amiable, patient look that went all the way back to their bull sessions at Yale. "What the hell are you driving at?"

"Simply that I keep getting back to what I thought as a kid. That the world is rotten, rotten to the core. That there never was any Garden of Eden. And that the only way we can find any life that's worth living is by seeking out and destroying the rot."

"I don't suppose you have very far to seek."

"No, it's everywhere, of course. And if you can't find it, look inside yourself!"

"And what is the reward for the victorious eradicator of rot? A harp in the New Jerusalem?"

Chip shook his head emphatically. "There isn't any reward. The fight is its own compensation. But maybe that's better than nothing."

Lars shrugged. Clearly he had had his quota of moral speculation for the day. "It all sounds pretty bleak to me. But I hope it helps you send the Barnheim wolves spinning down to hell."

When Chip returned to his office after this talk, which occurred at his now daily lunch with Lars in the officers' dining room, he sat at his desk for several minutes in what seemed to him a sudden stupor. He closed his eyes at last and shook his head to pull himself together. But no, this seizure — or whatever it was — was not going to go easily away. It was as if someone had approached him from behind and flung a black hood over his head and shoulders, securing it around his neck with the biting cord of depression. It was appalling that the entire structure of his confidence and happiness seemed to have been blown apart in a single conversation. But had not such things been known? Whoever, whatever it was that had been piling up a demolition arsenal in his moral basement must have been silently at work for a long time. And now the world was suddenly worn and gray. It was as if he were a Saul on the road to Damascus who would never get there. The vision had come too late. What vision?

He told his secretary that he would take no calls and see no one, and he spent the afternoon reading his files on the proxy fight. He was particularly struck by a passage from the brief of counsel to one of the directors of Barnheim, an attorney well known in Connecticut for his high-mindedness and distinguished public service.

"The management of Benedict appear to believe they have a mandate from on high to run a business that really belongs to the public. To keep Barnheim from realizing a sane and practicable plan of coordinating certain household industries in New England, the officers of Benedict feel justified in harnessing federal and state justice systems to their ruthless chariot so that judges and juries throughout the land must divert their time from the needs of our citizens to determine fabricated claims and evaluate character assassinations."

That evening when he came home he found Lars and Karen Alversen in the living room with Alida. Lars was at the bar, mixing drinks.

"How nice!" Karen's large blue eyes and big forehead gleamed with her frank welcome. "We thought you were never coming home."

Chip responded only with a brief nod and perfunctory smile. He took the drink that Lars handed him and went straight to the point.

"Has it ever occurred to you that we're shysters?"

"Leave that role to me, old boy. You'd better concentrate on being the client."

"No, seriously, Lars. Didn't we learn in law school that a good lawyer never initiates a lawsuit except to recover money or prevent an irreparable harm? Do any of our suits fall into either category?"

"Well, I concede the recovery of money may not be the real purpose. But what about the prevention of harm?"

"The purchase of our stock on the open market is hardly a harm. Didn't we put it there to *be* bought?"

"Not if it results in the destruction of an old and distinguished business."

"That you and I happen to believe the present management is a boon to Benedict doesn't mean a purchaser of our stock is bound to think so."

Lars seemed ready to give it up. He gazed for a moment into his glass. "All right, then, let's be good shysters. Let's at least win."

Chip turned abruptly to Lars's wife. "What do you think, Karen?"

"But, Chip, I'm hardly a businessman."

"You know right from wrong."

"I try."

"Then tell me what you'd do in my situation. Would you drop the suits?"

Karen glanced at her husband, not, Chip instantly felt, as seeking permission but to give him the chance to speak first in a matter that more directly concerned him.

"Go ahead, darling. Tell him."

"Oh, I'd drop the suits, yes," she replied, with only the glint of a smile. She had no wish to understate the seriousness of the matter.

"Even if it meant the loss of the company?"

"Well, there's always a price for doing the right thing, isn't there?"

"But such a great one, Karen!" Alida burst suddenly into the argument. "Think of the family. Think of my father-in-law."

"Lars told me you'd all be even richer if you lost."

"But we're not fighting just for the money!" Alida exclaimed indignantly.

"That does complicate matters, doesn't it?" Karen, sensing the embroilment of Chip and Alida, tried tactfully to withdraw. "Well, aren't you glad I'm not on your board?"

"No, I don't think I am, Karen," Chip responded gravely. "I like your directness. It clears the air. You're not devious, like Lars."

"Or sentimental, like me." Alida retorted. "Go ahead, say it! I don't know what gets into you, Chip, but you always have to go against everybody. Isn't it perfectly obvious that we're fighting for our very lives against a gang of pirates?"

"If it were obvious," Chip replied, "I shouldn't have said what I did."

Alida became silent at this, as she always did when she was frightened — he hated doing this to her, but how could he help it? — and the always diplomatic Lars changed the subject to that of his own golf score.

Chip was uncomfortably aware in the next days of the persistence of the hollow feeling inside of him. It was as if his substance were dripping away, oozing out of a leak; as if it could be only a matter of time before the Chip Benedict who attended so efficiently to his daily tasks became a finely wrought simulacrum of the business executive and community leader. And then there would come to him the image of a dummy that was no longer even a dummy but simply something that existed in the eye of the would-be beholder, like the clothes of the naked emperor. There were moments now when his heart would seem to pump sudden wrath. Was it nothing to have doubled the gross revenues of the company and brought prosperity to the town? Was it really nothing to have made Benedict more famous than his grandfather had?

"Why can I get nowhere with life?" he asked Lars at lunch.

"In life or with life?"

"With life. I suppose I've got somewhere in life. But it keeps turning back and slugging me. I tried to be my own boss at Yale and at law school, and it almost killed my parents. I tried to be a good soldier in the war, and I turned into a bloodhound. Then I decided, what the hell, I'd start all over again. I was going to be a good son, a good manager. And what have I become? A crook!"

"A crook!" Lars glanced about in mock alarm. "Lower your voice, please. Have your fingers strayed into the company till?"

"You know what I mean. You agreed we were shysters."

"A shyster is not necessarily a crook."

"He's a moral crook."

"Remember what Holmes said: the life of the law is not logic but experience. We have to keep up with the times. The word 'shyster' must be redefined each generation to keep it from taking in the most distinguished practitioners at the bar."

"But it's all downhill. Morally."

"Well, morals, too, my dear Chip, are hardly fixed things. They go up as well as down. We may no longer believe that a son is morally bound to pay his father's debts, but neither do we think a woman taken in adultery should be stoned."

"Are you telling me, Lars, that everything we're doing to save our management of Benedict is morally justified?"

"Well, perhaps you went a bit far in investigating the private lives of some of the officers of Barnheim. But we can cut that off."

Chip wondered whether he did not envy Lars. Wasn't it enviable to be able to see the foibles of the world so clearly and to accept so easily, even so gracefully, one's own helplessness to do anything much about it? Lars kept his moral fingernails as clean as he could; it would hardly help to plunge them into the mud. Nor would it clean the mud. But it was all right for Lars, because Lars had always been that way.

"Karen sees it more clearly," Chip said bluntly.

"Karen lives in a world of her own."

"But I'm wondering if that isn't the world I want to live in, too."

"Karen doesn't have to manage and defend large businesses. She can afford delicate scruples."

"Lars, all you're saying is that there are two codes: one for the active and one for the passive. I can't buy that."

Lars said nothing for a minute. Then he sighed. "You've been in such a funny mood lately that I've been wondering how to tell you something. We received another offer from Barnheim this morning."

"You're afraid I'll take it?"

"It's surely a hard one to turn down. The name Benedict to be retained. Something like Barnheim-Benedict, to be worked out. All officers, including yourself, to be given five-year contracts. And a stock offer that would almost double your wealth."

Chip laughed harshly. "It's as if God had bribed Saul on the road to Damascus!"

"You mean you're tempted?"

"It might be my one chance to live!"

"You are tempted."

"Wouldn't you be?"

"Perhaps. If Elihu Benedict weren't my old man."

Chip's brief elation collapsed under the fall of this black curtain. "Let's have a look at those terms," he said curtly.

17

CHIP

ELIHU BENEDICT was still only in his early seventies, but he was gaunt and gray, and there were long periods when he neither moved nor spoke. He liked to be taken every morning to his office directly below Chip's, hung with his beautiful collection of Fitzhugh Lane seascapes. Chip had prepared him for the interview with a memorandum on the Barnheim offer and the arguments in favor of its acceptance.

When Chip came in, his father told him calmly to close the door. The two sat in silence before the old man spoke.

"Let me see whether I understand you correctly, my son. You say that this offer will considerably enrich the Benedicts. You say that further resistance to the takeover might not only fail, but could leave us worse off than we now are. And then — and this is what interests me particularly — you say that the techniques of resistance are morally offensive to you."

"That's it, Dad. Is there any reason people should not be free to purchase stock as they wish?"

"Even if what they really wish is to dismember an old family business?"

"Well, that's a matter of opinion, isn't it? They're in business. We're in business. They think they can run Benedict more cheaply and profitably."

"And do you think they can?"

"Perhaps."

"Because our management in recent years has diminished the quality of the product to a point where it can be as readily produced by others as by ourselves?"

Chip stared into the impenetrable paternal eyes. He was not accustomed to this dry wind of detachment. "I suppose so, yes."

"And in order to enable us to enter the broad market of popular glassware, we had to go public. And once we had gone public, we had to anticipate that we might be bought out. So what have we accomplished?"

"We'll have made a lot of money."

"But we had a lot of money. And we had the pleasure of manufacturing beautiful things."

"All that is true, sir."

"And now we'll be rich. Period." Elihu looked away from his son. His voice was still devoid of any emotion. "I don't understand you, Chip. I don't know what motivates you. I never have. You build things up only to tear them down. Maybe you're a true man of your times. Maybe the idea of a small, family-run company that does one thing proudly and does it well is hopelessly old-fashioned. I have given you full rein and gone along with your ideas. You have turned your five talents into ten. You are a success. It's your world. You can live in it. My time is almost over. I'm just as glad."

Chip, looking at that long, immobile profile, knew that there was nothing to say. His heart ached with frustration. Was the lifetime of love that this man had given him to end on this note of desolation? Could he not throw his arms around the old man and cry, "Dad, I love you, I love you!" No. Because Elihu was too good for that. Elihu wanted more than that. He wanted a son who would run Benedict as he had run it. He knew that this would never be and probably never could have been. He accepted it. But it was bitter tea, and no amount of demonstration, no matter how sincere, no matter how heartfelt, was going to make it any sweeter.

"You know, Dad, that I'll do as you say. If you tell me to reject the offer and go on with the fight, I'll do it. I might even be relieved!"

"But I shall not tell you to do that, my son. I have no idea of resuming the duties and prerogatives of an office that I resigned of my own free will. You have assumed those duties, and you must discharge them as you see best."

"But you think me a callous opportunist," Chip replied bitterly. "Say it!"

His father turned back to him with eyes that contained no reproach, but rather a look of unexpected sympathy. "No, my boy, you're wrong. You belong to your time, I to mine. I am only sorry that you do not get the kick out of your time that I did out of mine. You're not happy, Chip."

"I'm certainly not happy about this."

"No, but you should be. By your own lights. If you believe in them."

"I don't know what I believe in, Dad."

"I wish I could help you, dear boy. But I can't. It's too late. I'm too old. But then I've never really understood you. Talk to your mother. Talk to Alida. But I think I need to rest now. This has been a trying experience. Don't worry. I'll get over it. Call Timmy, will you?"

Chip opened the door to call his father's orderly, and while they waited Elihu asked him about his future. "Will you work for the new syndicate?"

"No, I couldn't. Nor will I live in Benedict. It would be too hard, after being top dog here. I'll probably move to New York." He tried to laugh, but the laugh would not come. "I'll do good works to make up for my sins!"

But his father did not smile back. "Alida will like that. She's got New York in her blood. Though she has done a wonderful job here in Benedict."

Alone, Chip wondered how his father could be so wrong about Alida. He knew that the scene with her was going to be almost as difficult as the one with Elihu. He went directly home now from the office to get it over with. He found Alida in her garden and led her into the living room, where he told her of his decision. She listened, gaping, and then to his dismay she dropped into the sofa and started to sob.

"What are you doing to me?" she cried. "You can't just take a girl's life and snap it in two like that!"

"I didn't think you'd take it quite so hard. Perhaps I should have prepared you more for it. I know you feel that there hasn't been a proper communication between us. I've always found it difficult to be frank about myself. But now I'm trying. It's going to mean everything to me to get away from Benedict once this deal has gone through. I'm pretty sure I'll want to live in New York. There are all kinds of things I might go into there — hospital work, libraries, zoos. I know you've made a great life for yourself here. No one appreciates that more than I do. But you can do it again in New York." He hesitated. "I don't think I've ever asked a real sacrifice of you before now."

He could see that this gave her pause. She reached one hand doubtfully out to him, but then pulled it back.

"You say you've never asked a sacrifice of me. I guess that's true. Except for my silence, my not intruding. It's not easy for a woman to be silent, not to intrude. But now you're asking me to give up the only life I've ever loved and go back to one that I know I'm going to hate and despise!"

"How can you possibly know any such thing?"

"Because I do! Why can't we stay in Benedict? Even if we lose the company. You say we'll be richer. Why can't we stay and run the charities and the other things in town that nobody's going to kick us out of?"

"Live in Benedict after we've lost the company?" He marveled that even she could not see this. "Think of it, Alida! Have you no pride?"

"Not like yours, that's for sure."

"You can't seriously ask it of me!"

"Look what you're asking of me."

"But that's different. A man has to make certain basic decisions for himself. I want to go to New York where my law firm is. It's a bigger life than here. You can't expect me to stay in this backwater just because you feel cozier here!"

"Oh, so that's what it is after the Benedicts cease to rule. A backwater!"

"Exactly!" He was immediately convinced that she had stumbled upon a truth. "That's just what it is without the Benedicts. And the Benedicts would be nothing here without the company."

"So it's all a matter of pride and vanity," she retorted bitterly. "You didn't consult me when you surrendered the company to those pirates. Why consult me about moving to New York? Why not just tell me when it's time to go?"

He was silent, if only by an act of will. He moved to the window as he tried to control his temper. But he found that he was trembling all over. How dared she put her sentimental attachment to a few easily duplicatable activities in a small town against his whole future? Had he not given her everything? Oh, of course, he recognized with an angry shake of his head, she would argue no, that he hadn't given her happiness, that she had had to find that for herself in Benedict. But wasn't it her duty — yes, her wifely duty, or did that concept no longer exist? — to assist him with some show of cheerfulness in his resolution to move where he could be most useful, most fulfilled? It wasn't as if he were not providing her with every luxury, every opportunity for a braver, bigger life. It wasn't as if he were asking her to give up a serious profession, such as medicine or law.

The telephone rang, and he reached automatically to pick it up. He heard his mother's voice, flat, toneless.

"Chip? Come over, please. Your father's had another stroke. I think it's the end."

"It's Dad!" he almost shouted at Alida. "He's dying!"

"Oh, Chip!" She hurried over to put her arms around him. "Oh, Chip, my poor darling. I'm so sorry!"

But even in the frenzy of his need of her sympathy, he was able to push her off. "I don't think even you will want to stay in Benedict now!" he cried in anguish.

18

ALIDA

NINETEEN SIXTY-ONE, the first year of Jack Kennedy's presidency, found us settled in Manhattan in a large apartment on Park Avenue that we had rented furnished, as I had not the heart to dismantle our house in Benedict or the energy to decorate a new one. Our city abode was as expensively conventional as an elegant department store's sample rooms; it was full of bright chintz and handsome imitations of Colonial furniture, and Chip had a library with mahogany paneling and English hunting prints. But it was comfortable, and Chip at least seemed content. He went downtown every day to his law firm, but much of his time was devoted to public trusteeships. Of course, he was just what every charitable institution dreamed of: a board member who was willing to work as well as give, who could speak eloquently at meetings and read between the lines of a financial statement. Before our first year in town was up, he had been elected to the boards of the

Public Library, the Bronx Zoo and the New York Botanical Gardens. He was on his way to becoming "Mr. New York."

With me it was just the opposite. The bottom had simply dropped out of my life, and there was nothing that I wanted to do. Eleanor was at Yale Law School, immersed in her studies, which was perhaps just as well, for she and I continued not to get on. I think I tried, but her dry refusal to accord the slightest importance to anything that I cared about was certainly daunting. Dana, my darling, was in his last year at Saint Luke's, but Chip refused to let me visit the school more than once a term, for fear of my "mollycoddling" him. My literary agent (pretentious term, considering the exiguity of my output) had submitted without success to several publishers a short romantic novel. My publishing record at the age of forty-two was three short stories in magazines and a slender volume of sonnets.

I knew plenty of people in New York, but too many of them revived unpleasant memories of my debutante year. My parents were beginning to dote: Daddy's memory was largely gone, and Mummie's storytelling about society folk had become compulsive. Chip and I dined out a certain amount — he was always in demand — and we sometimes entertained, but I found myself allowing these parties to be done by caterers. It seemed that I had left my soul in Benedict.

I didn't know how to assess my resentment of Chip. There were times when he seemed to me a veritable monster of egotism and selfishness. That he should have so calmly accepted the rape of a business that had been the basis of our lives and of his parents' — with such fatal results to the latter — and now have embarked so cheerfully on a totally new career seemed to indicate more than a prodigious capability of accepting the inevitable; it seemed to suggest an actual spirit of cooperation with fate. Had Chip wanted Benedict to fall to the enemy? Had his ethical concern been mere quibbling? But even his poor dead father had not gone this far, and I tried to repress the suspicion. At worst his scruples must have been quixotic, not malicious. But what a price we had to pay for his quixoticism! And there he was, so to speak, his hands in his pockets, whistling.

He and I were more remote from each other than at any point of our marriage. Chip seemed to sense the existence of my doubts and difficulties, but he also appeared to have decided that only I could solve them for myself, that any interference on his part would be officious. He would tell me in the evening about the events of his eventful day, and his failure to question me about my own I could attribute only to his tact. The contrast between our days would have been too sad. We went to the Piping Rock Club on weekends, where Chip played golf or squash and I took long solitary walks in the woods. On Saturday nights he still made conscientious love to me. I suspected that he might have private arrangements for additional satisfaction in that area (God knows he had experience!), but I did not much care. It was like his new interest in being a public citizen — something that did not really seem to have much to do with me.

My problem was how to get through the days. During the war, when Chip was away, I had had a minor problem with alcohol. It had not been bad enough to be spotted by anyone but my all-seeing mother-in-law, and she had been kindness itself in her gentle warnings. What had appalled me then, and what appalled me now, was the prospect of appearing drunk to others. In my periods of greatest temptation I had managed to overindulge only in afternoons and evenings when I was quite alone. And even then the quantity that I consumed was not great, as I have never had a strong head. I used to recall Granny Struthers's dictum: "It's not a compliment to a lady to say she holds her liquor well." She might have revised this had she lived into our time!

I tried to arrange my day into zones that would offer the least ennui and the least temptation. I lingered over breakfast in bed with the newspapers. An early lunch at the Colony Club made for a short morning. I could usually find someone to eat with there, and company kept me down to a single cocktail. Few women at the club took more than one in midday. In the afternoon there was the blessed narcotic of bridge, at the Colony or at the homes of friends, and the evening was apt to provide a social engagement where I would be safe under Chip's observant eye. But if he was out of town, I would watch television alone and go to bed early after several (too many) libations. Fortunately he was not often out of town.

The cards were what really saved me. I had always played a respectable game of bridge, but now I conceived the ambition (never spurn an ambition!) of becoming expert. I found a teacher who would take me in the morning, which took care of that part of the day, and I soon discovered that I needed something better than the casual afternoon foursome that I had been able to put together, sometimes with difficulty, at the club. What I really needed was three regular players who were as good as I, or preferably a little better. And these I found through Suzanne Bogart, whom I had not seen since she and Chessy had left Charlottesville after the terrible episode of the cribbed Law Review note.

Suzy had changed a lot from the timid, pretty creature whom Chessy had brought to our midst at law school; she was now a fine, full, marble-skinned, rather stocky woman who seemed to be perfectly content with female society and had developed considerable self-assurance. She brushed aside the hostility between our spouses as if we had been two mothers discussing a spat of fisticuffs between their young sons.

"I don't see that what happened between Chip and Chessy need be any concern of ours. Wouldn't you like to join a bridge foursome that meets two afternoons a week? We just lost Anne Stone, who's had to move to Florida, poor dear. The other two are old pals of yours from deb days: Amanda Bayne and Dolly Jones."

Indeed, they had been two of my "disciples" in my foolish debutante career! Amanda Bayne had not married; she had survived her parents and lived rather elegantly alone in an apartment hotel. She was still pretty, though she had to work to be. She was one of those lacquered creatures, perfectly dressed, polite, amiable, with mildly artificial good manners, who seem oddly content with an existence of unvaried routine from which all the challenges that are supposed to make life worth living have been carefully pruned. It seemed characteristic that her perfect teeth had never known a cavity. Dolly, who had been born Dolly Hotchkiss and was now divorced, had been more ravaged by life. Childless and rudderless, she spent her evenings alone without a Chip to stand between her and the whiskey bottle. Daytime was her discipline; she managed to pull herself together for the card table.

We rotated our afternoons between Suzy's bleakly modern apartment, hung with Chessy's small but fine collection of abstract impressionists, Amanda's elegant, bibelot-crowded, high-ceilinged chamber at the Lamballe and my own Park Avenue abode. We never met at Dolly's, probably because she associ-

ated her own domicile with intemperance. Anyway, we never
served anything but soft drinks or tea. Suzanne would produce
the ice and bottles herself, I had a maid for the purpose, and
Amanda would ring down to the hotel restaurant for what she
needed, producing the necessary tip from a desk drawer that I
noticed was filled to the brim with quarters.

As I look back on our sessions, my three women companions,
pale figures all, seem to merge with the walls around them. We
never gossiped or quarreled over bids or criticized each other's
play. Rudeness, I have found, is more a characteristic of male
than of female players. Some men must always act the strutting
cock, even at the card table. But in our muted sessions I heard
little but the click of a played card, the swish of a shuffle, the
quiet enumeration of a bid, the subdued, almost apologetic
"double," the faint, disappointed "oh" at the appearance of an
unexpected trump, the permissible sigh of relief at the making
of a slam. And behind us, around us, I see Suzy's white walls
and the jagged lines and exquisite spirals of a Picasso drawing,
or the gleaming glass cupboard of Amanda's China trade
tureens and platters, or the fashionable, mauve decade portrait
of her grandmother by Boldini.

The real people were in my hand or on the board: the royal
families of the four suits, the imperial aces, the loyal soldiers of
the guard. We rarely used a pack more than half a dozen
times; we relished those easily sliding surfaces and the smart
tick of a stiff back as it was placed on the card previously
played. Time and anguish were suspended as I concentrated
on my contract, assessing the hands of my opponents, counting
my possible tricks, plotting ruffs and the establishment of a
long suit. I was in a world of consoling finiteness, where there
was nothing beyond the fifty-two cards and their infinite per-

mutations. I was pitted against the terrible deity of chance with the only weapon a human being could rationally expect: his capacity to make each card play for its greatest value. Call it peace, euphoria, a drugged existence — I was at least at ease as I played. Only when we put the cards away was life again empty and bare.

It was not long before Chessy Bogart made his appearance at one of our sessions at Suzy's. He looked very much as he had in Charlottesville, dark-complexioned, neatly groomed, but stouter, and with a voice that was almost a bark. His attitude towards me was familiar, almost aggressive.

"I suppose in your world, Alida, no husband dares show himself north of Canal Street before six. Chip will suppose I have gone quite to the dogs when he hears that I'm sometimes home in the middle of the day. Except, of course, that the dogs are just where he probably assumes I am."

Chessy, I learned, practiced law without any of the usual overhead. He had a few regular clients whom he advised about tax shelters, using any spare desk in their offices, and he took an occasional gamble with one of his own projects. Apparently he made enough to keep him and Suzy comfortable in their apartment, with a balance over for the purchase of an occasional picture. In the summer they visited friends or went to a seaside hotel. They had one son, who was twenty and who had gone to live in San Francisco. They did not speak of him.

If Chessy came in before we had finished, Suzy would let him take her hand. He was an expert player, much better than any of us, but his manners were vile.

"What *should* I have led?" I asked once, when he exploded over my opening.

"Any of the other twelve cards in your silly little hand!"

However, we took his abuse in good part. I think we liked having a man at our meetings, and his playing was bold and exciting. He tended to address most of his side remarks to me. Obviously he still hated Chip, and it gave him some satisfaction to be on friendly, sassy terms with me and to subject me to abuse about "self-righteous, small-town tycoons." I could not make out what sort of marriage he and Suzy had, but Dolly told me once in the taxi going home that they had twice been separated and on the brink of divorce.

It was in this period, during a winter visit to Saint Luke's School, that I learned something more definite about my own spouse's extramarital life.

Dana and I had always been close, perhaps too close. In the natural family balance it had obviously been Chip's role to make up to Eleanor for the growing distance between mother and daughter; the four of us should then have constituted two couples with greater possibilities of mutual understanding. But Chip had elected instead to compete with me for Dana, with the result that Eleanor got too little, and Dana too much, of both parents' attention. For all the boy's congeniality with me, for all our shared love of theater and art, for all our common appetite for laughter and gossip, Dana had a rather cringing admiration for his father, punctured by almost hysterical fits of shrill defiance. To tell the truth, I preferred the latter, for there was something of the spaniel waiting coyly to be stroked and patted in Dana's way of looking at his father when he wanted to be praised. Something effeminate.

By which I do not mean homosexual, though Dana sometimes seemed to invite this inference. His blond, willowy good looks, his damp gray eyes, his emphatic stresses of speech, plus the presence of a strong father and a possessive mother, undoubtedly led many of our friends to suppose the boy a classic case of inversion. But he was, and still is, much attracted to girls. I have even suspected that he uses the feminine aspect of his personality as a way of creeping close to them before they realize his true intent. Not that I object! One child is quite enough to have contributed to that other world. I mention the doubts that Dana aroused only because I believe he aroused them in Chip, which may have been why the latter so forcefully opposed Dana's going to college in England. The three of us had a rather violent dinner at the Parents' House.

"If I'm going to specialize in English Romantic poetry, Dad," Dana argued, "wouldn't I do better to go where it was written? Can you think of anything more appropriate than to spend a vacation hiking in the lake country or visiting the British Museum to view a Grecian urn?"

"I can send you to Camden, New Jersey, if you want to read Walt Whitman."

"But, Dad, Whitman didn't write about Camden. He wrote about America. I'd have to travel from coast to coast!"

"I'd be glad to stake you to that. The point is, Dana, you need to be more Americanized, not less. Look, I'll send you to Oxford *after* you've graduated from an American college. Any one you please. Any one you can get into, that is. Is that fair?"

"No!" Dana was suddenly shrill. "Because when you were young, you had your own money and could thumb your nose at your old man! I can't. Is that fair?"

"Well, I guess I learned something from my father's errors."

"You mean you planned to keep me a beggar? I thought as much. Mummie, are you going to stand by and let him do this? Won't you take my side?"

"Darling, what good would it do you? I don't pay the bills.

Besides, you know your father's not going to change his mind. Don't you recognize that expression of his by now?"

"So! Mrs. Pilate calls for a bowl to wash her lily-white hands in!"

Chip had to fly to San Francisco to a conference of charitable trustees early the next morning, and Dana and I took a walk before chapel. Tight-lipped and sultry-eyed, he told me about the ballerina his father was supposed to be keeping.

"You've turned yourself into a carpet, Ma. And I suppose carpets can't complain when they get trod on."

I returned to New York, feeling more numb and useless than ever. And it was on the following Tuesday, while Chip was still away, that, arriving at Suzy's at three o'clock, I was met by Chessy at the front door.

"Suzy's been called to Greenwich. Her mother's had some sort of a seizure. She may be gone several days."

"I'm so sorry. I hope it's not serious. Is there anything I can do?"

"Is there ever?"

"Then I'll take myself off."

"No, stay." He opened the door wide and stood aside to let me pass. "I telephoned Amanda and Dolly, as Suzy asked me to. I didn't telephone you."

I made no move. "Did Suzy ask you not to?"

"No, that was my decision. I wanted to see you alone."

This disappointed me. Surely he could have taken a little more trouble about a seduction that was to be his obvious revenge on Chip. But then, surprisingly, he continued: "I thought you needed a bridge lesson. Rather badly, in fact. Don't worry. I make no charge."

And that is precisely how we spent the whole long afternoon

and early evening. Chessy had never been more lucid. He analyzed hand after hand, and it seemed to me that my mind embraced a whole new dimension of the game. If he was a great player, he was a still greater teacher.

That we should go out for dinner together afterwards seemed the most natural thing in the world. I supposed that the evening would end with a proposition, but I was perfectly willing to reserve my decision about that until the time came. Certainly I did not find Chessy romantic, but he was busy and masterful, and it was not unpleasant to feel myself competently handled. And I'm afraid there was something titillating to me in his loathing of Chip. Chessy had behaved so far like a gentleman; surely I could behave like a lady. And so long as we both maintained these roles, did it, at this point in my life, very much matter what else happened?

We dined at a sawdusty steak house where they served very large, very dry Martinis. It was not long before the subject turned to Chip and the Benedicts. Chessy's curiosity about my life in the factory town seemed to last the whole meal. He was very funny and sarcastic about my in-laws and what he called the Benedict "mystique." Only towards the end of our meal did he move to a pronouncement of judgment.

"What in your opinion, Alida, is really wrong with your lord and master? For something's got to be wrong with a guy who blew up the family fort after he'd filled his pockets."

I debated this. "May it not be simply that he's too much of an idealist?"

Chessy had a stare of deadly effect. He could keep his large, dark, unblinking eyes fixed on one for minutes at a time, his lips half-open, as if in wonderment at one's constantly renewed naïveté.

"Chip an idealist?" he repeated. "Surely you can't have been brainwashed to that extent. Was he an idealist back at Saint Luke's when he denied me to his grandfather?"

"But you had no right to implicate him!"

"I was only trying to save another boy's skin. It wouldn't have hurt him to tell the truth. And then we'd all three of us have been cleared."

"Chip says you never understood his grandfather. You'd have all three been expelled. So what good would it have done you?"

"The good that it does a man to see his friend stand up and tell the truth."

"Even if that truth would have killed Mr. B?"

Again Chessy let me have the full benefit of that stare. "If you really believe that, Alida, then you have been brainwashed. Mr. B, as you call him, had a singularly sharp nose for the dirty things that boys do with one another. It makes one wonder about his own schooldays. Oh, he would have thundered about it, all right. He would have roared and shouted. But in the end he would have raised those disingenuously innocent eyes piously to the heavens and cried, 'Lord, thy will be done!' Hypocrisy, as usual, would have won the day."

"We must agree to disagree about that."

"How smug can a woman be?" he demanded angrily. "Did you know the late headmaster of Saint Luke's School?"

"No."

"And have you ever heard anything about him except from his beloved daughter and grandson?"

"I suppose not."

"I know you were not burdened with the disadvantages of a college education, but no doubt you know the meaning of the word 'hagiography'?"

"Yes. Even without four years of football games and whiskey."

"Then you should have learned that the Benedicts are adept in the fabrication of halos. It is a trade, indeed, to which they seem to have apprenticed you. You will graduate with honors when you have fashioned one for Chip."

"Oh, come, Chessy. I know Chip has his faults, but . . ."

"Faults!" Chessy raised both hands. "You don't say the devil has faults."

"Now you're being absurd."

"Let us consider that." Again that stare! But now I looked away from him impatiently. "I submit in all sobriety," he continued in his most gravelly tone, "that your husband has dedicated his lost soul to the destruction of his fellow man."

"Must you go on so?"

"And his fellow woman! Do you not care to be warned, my dear? By one who knows? By one who learned the hard way?" His stare hardened into a glare.

"All right," I said, cowed. "Go ahead."

"Primo!" He held up a solemn forefinger. "The destruction of Chessy Bogart. Initiated at Saint Luke's School and completed at the University of Virginia. When Chip at Yale recognized that his victim was only scotched, not killed, he had to devise a further strategy. It took him three years, but it worked. Oh, brilliantly!"

"You seem to forget that I know about that. If you were so innocent, you could have gone to the Honor Court."

"Ah, but that was precisely the brilliance of his scheme!" Chessy struck the table with his fist so hard that people looked around. He ignored them. "Before the Honor Court, with a shining witness like Chip against me, my innocence was not sure to prevail. It would have been foolhardy of me not to take the safer alternative that Lucifer offered. But what he knew was that my leaving law school on the lame excuse of a healthy mother's heart would raise questions that would never quite be settled. Small wonder that my law career has been less than distinguished."

"It seems to me rather far-fetched to blame that on one incident."

"One! Have I not told you, woman, there were two?" His middle finger joined the index in his again raised right hand. "But now let us pass Chessy. Chip was merely sharpening his teeth on me. Let us proceed to his major crimes. Surely even one as mesmerized as yourself can recognize the fiendish success of his campaign against his parents. What timing! It was sheer genius. First, the poor old darlings are subjected to a series of calculated rebuffs. They are made to admit that their lovely boy owes them nothing, for it is *after* he has essentially broken with them that he becomes a successful law student and a war hero. And then, when they have been weakened and humiliated, what does he do? He forgives them, opens his arms and returns to the home town to become everything they've dreamed of. And then, when they have given him all — Glamis, Cawdor, the crown itself — he quietly lowers the drawbridge to the enemy and escapes to New York, his pockets crammed with gold. Small wonder it killed the old man. I was only surprised it didn't kill them both."

A horrid little scratch of suspicion in the pit of my stomach made me twist. "But Chip had his reasons for that. There was some sort of legal ethics question involved."

"With Chip ethics are always involved. Ethics come out of his ears. Ethics, my poor deluded girl, are his stock-in-trade. Which brings me to his next victim."

"No, please, Chessy. I've heard enough."

"You don't want to hear what he did to Alida Struthers?" I could only stare at him now, as if he were a mesmerist. "Alida was a brilliant, beautiful girl who had everything but a purpose in life. Such a person is very difficult to destroy, because she has nothing she really cares about that one can take away. But that need not trouble the devil. *Give* her a purpose so that one can smash it! And is that not precisely what your loving husband did? Moved you to Benedict, put a scepter in your hands and then — when you had learned to enjoy wielding it and were a bit too old to acquire another — he tore it from your grasp!"

"Oh!" I closed my eyes in pain. "Oh, Chessy, don't!"

"But he's not through with you yet. He may have his little ballet dancer, but that's not it. He probably knows that you know that she's not important to him. For who is? Lucky for her, anyway, for if she *were* important to him, he'd find a way to blight her career. No, Chip knows where you've been playing bridge and who with."

"Why not? I've made no secret of it."

"But he sees what will be your ultimate humiliation!" Chessy's stare seemed to extend itself now into a beam of light, and he brought out his next sentence with a rasping laugh. "To be screwed by Chessy Bogart!"

I stared back, like one hypnotized. I realized with a shock that I must have been thinking about this for weeks. "You mean we have no choice?"

"That's it. No choice. Two victims of Satan Benedict!"

He paid the check and we went back to his apartment without further discussion. It was the only night of adultery in my married life. I say night, rather than act, because we performed the act furiously no less than three times. I had no love for Chessy, and he certainly had none for me, but there was a tense, desperate satisfaction in what we did. I found him too concentrated, too busy, a bit ridiculous, really, and I'm sure he found me bossy in trying to take the lead. But I spent the whole night there, and when I left, after a cup of coffee in the morning, he did not seem the least put out that I told him that the experience must have no sequel.

"We did what we had to do," he observed gravely. "Will you tell Chip?"

"I don't know."

"Well, just so long as you don't tell Suzy!"

It was a number of weeks before I did tell Chip. He gave me a long, cool stare and then shrugged.

"Well, I can't say I haven't deserved it."

He didn't care! So once again he cut me down.

19

ALIDA

ONE RESULT of my telling Chip about the episode with Chessy was the total discontinuance of our sexual relations. He made no comment on this, nor did I; he simply thereafter spent the nights in a cot in his dressing room. I do not know why he felt himself entitled to any sense of outrage, or, for that matter, whether he did so. He had always, so far as I could make out, been devoid of the least sense of jealousy. It was more probable that he considered that I had been contaminated by the touch of the loathed Chessy and was now too unclean for him. I was certainly not going to protest, as I did not wish to give him the least impression that I objected. Our marriage had deteriorated to the lowest point where it could still endure.

The war in Vietnam was now raging hotly and the protest was nationwide. Dana, who had just graduated from Yale, had postponed any idea of working until he decided what to do about the draft. His number was imminent, and he was threatening to leave the country. He and his father had had a furious row about this, in which Chip had used the word "treason," and now Dana refused to come home, spending his time visiting friends of like persuasion, and, I fear, on drugs. Eleanor had given up her job in Legal Aid to work full time for an antiwar group. She came to the apartment one night when Chip was away to suggest that I should work in her office. I demurred.

"Why not, Mother? You're against the war, aren't you?"

"Why do you assume that? Your father certainly isn't."

"Oh, it's been clear for quite a while that Daddy's being for something is almost enough for you to be against it. Anyway, it's high time you stopped being an old-fashioned female chattel and started thinking for yourself. Come out of the doll's house, Ma! You might even enjoy it."

Eleanor was not a lovable girl. She had the wide face and small features of my mother (her opposite, however, in every other conceivable respect), and she was putting on a good deal of weight. She did nothing about her messy brown hair, dressed plainly and spoke in a voice of seemingly permanent exasperation.

"I'm perfectly capable of making up my own mind," I replied. "But yes, I think I do disapprove of the war. Why should we care if the South Vietnamese go communist? At least, why should we care more than they do?"

Eleanor nodded like an approving schoolteacher. "I guess that'll do for a start. Keep an open mind, and we'll make you a zealot. But seriously, Mother, the work would do you good. If you go on with your regime of cards and gin, you'll end up in an institution."

"Eleanor! What are you saying?"

"Well, can you deny it?"

Could I? I was thunderstruck. It had not crossed my addled and preoccupied mind that I could present such a picture of futility to my indifferent and largely absent daughter. And then, very suddenly, it struck me that I couldn't bear to have her think what she was thinking. Anything was better than that.

"All right! I'll work for you."

"Splendid. Come to the office tomorrow."

"What will I do?"

"Well, we'll start by giving you reports to read. And when you're indoctrinated, you can begin addressing letters."

"But I can't even type, Eleanor!"

"You can write out the envelopes, then. Never mind, I'll find something. Maybe you can answer the telephone. The great thing is to do what you can."

I actually went to Eleanor's office the next day. It was a small affair, one floor of an old brownstone, dirty and cluttered, but the young, chain-smoking people who filled it were friendly and enthusiastic and greeted me warmly. A nice young man taught me about the telephone, and I even wondered whether I had not found my niche at last.

Chip was roundly disgusted when I told him about it that night.

"What the hell do you think you're doing?"

"I'm doing what I want, for a change. I'm doing my own thing."

"But have you thought it through? Do you honestly and truly feel yourself justified in trying to hamper your government where the very lives of our soldiers may be at stake?"

"I don't see why it wouldn't save their lives to stop the fighting."

"And what about our national honor? What about our commitment to world freedom?"

"I don't want to discuss it, Chip. You always throw facts at me that I can't rebut. I know what I *feel*; that's the point."

"But I've got to make you see it!" He was suddenly very agitated, more than seemed warranted by what he obviously deemed my ineptitude. "Can't you take in that this is the first real moral challenge we've had since Pearl Harbor? And that we've actually elected to meet it without using the bomb? That we've chosen to fight not a war, but a duel, and with prescribed weapons? We, who could annihilate Hanoi with a single blow! It's ... well, it's magnificent! It restores honor to a cynical globe."

I declined to reply to his argument, which struck me as almost irrational, but I did think it might be a good idea to have a family confrontation on the issue, and I invited the children to dinner the following night for this announced purpose. They at least would be able to answer him. Dana had just come back to New York, and he agreed, reluctantly, to come. Eleanor, insisting that it was a waste of time, also accepted. After all, I was working for her; she owed me something.

My idea was that we should first have a very good dinner, just the four of us, at which the war would not be discussed, and then retire to the library to have it out. Eleanor was rather sullenly silent during our scantily enjoyed meal. Dana drank too many cocktails and told a couple of silly stories. Chip, of course, was utterly at ease. He filled the silences with a rather interesting account of new exhibits at the Bronx Zoo. I knew with a sinking heart that he was not going to lose his temper. He was determined to win, and, of course, as usual, would win — at least the debate. Dana and Eleanor were bound to get fretful. I was already beginning to regret my idea.

When we had taken our seats in the library around a table with coffee cups and brandy glasses, Chip gravely opened the discussion.

"You seem to be running a considerable office, Eleanor. Do you mind telling me how it's financed?"

Eleanor, smoking and inhaling deeply, gazed at him with an expression of barely restrained irritation. "I thought you'd ask that. How is it relevant to the war?"

"It's relevant because we're talking about the war *and* us."

"Oh, Chip, you know Ellie's paying for it!" I broke in impatiently.

"Pardon me, Alida, I did not know it. I suspected it, of course. But Eleanor most certainly did not see fit to consult me about any proposed dissipation of family funds."

"Family funds, Dad? Didn't Grandpa leave me that money? Haven't I a right to do with it as I choose?"

"A legal right, certainly. But that money was left to you by your grandfather at my request. It was part of an overall family estate plan. It was never intended that it should be dissipated across the nation to sow dissension and foster treason."

Chip's tone was so matter-of-fact that the dynamite in his last words took us all by surprise. Eleanor laughed scornfully.

"I doubt the Benedict money was ever better spent."

"How come, Dad," Dana put in, "that Eleanor can blow her money and I can't touch mine?"

"Your grandfather and I decided that I should have discretion over your income and principal until you were thirty, Dana. We thought there was an element of emotional volatility in your nature that would take time to straighten out. We believed that Eleanor was stabler. We were wrong. About Eleanor, that is."

"Oh, Chip, don't be so cold and detached! These are your children, after all."

"I am being deliberately detached, Alida. I hope I am not being cold. I certainly don't feel cold. In my opinion a man who is old enough to contemplate deserting his country in time of war is old enough to be told the truth in matters of financial planning."

"Let him go on, Mummie!" Dana cried, furious. "Give him all the rope he needs to hang himself."

As I saw Chip's cold gaze upon his only son, I felt a sudden panic as to what his real motives might be. Did he want to goad his children into a breach?

"Let's not fly off the handle," Eleanor intervened. "Let's get on to the war itself. Are you prepared to tell us, Dad, that in your considered opinion it is a wise war?"

"Wise? Perhaps not. Had I been President, I should never have instituted so massive a military presence on the Asian mainland. It can hardly be justified on economic grounds, and probably not even on grounds of national security."

"If you really believe that," Eleanor followed up in astonishment, "how can you defend such wickedness?"

"You're begging the question, Eleanor. I never said it was wicked. I do not believe that it is wicked. On the contrary, I think it's rather noble. I . . ."

"Noble! That holocaust!"

"My dear, will you let me finish? To me there is something fine about coming to the rescue of the little guy who's getting kicked around. Stepping in between the victim and the bully, even when the victim happens to be no great shakes. That to me is the perennial role of America. We kicked the British out in 1781. We rescued our seamen from impressment in 1812. We freed the slaves. We liberated Cuba. We beat the Kaiser out of Berlin and drove Hitler to his bunker. We saved South Korea. We . . ."

"Ta-*ta*, ta-ta-*ta*, ta-ta-*ta*!" intoned Dana mockingly.

"Really, Dad, can't you save it for the Fourth of July?"

Chip was imperturbable. "Very well, children. I'm a tin-pan patriot. What are you? What do you believe in?"

Eleanor was clear. "I believe in allowing other countries to make their own decisions about their own political problems. I do not believe in teaching democracy to ignorant peasants by blowing up their huts and rice paddies."

"Or drafting the youth of America to die in undeclared and illegal warfare!" Dana added.

"All I am saying," Chip insisted, "is that Hanoi is forcing red rule on a people that have neither asked nor voted for it. It strikes me that that is an evil thing to do. To oppose an evil thing, even by force, may be impracticable. But to me it cannot be wrong. If a thousand men die to prevent the murder of one, it may be foolish, but it is still fine!"

"If they're volunteers!" Dana exclaimed. "But should you draft them to die in vain?"

"That, I admit, is a point," his father conceded. "But in these matters I believe one must obey one's government. Disobedience can be justified only by some grave moral cause. If it is a question of judgment, the individual should not pit his against his country's."

"But lack of judgment," Eleanor argued, "can be carried to an extreme where it becomes a crime."

"I shan't be drafted, Dad. I promise you that! Even if I have to skip the country!"

"I did not expect to persuade either of you to a different

view," Chip said gravely. "This conference was your mother's idea. But it gives me the opportunity to tell you both that I deem it my duty to counteract, insofar as I can, the unpatriotic acts of my children by my own, I hope more patriotic ones. I intend now to offer my services to the government in any capacity in which it sees fit to employ them. And I shall contribute to patriotic causes a sum at least equal to what Eleanor has spent."

Chip rose and left the room abruptly after making this speech, and he did not return that night. I found out later that he had taken the shuttle to Washington. What he was doing there I neither knew nor cared, for in the next week my mind and heart were entirely taken up with my son. Dana's draft number came up, and he left a note with my doorman that he was catching a plane to Stockholm.

20

※※※※

CHIP

WHEN CHIP accepted the commission of Special Assistant to the Secretary of State, with the particular mission of engendering support for the American cause in Vietnam among the nations of Southeast Asia, he and Alida had the most violent scene of their marriage. It took place when he returned from a trip to Washington unexpectedly late at night to find her before the television set with a bottle of whiskey. He realized too late that he should have postponed discussion of his new job until morning.

"You can't be serious!" she cried, her eyes flickering with a kind of panic. "But what am I saying? You're always serious. You were born serious. You're doing this to spite me!"

"I guess you'd better sleep on it. We'll talk in the morning."

"We'll talk right now! What do you think this will do to your children? To have you running a war they're risking their very lives to oppose!"

"It won't help to be melodramatic, Alida. A man has to do what he believes is right."

"A man! That's all you can think of, isn't it? Your masculinity. And now you've got to prove it again, for the umpteenth time, by showering bombs on helpless peasants."

"That's an absurd oversimplification."

"Oh, I know, you're fighting the red menace. You wouldn't listen to the children when they tried to talk sense into you. What are you trying to do, Chip? Destroy them?"

He glanced in distaste from that angry, pouting face to the empty glass on the table. Alida's beauty had been eroded by her indulgences; there were bags under her eyes, and he could detect already the threat of a second chin. A gust of anger at the thought of the waste of it all rustled through him. But the sudden storm that followed it in a flash and that now tightly gripped every part of his throbbing being was a passionate resentment.

"My children! When have they bothered to give me the smallest consideration? When Eleanor blew her money, did she take the trouble to consult me? When Dana decided to disobey the law of the land and slink off to Europe to avoid the consequences, did he see fit to discuss it with me?"

"But, Chip, you made them feel it was hopeless to argue with you!"

"Because they knew they wouldn't convince me. It's true they couldn't have. But it's equally true that I hadn't a prayer of convincing them. At least I tried. At least I kept the doors open. Until they slammed them in my face!"

As he spoke, a sobering question struck him. Did he actually dislike Ellie and Dana? Dislike his own children? But yes, he did, and why not? Could any man, after years of patience, help giving in to a revulsion of feeling when he never met anything but rebuff? Oh, the smug, smirking condescension of youth!

"I promise you one thing, Alida. I'll always be ready to take them back. Always ready to support them financially, no matter what they do. But for the moment I'm fed up with both of them."

"And with me, too, I suppose."

"I thought there the shoe was on the other foot. Are you coming to Washington with me?"

"Do you want me?"

"Of course I want you. I've rented a house, fully furnished. It even has a couple that go with it. All you have to do is lock the door here and open it there."

"Taken a house!" she cried, exasperated. "Taken a house without consulting me? Is that your way of persuading me to move?"

"I've taken the house you said you wanted to live in if you ever had to live in Washington. The yellow brick one on S Street that Lars and Karen had when he was in the Pentagon. It even has a little pool in the garden."

A pause showed that she was touched, in spite of herself. "Oh? That *is* a lovely house."

"How about it? Will you come?"

"Give me time to think it over."

"All the time you want. But I'm starting on Monday. However, that doesn't matter. We can run two households as long as you need. Georgetown will be there waiting for you."

"Oh, Chip, I'll think it over, of course, but won't you, too? Is it absolutely imperative that you support this hideous war?"

But he had no idea of getting into another fruitless argument, and he dropped the discussion, suggesting that she had better go to bed. The next morning he left for Washington before she was up. It was evident that they would not meet again before he had taken his oath of office.

He was not sorry to leave New York. He had discovered what he had not been wholly surprised to discover: that the fiduciary of a charitable institution, in the absence of an administrative crisis, was expected only to give or raise money. This, however, had been acceptable to him, and he had thrown himself into the job with all of his energy. What he had been less willing to accept was the tendency to vulgarization in the arts and sciences. Culture had become "big business," with big shows for bigger crowds, and Chip had begun to feel that he might as well be back in the glass business, making shabbier products for higher prices under Elihu's disapproving eye. The fact that that eye had been removed to a higher sphere would not have made it less disapproving.

What was it but another confirmation that the world was made up of alloy? That the poor Albigenses, whose brutal extinction he had deplored as a boy in Albi Cathedral, had been right, and that the creating force had built whatever was out of badness? How could he escape the conclusion when he saw all around him the ineluctable evolution of nobility into fatuity?

He had overstated his case for the war, deliberately, to the children. Certainly he had little enthusiasm for its continuance. Common sense and discretion called for an early pullout. But so long as the powers that were had decided against it, was it a crime to get a kick — all right, call it just that! — out of hacking at the green scaly neck that bore the head of the dragon? Gerry Hastings had said the enemy was a state of mind. Well, surely Moscow and Hanoi were aspects of that state. If there was value in nothing but the opposition to evil, at least one could oppose!

In his first six months at the Department he was so busy that it hardly mattered whether or not Alida moved to Washington. His existence seemed to have changed from a slow silent movie to a hectic newsreel. He had to read every intelligence report from every embassy, consulate and military post in Southeast Asia; he had to peruse every letter volunteered from a traveler or businessman. He was sent on a flying trip to Singapore, Bangkok and Saigon. When he was not reading, he was dictating, endlessly turning out memoranda on different ways of justifying the American presence. In Washington he worked nights and often weekends. His life had become a blur of airports, uniforms, jeeps and long, shiny limousines, of gravely shaking heads bent over maps, of paper, paper, paper.

Alida did at last come down to Georgetown, but she kept the New York apartment and spent more than half of every month in it. She had given up her job with Eleanor because of her nervous tension over Dana, and she said that she could not survive without her bridge sessions. Her drinking was now so much worse that any social life was out of the question. After a few cocktails she would denounce the war in terms that made it desirable that none of his associates be present. Having at first tried to loosen her ties to Manhattan, Chip now began to look forward to her departures to the north.

His only real friend was his secretary, with whom he spent most of his time. Violet Crane was twenty-nine, with a fine full figure, strong features, curly blond hair and sympathetic, yellow-tan eyes through which radiated a character so warm as to make her everybody's friend. She had a tendency to be disorganized in small matters, mislaying her purse, leaving her coat in the cafeteria, always forgetting her cigarettes. But her work was first-rate, and she was willing to put in any number of hours.

Chip soon discovered that her background was not unlike Alida's. She was listed in the New York Social Register, but she had no income other than what she earned.

"Mummie likes to call us *nouveaux pauvres*," she told him on the first night that he took her out to dinner after work. "But it seems to me we're rather *vieux* in that *galère*. You have to go back a couple of generations to find the first butler."

"What made you join the Department? It can't have been, at your age, an impassioned belief in the war."

"No, although I'm certainly not opposed. What do I really know about it? I leave those things to the Special Assistant."

"That's more than his children do."

"Ah, but I feel sorry for them! They're going to regret having been so disagreeable to you. I read an interview with your daughter at the time you took the post. It wasn't really a bit nice. But she'll grow out of it."

"She's the same age as you, Violet."

"I guess I feel older because I didn't have a father. At least one who was available. Someday your daughter will know how blessed she's been."

There was a candor in her tone that barred any suspicion of insincerity. Yet he couldn't help asking, "You're not just being nice to the boss?"

"Why shouldn't I be nice to him? He's a very good boss."

When he stopped his car by her apartment house, she behaved perfectly. She didn't hurry to get out to avoid the possibility of his seeking to come up; she appeared not even to envisage the possibility of a vulgar finale to their evening. She sat for a moment, straight upright, like a little girl in pink satin about to leave dancing school. Then she turned and said, with a quaintly natural formality, "Thank you, Mr. Benedict, for my pleasant evening. I much enjoyed it."

"Am I too old to be called Chip?"

She considered this, her head to one side. "Certainly not too old. That's ridiculous. But I think it had better be Mr. Benedict in the office. Good night, Chip."

It was a warm spring, and Alida had been in New York for three weeks running. When he asked Violet for dinner in his garden by the pool, she accepted, again without embarrassment, but when she arrived and discovered there was no Mrs. Benedict, she seemed for a moment nonplused. And then, taking in the little oval pool and the small garden of rhododendrons, she suddenly clapped her hands.

"How lovely it all is!"

"Alida is in New York. Let me say at once, Violet, that Alida is usually in New York. That's beginning to be the way things are."

"What a shame!"

"I suppose so. But it needn't keep us from having a pleasant dinner together, need it?"

"Why on earth should it?"

There had been an idea that they would do some work after dinner, but with the second Martini Chip dismissed it. He was having too good a time. Violet, it was true, was less at ease than she had been at the restaurant, for his invitation on that night could have been attributed to simple friendliness, whereas a dinner at home without his wife had all the aspects of a proposed affair. But she too was obviously enjoying herself, and she seemed determined not to spoil any minute of their evening by a fussy or prudish concern over how it might end. She talked with animation and humor about herself and her life, but only in answer to his questions.

"You're like Alida," he commented. "Old New York."

"Not really. I'm Hungarian and not even very old Hungarian. My real name is Belik. My father was some sort of a count, or at least he claimed he was. He came to New York in the early years of the depression and thought he'd found a permanent meal ticket in Mummie. And he might have, too, if he hadn't mistreated her so."

"What did he do? Beat her?"

"I don't know. She never talks about it. She simply shivers if you mention his name. I guess he was pretty bad, but then she's pretty timid. It must have been a hopeless match from the beginning. Sometimes, when Mummie's being a bit too 'old New York,' as you put it, I feel a sneaking sympathy for him."

He thought he could make out the hint of a muscular male Hungarian parent in her strong, well-shaped limbs. But anything mean or brutal in Count Belik had certainly circumvented her.

"So she divorced him?"

"Well, her family did that for her. She hid away with me and my brother until a settlement was made. Father was willing enough to sell us for a good slice of her tiny fortune."

"He didn't mind your giving up his name?"

"Why should he have? It probably wasn't his real one. So we took Mother's and never saw him more. But surely all this can't interest you."

"It does, Violet. I want to hear your whole story."

"Really? You mean, the boss should know? What more can I tell you?"

"How you were brought up."

"In an old-fashioned apartment hotel. They weren't so dear in those days. I shared the bedroom with Mummie, and Brian had a maid's room. It was on Central Park West, not fashionable, of course, but we went to fashionable schools, Brian to

Buckley, for a while anyway, and I to Brearley. And all the summers we spent with Granny Crane in her little cottage on Washington Street in Newport. Oh, yes, we were always genteel! Only it took a good deal of effort to keep up with the richer cousins. Well, not keep *up* with them — that was impossible — but keep enough in sight so that we wouldn't be forgotten and might sometimes be asked to parties."

"But you went to college?"

"Yes, an aunt sent me to Vassar. Oh, I have nothing to complain about. I enjoyed my youth. If only Mummie had been a bit stronger! But she was always such a white scared little thing, huddled over her bric-a-brac, dreaming how different her life might have been if she'd never met Father."

"Couldn't she have married again?"

"You don't know her! She felt that a lifetime of expiation would hardly make up for the trouble she had caused her parents. And for just one misstep! How could it have happened? she must have always asked herself. How could she not have married a nice bunny rabbit like herself? What fiend had placed that Hungarian in her path?"

Chip, leaning back on the settee, sipping his drink, felt a pleasant calm slipping about him, like a silk kimono draped by competent hands over his shoulders and back.

"What about your brother? Did he turn out all right?"

"Alas, no. It may have been the trauma of the divorce. Or maybe there was some terrible scene; I don't know. Father had ghastly standards of how masculine a boy should be. He may even have beat him. Anyway, Brian was a nervous wreck. He never could get through any school or college, and he's been in the Stauffer Psychiatric Clinic in Worcester for five years now. I sometimes wonder if he'll ever get out."

"That must cost your mother a pretty penny."

"It takes every one she's got! Each year we have to sell something new, the Kensett, the Copley. Soon there won't be anything left. Thank God there's a small Crane trust that Mummie can't touch. But what am I saying?" She put a hand to her lips in dismay. "You'll think I'm looking for a handout!"

"Violet, please, don't be gross. What I don't see, with all this sadness, is how you ever got away."

"To Washington? It was that same aunt. She's Mummie's sister and a perfect darling, not at all like Mummie, ever so much stronger. She told me to give up my job at Scribner's and get out of town. She said it was my only chance."

"She was quite right."

"When I told her I couldn't leave Mummie, she insisted. She promised me she'd look in on her every day. And so I finally decided to come down here."

At dinner he told her about the Benedicts and about Alida, Eleanor and Dana. He told her that his marriage was really over, which he had not acknowledged to himself until then. They drank a bottle of wine and then a good deal of brandy, but he noted with approval, when he drove her home, that she was sober. They said good night in the same way that they had done before, but he knew, and he was passably sure that she knew, that it would not be so on the next evening they spent together.

Nor was it. He had sent the couple off for the weekend, and he and Violet had the house to themselves for two days and nights. She gave herself to love with a freedom and a gaiety that he found delightful. She was not totally inexperienced in the art — she told him that she had had one other affair, three years earlier, with a married literary agent that had lasted a year — but Chip suspected that her partner had been clumsy, for she seemed amazed and exhilarated at what he aroused in her. The only thing that disturbed him was that she was obviously very much in love, but she seemed at the same time to sense that this would disturb him, that it might spoil their "idyll," like a whiff of bad breath or some revelation of coarseness. She gave the appearance of making light of their lovemaking — or of trying to — by keeping her terms of affection moderate and half-humorous. It was as if she were watching him out of the corner of her eye to be sure that her remarks were in tune with his.

"You needn't take me home," she announced on Sunday night. It had been agreed that she would leave before the couple returned. "I'll get a cab, and if not, I can walk. It's a lovely night."

"But my car's right outside. It'll take me only ten minutes."

"Please, Chip!" There was a sudden note of near panic in her tone.

"But, Violet, my dear, what's wrong?"

"Because I know you want to work! And because if I'm an importunate bitch, you'll give me up. And I don't want you to give me up. Not just yet, anyway. Oh, of course, you'll have to, in time. You have a whole other life — I know that. But I do want a little more of you first. Oh, yes, I do!"

And she almost ran out the door.

At the office her conduct was perfect. Never by anything so vulgar as even a private wink did she suggest that their relationship had changed. She was as pleasant as ever, possibly a touch more businesslike, and she seemed determined to work even harder than before. Only when it was time to quit did she, by her instant acquiescence with any plan he offered, betray the fact that she had placed her every minute at his disposal. He was convinced that if he did not take her out, she would spend the evening alone in her room. The completeness with which he had all at once filled her life was disconcerting. But what could he do about it if she never complained?

One Saturday night, when they were having a drink at Chip's before going out to dinner, Alida called from New York to inform him that she had just been talking to Dana on the transAtlantic telephone. Had Chip sent him any money?

"None," he retorted, amused by Violet's intently listening countenance. "Nor will I until he comes home and signs up for the draft."

"How typical of you! Of course I'll have to give it to him."

"Do as you see fit. I don't begrudge him the money. But as a government officer I must decline to support a draft dodger."

"He's not dodging anything, Chip. He's taking a moral stand against an illegal war."

"It's a question of terminology."

"Eleanor's in San Francisco. She addressed a rally on Monday of three thousand people."

"I always thought she'd make her mark."

There was a silence, after which Alida's voice rose almost to a scream. "You snotty bastard, I'm leaving you! I meant to, months ago — I was going to write you a note — and then I lost my nerve. Well, I shan't lose it again. I'm leaving you, I tell you!"

"You'd better talk to Lars about that."

"I shan't talk to Lars! I'm going to retain Chessy Bogart."

Chip felt his throat clotted with instant rage. "If you do that, you'll regret it for the rest of your life."

"You're afraid of him because he knows what you're up to. Well, you'll see!"

"Alida, you've been drinking. Call me in the morning when you're sober."

"I'll never call you again as long as I live!"

Chip hung up and turned to Violet. "She says she's leaving me."

"You mean she knows?"

"Knows what?"

"Oh, Chip, *what*? About you and me? Or have you been such a philanderer that it no longer matters to her?"

"I'll thank you to keep a civil tongue in your mouth, young lady. No, she doesn't know a thing about you and me."

"How can you be sure?"

"Because she'd have flung it in my face if she had. Alida's a very direct woman."

"Well, I'm glad anyway I'm not the cause! Do you think she'll divorce you?"

"Do you hope she will?"

"Of course I hope she will!"

"So that I'll be free to marry you?"

"Oh, my God! *Would* you?"

"Don't you think twenty-two years is rather a gap in our ages?"

"Oh, that doesn't matter when the man's as rich as you are."

Chip laughed in delighted surprise. How could she so consistently hit the right note? "So that's what you've been all along? A gold digger?"

"Well, you can hardly blame a girl who's never even seen a gold piece. Anyway, I put my cards on the table."

"Oh, that was just your subtlety."

But poor Violet couldn't keep up the game, after all, even though she could see how much he enjoyed it. There were sudden tears in her eyes. "I couldn't fool you if I tried, and you know it. I'm too much your woman. It's obscene! You should have seen Mummie's face when I told her about it."

"You told her? My God, when?"

"Last Sunday, when I went up there. She must have sensed that something was going on, because she was nosy, which isn't like her. So I told her, yes, I was living with a married man, old enough to be my father, who had no intention of ever marrying me, and that I planned to go right on that way! I was going to be like Irene Dunne in *Back Street*, following John Boles discreetly when he went abroad on important missions, always in the background, always hidden from the public and family. And when he died at last, and his scornful children came to pay me off, they'd be appalled to find me a broken old hag, dying of grief!"

"I remember that movie. Margaret Sullavan did a remake of it."

"With Charles Boyer. I must have seen it four times. I always imagined it would be my life, and I didn't care!"

"Your mother must have been horrified."

"Oh, she was. She said I'd made myself cheap, that you'd never respect me. She said that if you ever did get your freedom, you wouldn't marry me. And maybe you won't. Why should you? But I'm warning you, Charles Benedict, if you ask me, I'll accept. I'll be your mistress or your wife. Or neither. It's all up to you!"

"I can't figure you out, Violet. You may be the frankest, most honest woman who ever breathed . . ."

"Or else a 'super subtle Venetian'!" she finished for him with a shout of laughter. "You see, I even know when you're going to quote Shakespeare!"

21

✕✕✕

CHIP

WHEN IT BECAME KNOWN that Alida would not return to Washington and that a separation, and possibly a divorce, between her and Chip was imminent, Matilda Benedict, to the astonishment of her offspring, made a great decision. She announced that she was leasing a house in Georgetown for a year.

"It seems to me that everyone is deserting Chip," she told her protesting daughters. "I intend to hoist my flag at his very doorstep!"

But when Chip telephoned to convince her that he was perfectly all right alone and that he worked so hard as to leave little time for family visitations, she was less embattled.

"Don't think your old ma is coming down to try to muscle in on your life," she assured him. "Nothing could be further from my purpose. I'm bored with myself and bored with Benedict. I need a change of air and maybe one or two new friends, and if you can drop in for a drink once or twice a month, that is quite all that I shall require."

And indeed she seemed determined to be good to her word. She redecorated the living room of the charming little Greek Revival house that she had rented and renewed her friendships with some retired diplomatic couples living in the neighborhood. She never called Chip, but waited for him to call her, and when he dined with her, which he found himself doing, quite of his own accord, at least once a week, her conversation was cheerful and interesting. He found her particularly sympathetic about the war, which she regarded as a tangled mess but one from which the nation could not retreat with honor.

One night she asked him: "Why don't you bring your secretary here for dinner? I hear she's a wonderful girl."

"Who's been gossiping about me?"

"Nobody's been gossiping about you. Alma Rand mentioned Miss Crane. She said her son-in-law described her as your girl Friday and one of the best workers in the Department."

"Well, he ought to know. Jim and I work together daily. Sure, I'll ask Violet to dinner. Only don't get any ideas."

"What ideas should I have? Surely Alida doesn't expect the handsome husband she's left to live like a monk!"

Chip looked at his parent with astonishment. "Don't tell me the sexual revolution has hit your generation, Ma! I hadn't thought it had reached mine yet."

"Yours! You're a mere child."

"A child of fifty-one."

Amused by his mother's new liberality, he invited Violet to dine there on Saturday. But she seemed terrified.

"Oh, Chip, did you make her?"

"It was entirely her idea, not mine."

"What do you suppose she wants of me?"

"She knows that you and I work together. She'd like to meet you; that's all."

Matilda handled her guest with the greatest ease and kindness, and the evening passed agreeably for all three, except for a somber discussion at the end of a reported massacre of Vietnamese peasants by trigger-happy Americans seeking out the Vietcong.

"I'm sure it will turn out to be much exaggerated," Matilda said.

"I'm afraid not, Ma. I've seen the reports. I don't know what devil gets into our boys."

"Do you suppose it's drugs?"

"One would almost like to think so. Anything rather than they could do it in cold blood."

When he took Violet home later, she wouldn't let him come up. "I'm sorry, darling, but it doesn't seem right. After dining with your mother."

"I never heard anything so prudish! You'll make me sorry I took you there."

"Oh, it's only for tonight, I promise! You see, when she took me upstairs before we left, she asked me to lunch tomorrow. Just the two of us. She wants to get to know me better. It was so darling of her, and I'd hate to think that I'd done anything she'd disapprove of in the meanwhile."

"How do you know she'd disapprove?"

"Oh, Chip!"

"Seriously, don't you think a woman her age can grow with the times?"

"Not that fast. Oh, darling, it's just for tonight. Forgive me! And there's something else, too. Are you sure you're really in the mood?"

"What makes you think I'm not?"

"That terrible slaughter. It's been on your mind all day."

"That's pretty sharp of you," he admitted. "It hasn't been on yours?"

"No."

"Why not?"

"Because there's nothing on my mind but you!"

Driving home, he reflected on her acuity. He had not realized that he had so obviously betrayed the horror he had felt over the massacre. He had seen corpses on his visit to Vietnam, and the sight of them had simply aroused his ire against the merciless killers from the north. How, he had asked himself, could it be worth any man's while to do that to another man in the cause of a doctrine that would only plunge the world into uniform gray dullness? How could men kill and maim other men for that? But now it was our men who had done this, and done it for what? Not even to spread dullness. For kicks?

On Monday he lunched at the Pentagon with Gerald Hastings, disgusted by his desk job in navy personnel. But Gerry was sixty-two; he could not very well expect a sea command. As he listened to Chip's complaints about the massacre, sitting at a corner table in the officers' dining room, his glum stare was that of a teacher who wonders whether he will ever come to an end of student intransigence.

"What earthly difference does it make, Chip? Has there ever been a time when there weren't men like that? What can you expect when you have to use conscription to raise an army?"

"So that's all it is? A question of reserves as opposed to regulars?"

"That's all it ever was. Do you remember, on the Normandy beach, when that German prisoner spat on one of our dead?"

Chip was startled. He had not thought of the episode in years.

He saw now, in the early morning light, the ragged gray line of German prisoners waiting to board the LST through its gaping bow doors, like ancient offerings to the Minotaur, and the stretchers on the beach in which the American corpses had been laid, borne back from the fighting area. "They shot him, didn't they? But he had outraged them!"

"Was it any less a war atrocity? Do you shoot a man for one expectoration?"

"But surely, Gerry, there's a difference between a cold-blooded slaughter of civilians and the shooting, almost in the heat of battle, of an insolent foe?"

"A difference in degree, of course. No difference in principle. And I thought principle was what you cared about. My point is that no regular officer would have been guilty of either the massacre or the assassination. Those are things that happen in modern war when you have to use civilians. They are unfortunate irrelevancies."

"But that's just what I'm questioning. It seems to me that they're more likely to happen in a war that doesn't have the moral support of the public. I'm afraid the innate evil in war can corrupt even the bravest soldiers unless it is controlled by some kind of moral fervor. We had that moral fervor in our other wars. Once it's missing, there's nothing to redeem the bloodshed."

"My dear Chip, you're talking twaddle. The moral fervor you speak of is a mere coincidence, depending on whether or not the public happen to agree with their government as to a particular war. If the war is a bad one, like a war of aggrandizement, no amount of moral fervor can justify it. Did German public enthusiasm justify the invasion of Poland? Of course not. Only a moral *cause* can justify a war. And no cause has ever been more moral than in this one, where we're fighting for no conceivable material gain. Haven't you said so yourself?"

"But that is not how most people see it."

"How many French peasants understood what Joan of Arc was up to? We're facing a world threat, Chip. How can you, of all people, be so concerned with radical dissidents on the drug-soaked campuses of Academe?"

"When you put it that way," Chip answered, shivering at the sudden bleak wind in his heart, "I begin to see that that is just the way I *have* been seeing it."

"Your trouble, my friend, is that you can never keep your mind on the main point. You are distracted by things that don't basically matter. It was the same way, if it's not too painful to remind you, with your glass company. Instead of keeping your mind on the essential point of saving the family business from a gang of pirates, you allowed yourself to be put off by the way one or two pirates were being roughed up. That's no way to fight a war, Chip."

"Tell me, Gerry, would you use nuclear force, if necessary, to win in Vietnam?"

"Without hesitation."

"Regardless of consequences?"

"The consequences are matters to be taken into consideration by the men who seek to enslave the world. You have heard cynical young people say they'd rather be red than dead. Well, I wouldn't!"

"That's all very well for you, but don't you hesitate to make that decision for them?"

"Not at all. Because I think being red *is* being dead. Besides, my policy would involve no such holocaust. The Soviets don't want to blow up the world any more than we do."

"You hope!"

"Well, there's always a risk in any policy. To my mind the greatest risk of all is to lose a war."

Chip decided not to go back to his office that afternoon, and he sought to underline the importance of his resolution by failing to call Violet and by making his way to the zoo, where nobody in the Department would have dreamed of seeking him. He visited the sleeping lions; he followed the plunging of the ever-restless seals; he fed the sparrows and pigeons; and he watched the two bald eagles flap endlessly back and forth between the perches at either end of their massive aviary. It seemed to him that these huge birds expressed the dilemma of the times. What could they do but fly helplessly to and fro between the moral cause and the practical horror, encaged in the limitations of the soul? Our national emblem might dream of an azure sky under which it could endlessly and magnificently soar. But there was no way it could break through those bars.

He must have stayed by the aviary for half an hour. Then he shrugged and strode away. What did he feel as he unloaded a conscience that was older than half a century? Relief? If this was failure, he would make the most of it.

Half past five found him at his mother's. She was having tea by herself and was enchanted by the unexpected visit. Looking at her seated before the silver tea tray, and viewing the orange sunset light in the garden window behind her, he felt again the serenity that he had experienced the first time Violet had come to his house. The room was prettier than one might have expected from one of Matilda's austerity. There were handsome, chaste Empire things, a mirror surmounted by two small golden swans and three of his father's finest Fitzhugh Lane seascapes. Alone and old, his mother seemed to have come to terms with a long-repressed aesthetic side of her nature. He relished again the feeling that no one knew where he was, that he and his mother were strange allies, surrounded by the debris of shorn fetishes.

But now she dispelled this. "Violet called. She wondered whether I had heard from you. She said you hadn't been at the office since before lunch."

He said nothing.

"Aren't you going to call her?"

"Must I?"

"But she was worried, darling."

"She doesn't own me, Ma."

"Very well, dear."

He got up to take the cup she now handed him. "Isn't it a rather peculiar role for you to be playing? The sponsor of adultery? What would your father have said?"

"My father would have used just those terms. He would have scolded me properly. But I think that by seventy-five one should be able to make up one's own mind, don't you?"

He smiled at the quick flash in her eyes. "Oh, *I* do, yes. I was only wondering what had changed you."

"You really wish to know?"

"I wish very much to know!"

"Then I'll tell you." Matilda put down her cup. "I've had many failures in my life. I failed with your sister Flossie. She's unhappy and goes to a ridiculous guru, who makes things worse. But I'm helpless in the matter, and I accept my helplessness. I failed with Margaret. She has made a life for herself with her advertising agency, but she has not married, and now I fear she never will. Had I supported her in either of her relationships with the only two men she ever cared about, she might have married, and happily. But no, I disapproved of her having affairs and would have nothing to do with it. Elaine has been happy, it's true, but she has made her own happiness. I can claim no credit for that. But my greatest failure, my child, has been with you."

"Oh, no, Ma. No."

"Oh, yes. From the very beginning, I could see that you were struggling with yourself, and I was always afraid that you were struggling with something bad in yourself. That was the puritan in me. A struggle had to be like that huge George Barnard statue they used to have in the main hall of the Metropolitan and that now, I think, is in the cellar. It represents the two natures of man, one good and one evil, wrestling with each other. What I couldn't see, and what my poor father could never see, was that a child might be simply struggling to be himself — to let his real self, like a caged bird, go free. I had always to be hurrying in with moral reinforcements to help the 'good' side of your nature in the wrestling bout. I threw in my father and his school and Bulldog at Yale and the family business — oh, everything I could get my hands on — to keep you on the straight and narrow. And when Alida frustrated my plans and got you, I went on as if the whore of Babylon had won out! Poor dear Alida, who was really much more 'got' by you."

"Much. But you let her come over to you."

"Oh, yes. I made her an ally. And I thought I had won at last — or really that you had won — when you settled in Benedict."

"And then I pulled that to pieces. You must have felt that the evil figure in the Barnard group had at last pinned the good one's shoulders to the mat!"

"I might have, had it not been for your father. He had always foreseen something like that. He told me once: 'You and

Chip have a lot in common. You're both puritans without a god.'"

In the silence he stared. "Have you no god, Ma?"

"Do you know, I've hardly ever stopped to think of that?"

"Then Father was right. We have much in common. Why couldn't he have helped us more?"

"Because that wasn't his way. He had a horror of interfering in people's lives. His own father, you see, had been a great meddler. So he believed that all he could do was love — and keep his hands off."

Chip shook his head. "It wasn't enough."

"No, it wasn't. But it's too late to alter that. What it's not too late to alter is me. That's why I came to Washington. I was determined to do something for you if it was humanly possible."

"I thought you wanted to save my marriage."

"I was resolved to have no preset ideas, to focus on your happiness alone. I promised myself that I would leave all moral questions to you. That I should be concerned only with what *you* wanted. Oh, I was going to be a grinning madame, if necessary, before the doors of pleasure!"

The picture of Matilda, gaunt and skinny, yet with eyes so full of fire, in such a role provoked him to uncontrollable mirth. He let out a little yelp of laughter.

"Call me an old fool!" she cried indignantly. "Call me anything you like! But admit I'm on my boy's side at last. You don't have to love Violet just because the poor girl's obviously dippy about you. You don't have to love anybody! But you do have to recognize that whatever you do — divorce Alida, make up with Alida, marry Violet, give up Violet, prosecute the war or resign from the government — I am backing you to the hilt!"

He went over to put his arms around her skinny shoulders and to hug her. It amused him that even in the throes of her obviously sincere passion, she still did not quite like this. "What makes you think I might resign my office?"

"Violet said so."

"Did she? Maybe she knows me better than I know myself."

"Any woman in love does. Why don't you call her, Chip? She was so worried!"

"Shall I ask her to dinner here? Have you enough for three?"

"Oh, plenty! But wouldn't you rather take her out? Of course you would. You don't want me."

"Ah, but I do!" And the vision of the three of them in that room, sitting by the fire that he would presently light — for it was getting chilly — drinking the cocktail that he would presently mix, was suddenly very agreeable. "I think what I want right now is to see Violet here, in this room, with you."

As he walked to the narrow front hall where the telephone was, he felt a tightness around his heart that was both uncomfortable and oddly pleasant. So that's what it's like, he whispered to himself in surprise. That's what it is like to be free. Free of one's self. To exist, or at least for a while, anyway, not to live. Not to live, at any rate, as he'd always been living.

Violet was still at the office. For all her discipline, she couldn't restrain a little cry of delight. "Oh, you're all right!"

"Of course I'm all right. Mother wants you to come for dinner. Right away."

"Give me twenty minutes!"

The evening developed just as he had wanted it. Both women seemed to sense that he had no desire to talk, that he sought for once to be inert, passive, to listen to any chatter they cared to exchange. His mother was at her very best, marvelously funny about the life of the only daughter of a widowed minister in a New England boys' school. She told stories of Saint Luke's that he had never heard before. And Violet, warming to the older woman, enchanted at being so accepted, was amusing about her own mother's fears of the perils of dancing school and subscription balls for subdebutantes. At first there had been a slight constraint in their exchange, as if they were conscious of putting on a kind of performance for him, but this wore off as they became sincerely interested in each other's background, and he had no objection to the possibility of an alliance between them, even if, like all female alliances, it had some degree of exclusivity.

In his relaxed mood, a drink in hand, he had an easy sense of numbness, as if he had survived some great catastrophe, but only as an incapacitated observer, propped up, so to speak, in a wheelchair in a sanitarium, listening to the prattle of these two, who represented, in some curious fashion, all that had survived. Yet that all was somehow going to be enough; that was his odd conviction. The terrible fires that had raged all his life, spitting and crackling within him, outside him, had gone out at last, and the black ugly smoke of hate had been blown away until it was only a small cloud on the horizon. All he had to do now was to accept their love. Was that going to be, like everything else, impossible?

Very likely, but at least he could try. Or better yet, he could learn to stop trying.

"Chip," his mother said severely, "I don't think you should have another drink. I'm sure Violet agrees with me. You've had three since dinner."

"Very well, Ma, I shan't have another. But suppose I mix one for you and Violet? I think you both deserve it!"

22

×××××

ALIDA

It was Chip's sister Flossie who told me about Violet Crane. She had hated Chip ever since the row over the glass museum, and I could almost hear the smacking of her lips across the telephone wire.

"Mother's actually sponsoring the whole thing!" Flossie went on indignantly. "It's revolting. I suppose the kindest thing you can say about her is that she's senile."

"Does Chip want to marry this girl?"

"She's no older than Ellie. But you know what kind of fool there's no fool like. All I can do is warn you, Alida, to get hold of every penny you can of Chip's money before Miss Gold Digger gets her hot little hands on it. Do you know how her type uses the marital deduction argument? They purr and cuddle up and whisper: 'Darling, oo don't want oos money to go to Uncle Sam, do oo? So leave it all to poor little me and pay no hahwid taxes. Don't worry about oos children; *I'll* take care of them.' In a pig's eye, she will! For a pig is what she is."

"Have you met her, Flossie?"

"For what do you take me? Of course I haven't met the slut. Have you got a lawyer, my dear? A sharp, fighting lawyer? You're sure as hell going to need one."

"I haven't as yet. I was thinking of Chessy Bogart. I told Chip, but he got furious."

"Well, who cares? Bogart's my man! Unless you can find one who'll make Chip even madder."

"I don't want to make him too mad."

"Why ever not?"

But I never did retain Chessy. Before I had made up my mind to call him — and I had a good many doubts about doing so — I had a call from Lars. He said that Chip had told him that I was threatening legal proceedings, and he begged me to let him see me before I did anything. I could hardly refuse such an old friend, and that very afternoon he presented himself in my library. He was very grave and declined the drink I offered him.

"Chip tells me you're planning to retain Chessy Bogart. I hope you haven't done so yet."

"Won't you represent Chip?"

"I don't see how I can. Having known you both so well and so long."

"Oh, come, Lars, you know your first loyalty is to Chip. Admit it. I'm not going to take it personally."

"I don't know just what my first loyalty amounts to. Certainly I am devoted to Chip. But Karen and I are also both devoted to you, too, and, what is more, extremely concerned about you. The only way that I could properly represent Chip would be if I represented you as well."

"Me? Wouldn't that be a conflict of interest?"

"Not if both sides consent. It's often done."

"But I have no idea of consenting! I want my lawyer to be entirely on my side."

"But I would be. Because your side is Chip's. And I'll tell you something else. I'll charge no fee, either to you or Chip. When we've fixed upon a settlement, I shall insist that you submit it to an eminent domestic relations lawyer of your choice — Chessy Bogart excepted — and ask him whether you could do any better in a more adversary proceeding."

"Why Chessy excepted?"

"Because he hates Chip. He wouldn't be fair. Chip is perfectly willing to give you anything you want — within reason. And even beyond reason, if the settlement's in trust and will go ultimately to your children. So there's no point going through the expense and dirt of a public proceeding, is there?"

I think at that moment I almost hated Lars. What was he doing but depriving me of the only satisfaction that an injured wife wants?

"But Chip has behaved outrageously!"

"With this girl? What did you expect when you left him alone in Washington?"

"It was his idea to go to Washington! Just as it was his idea to leave Benedict! What's a woman expected to do? Travel all over the globe after her wandering, philandering husband?"

"What about your philandering with Chessy?"

"Oh, he told you about that, did he? Well, he'd never have known it if I hadn't told him. Can you compare a single roll in the hay with a lifetime of adultery? Oh, yes, I suppose you and Karen could. To the truly chaste there are no degrees in carnality."

Lars smiled. Had he not been possessed of considerable charm, his condescension would have been intolerable. "All that would make no difference, Alida, if you and Chip really loved each other. But as long as that is all over, what's the point of recrimination? Isn't it wiser for you to let each other go and get on with your own lives? How does it help to nurture hate and self-pity?"

"What life do I have to get on with?" I was also about to ask him what made him so sure that I no longer loved Chip, but some tattered shred of pride prevented me. I thought of Karen and Lars, like the good in Elinor Wylie's plea for Cressid, going down to their marble vaults, their heads erect, their eyes serene, their shining raiment unspotted. And what was left of me but a shivering, naked, crouching figure whose G-string of a soul-saving personal resentment had been brutally snatched away?

"You have a great life to get on with," Lars insisted. "You're only in your forties, and you're still a beautiful woman. You have a son who needs you and money to do useful things with. Frankly, I think you've been always a bit in Chip's shadow. You'll find yourself at last on your own two feet. The great thing is to let the bitterness go. It isn't easy, I know. It takes character. But I think you have character. Why don't you take a giant first step by allowing me to start drafting a separation agreement?"

"All right, all right!" I covered my face with my hands.

"You'll find that you have everything you need."

"I don't want anything! Tell Chip I'll give him his divorce and he can keep his money!"

"That, of course, is an emotional reaction that will pass. Neither Chip nor I will allow you to be anything but a rich woman. But here's a better idea. Why not tell him yourself? Tell him that you'll let me have a try at what I propose."

My hands dropped to my sides. "You mean telephone him?"

"No. Tell him directly. He came here with me. He's down in the lobby. We agreed that if you were amenable, I'd ask him to come up."

"How can he be here? I thought he worked night and day at the Department."

"He's quit his job. As of yesterday."

"But why?"

"Apparently he's seen the light."

"No!" I spoke almost in a whisper.

"I'll send him up and be on my way. And believe me, Alida, you've made a very brave and a very wise decision."

I turned abruptly away from him and walked to the window and looked up at a dirty gray sky, for minutes, it seemed, on end, until I heard my husband's familiar firm step in the hall. When I turned to greet him, I thought my heart would burst. He was as handsome as the day when I had first seen him in the ballroom of the Bar Harbor Swimming Club.

"Lars tells me you've left the Department!"

"I won't say 'Better late.'"

"You really and truly have changed your views?"

"At long last."

"And are you sorry? Are you repentant?" But what was I saying? I was desperate in my misery, my abandonment.

"Repentance is a sterile thing. I did what I thought was best at the time. Now it's over. We go on. That's all."

"We?"

"The people who made the errors."

"Not you and I?"

"What do you mean, Alida?"

"Is it too late for us to try again?"

His eyes flickered; obviously, he had not foreseen this. But what could break his resolution? What ever had? "I'm afraid so."

"This girl, this Violet . . . Is she pregnant?"

"No." How he must have despised me!

"But she will be?"

"You mean after we marry? I hope so."

"You'll have lots of babies? Lots and lots?"

Had he not been so controlled, he would have blushed for me. As it was, he simply replied: "We'll have as many as Violet wants. I think she'll make a good mother. I may be old to start being daddy again, but with any luck I should live to see them grow up, and if not, Violet can handle it."

"Oh, I'm sure you'll see them all grow up!" I cried bitterly. "I'm sure they'll make you a grandfather, which Eleanor and Dana probably never will. And I'm sure you'll get on with them better than you did with our children, because, damn you, you *can* learn by your mistakes. While I . . ."

I could not go on. The sudden appalling vision of the man's strength, like some ineluctable glacier, moving on relentlessly over the frozen bodies of his first wife and offspring, moving on from a past that crumbled to nothing behind it, with hardly a memory, certainly not a regret, robbed me of even the desire to protest. I saw him now as a statue, shining, glowing, unveiled, with alabaster limbs and one arm, like Perseus' upstretched, holding the head of Medusa. And what *was* Medusa? Myself? Oh, no. I was simply one of the fallen chips from the block of marble out of which he had been sculpted. My mind reeled. I closed my eyes. I saw the features of the beheaded monster. Whose were they? Whose but his? How banal, how obvious! How true.

"Do you want to stay here tonight?" I asked politely.

"No, thanks. I think it's better from now on if we regard it as your apartment. I told Lars to prepare the papers for conveying it to you. I'll be staying at the Union Club."

"And Violet?"

"She's with her mother. I'm dining there tonight. To meet Mrs. Crane. Wish me luck."

"You won't need it. When have you ever?"

When he had gone at last, I thought I would collapse. Or at least I thought I wanted to collapse. I suppose it was only anger that kept me erect, anger at the ghastly vision of the life that I had simply flung away for this man while he was all the while preparing himself, however unconsciously, to be a better husband and father to a second family. For that, horrible as it was to admit, was just what he would be; he had learned enough, damn his eyes, from the experience of his multitudinous sins. It would be my ultimate humiliation to hear him praised!

Anger, anyway, I would have to cultivate. Anger might save me from the temptation of trying to soil his happiness and good fortune by depositing the reproachful carcass of Alida Benedict, a suicide or victim of drugs and liquor, on the doorstep of his child bride. What would he do but call a garbage truck? No, I could not let myself go the way he and Eleanor were so smugly sure I would go. I had still one ally, an ally all the stronger in that his need of me was as great as my own of him.

I went to my desk and scribbled out a desperate cable to Dana. I told him that I had agreed to a divorce and that his father was planning to remarry. I begged him not to object if I were to fly over to Stockholm and stay in a hotel in his neighborhood. I promised not to interfere with his life there. I ended with the words "Darling, I need you. Please!" But I wondered whether, in the sternness of his dedication to a cause of which I had been at best a wobbly support, he would see fit to stretch out a hand. It would be just my luck to see puritanism take its last twisted stand in both my children.